CLAIMED

A HAVEN REALM NOVEL

MILA YOUNG

Thank you for purchasing a Mila Young novel. **If you want to be notified when Mila Young's next novel is released**, please sign up for her **mailing list** by <u>**clicking here**</u>.

Your email address will never be shared and you can unsubscribe at any time.

Join **Mila Young's Wicked Readers Group** to chat directly with Mila and other readers about her books, enter giveaways, and generally just have loads of fun!

Join the Wicked Reader's Group!

A NOTE FROM MILA YOUNG

I've had so much fun writing these fairy tale retellings and I hope you enjoy them just as much.

Each story in the Haven Realm series is a standalone novel and can be read in any order, though the more tales you read, the more likely you'll meet familiar characters.

These are adult fairy tale retellings for anyone who loves happily ever afters with steamy romance, sexy alphas, and seductive fun.

Join My Wicked Reader's Group!

Enjoy!

Mila

Wickedly Ever After

HAVEN REALM SERIES

Hunted (Little Red Riding Hood Retelling)
Charmed (Aladdin Retelling)
Cursed (Beauty and the Beast Retelling)
Claimed (Little Mermaid Retelling)
Entangled (Rapunzel Retelling...to come in May)
Wicked (Snow White Retelling to come in June)

More on the way...

HAVEN REALM

The realms of Haven warred for ages upon ages, laying devastation upon its lands and its residents alike. To put an end to the death and destruction, the realm was divided into seven kingdoms, one for each race, ruled by nobility, entrusted to maintain the truce. Over centuries, kingdoms rose and fell as the power of the ruling noble houses waxed and waned. And the peace between the lands persevered. But a corruption is growing, bringing darkness to the realms, and threatening the return of war and suffering to Haven.

HAVEN REALM
and the Seven Territories

CHAPTER 1

"*O*n my count." My cousin Taura's voice resounded in my mind. "Three. Two. One."

Taura, Gellian, and I tipped the preserved bladders made from the skin of sea cucumber upside down and swallowed the liquid inside. The brew burned down my throat and set fire to my chest. We slammed the empty vessels on the tavern's counter and laughed.

Taura grabbed my waist and one of my hands and twirled me. I loved the feel of the water on my skin—caressing it, soothing it, energizing it. A haze of bubbles floated all around us.

"Whoa," I said as the merrum hit my blood, charging my pulse and leaving me a little unsteady on my fins. I held on to the counter for balance.

Outside the window of the bar, scores of lemon-colored butterflyfish crossed the reef, most likely headed for the stony coral patch they grazed on. I blinked, trying to make them stop swirling.

"You're a lightweight," Gellian joked, downing another drink like a true party animal.

Taura's brown eyes filled with concern. "Have some cala-mari rings," she said, offering me a seaweed basket filled with the delicate treats.

I nibbled on a few.

On the table in front of us, a Sharkrider threw down his handful of cards and pushed the table away. As he stormed out of the bar, he slammed into a deep-sea fisher slow-dancing with a harvester.

"Watch where you're going, ya' guppy!" shouted the diver.

The Sharkrider spun around and loomed over the diver. "You got a problem?"

I tensed, bracing myself for trouble.

Taura squeezed my arm, her pale forehead scored by apprehensive lines.

Gellian's blue eyes sparkled. My best friend likened a good tussle to sport. Told us the violence turned her on. That's where we disagreed. A fight always brought down the mood and ruined our party. Blood? No, thanks.

"You should apologize to my lady," said the diver.

"Shellfish off." The Sharkrider's nostrils flared, spitting out bubbles.

The bartender intervened, pulling a long trident from underneath the counter. "Time to leave," he said, soaring across the bar and jabbing the weapon at the Sharkrider's chest.

The wild merman narrowed his eyes, grunted, and then stormed out, generating a current that whisked my hair across my face.

Good riddance.

Shark Bait bar was a real dive. Seedy characters, ruffians, and lawless Sharkriders frequented the place, gambling, chewing sea tobacco, drinking, getting rowdy, and causing fights. Dim lighting illuminated the old and cracked furni-ture. The waiter behind the counter looked about two hundred years old...probably from all his partying. Inside, the place stunk of mersweat and sometimes of blood when a rumble broke out...like we needed to attract the real sharks. A half-drunk band played screeching rock tunes in the corner. The little hole-in-the-wall bar was a stark contrast to the bright, exploding color of the reef outside the windows.

But I loved it there. They served the best merrum in Tritonia, and no one would ever think of looking for a merprincess here. Several times in the moon cycle, I'd sneak away to the bar to escape my father's kingdom.

Poseidon. If King Triton knew I came here, he'd have a fit. I'd be locked up in my quarters for a month. Possibly assigned a guard and never let out of anyone's sight. My father was a conservative king. Partying, mermen, merrum, and dancing were not activities fit for a princess. Noooo. We had to attend all formal events: meetings, celebrations, negotiations, war councils. Basically, sit and look pretty. Offer up intelligent conversation. Flatter the noble guests at court. Soothe wounded egos when conflicts arose. Even solve difficult strategic and political problems in the realm. Sometimes, my duties exhausted me, and I just needed a reprieve from it all.

At Shark Bait, I could be myself. Relax, dance, drink, play, and get rowdy. All the things any self-respecting, twenty-two-year-old wanted to do.

"Sea god," said Taura, running her fingers through her limp, red curls. "Eight degrees to your right. A hot Sharkrider is checking you out, Cousin."

Gellian pulled up her corset, highlighting her boobs, and pouted her crimson lips. "If you don't go talk to him, Nyssa, I will."

I didn't doubt that. Gellian was like a walrus when it came to mermen. If she saw one she fancied, he was hers, whether he liked it or not.

Completely the opposite of me. I turned into a blabbering, embarrassing mess when it came to talking to a handsome merman.

Still, curiosity got the better of me, and I casually glanced over my shoulder. What waited for me made me nearly fall off my chair.

Poseidon. They were right. Some hulk, muscled from head to fin and complete with tattoos and long, wild black hair was giving me the sexy, come-hither, I-want-to-mate-with-you eyes. Not that I'd ever done that. My purity remained intact. Mainly because I hadn't met anyone who'd taken my breath away and made my heart sing....and because my father would murder the merman if he found out. Facing the threat of having their mersac cut out wasn't exactly a turn on.

Taura shoved me in the arm. "Talk to him."

"No way," I sent to her.

All merfolk communicated telepathically in water to one or many recipients. Outside the comforts of the sea, we spoke like normal humans. Although, if we didn't practice using our vocal cords often enough, they tended to dry out and get lazy, like slack muscles, making talking a bit hard.

"No one in here cares that you're a princess." Gellian leaped off her seat to primp my long, silvery hair.

"I'll just embarrass myself," I mumbled, admiring the sea leather sash crossed over his powerful chest.

"Not with a bit of liquid courage," said Taura, wiggling her slim hips as she swished over to the bar to order another round of shots.

I buried my face in my hands. What was I getting myself into? I turned to serious mush around mermen... Mush of the squashed jellyfish kind. No one wanted to see that, least of all the males.

"Sea god," said Gellian. "I wish I had your violet eyes."

Eyes the color of mine were very rare among merfolk. Only my father, two other merfolk, and I shared them. They certainly attracted a lot of attention from the males. But I hadn't met a male who could stare into them instead of gazing at my buxom chest.

A few moments later, another merrum appeared beneath my nose.

"Drink this." Judging by my cousin's pursed lips and the way she shoved the drink into my hand, she wasn't taking *no* for an answer when it came to both the drink and me talking to the Sharkrider.

I glanced out the window at the seahorse doing his mating dance for his lady amidst the sea grass swaying in the current. *Sea god!* Was that a sign? Determination brewed in my belly, and I threw back the shot before I could talk myself out of it. I let out a hiss as the liquid burned my throat. But for some reason, my bottom remained stuck to the chair.

"Just go."

My cousin shoved me off the seat, and I stumbled in the water.

I collected myself, smoothing my hair, hoisting my boobs in my corset.

The Sharkrider smiled at me, lighting a fire inside me, and before I could stop, my fin—which had a mind of its own —propelled me over to him.

Poseidon. What was I doing? I must have been mad. My whole body quaked. Nerves coiled in my belly. But I couldn't turn back now.

"Hi there, Sugarfins," the Sharkrider said.

He had this dark, smoky, baritone voice that made my knees shudder. His gaze caressed my chest and body.

I got lost in the golden flecks in his brown eyes.

When I didn't say anything, he chuckled, rubbed his broad nose, and asked, "Can I buy you a drink?"

Still nothing. My throat thickened, as if someone had poured a whole bunch of sand in it. *Poseidon. Say something!*

Someone bumped into me, dislodging the blockage in my throat.

"Sorry, darling," muttered the diver from earlier.

I didn't glance his way. The strong line of the Sharkrider's jaw captivated me. "Sure," I squeaked at him, imagining his lips leaving sweet kisses along my collarbone.

"What'll you have, Sugarfins?" he said, running a finger along my cheek.

I shuddered.

My gaze glued to the bulge of his arms. "Flexed muscles," I replied, lost in thought.

Fire scaled up my spine when I realized what I'd said. *Poseidon.* There I went, embarrassing myself already. Every cell in my body screamed at me to return to my table, have another five drinks, and receive consolation from my best friends all afternoon. But my fin wasn't having it.

His husky laugh stroked my insides. "Later. When I take you home, Sugarfins."

Take me home? That was a bit forward. We didn't even know each other yet. Maybe I should have let Gellian eat him up.

"Merrum, please." My words rushed out.

"Back in a flash." The Sharkrider gave me a cocky smile and left to order our drinks.

Damn. He was just as handsome from the rear. Well-built shoulders and back. Thick, powerful tail and long fin. A body finely honed, most likely from all the work he did, catching and training sharks.

When I turned around, Taura and Gellian gave me four thumbs up.

Soon, the Sharkrider returned with my merrum—a much larger offering than the shots Taura had been plying into me.

"Spank you," I said.

He laughed again, and I gasped, clasping my mouth.

Shellfish. That was a little in-joke with my girls. Damn this liquor. It was loosening me up and making me even more shameful than usual. I prayed to the sea god to end my streak of embarrassing myself.

He leaned into me, and my pulse scaled ten beats.

"You're into that, huh?" he asked.

What? No way! Not that I'd ever tried. But getting my ass spanked didn't sound pleasant.

"No," I said, a little too fast and dismissive.

The Sharkrider's thick black brows pinched.

Poseidon. Just shut up now before you say something stupid.

"Haven't seen you 'round here before, Sugarfins." He took a sip from his seaweed beer. "Where you from?"

Shellfish. It wasn't like I could admit I was Triton's daughter. Second in line for the throne after my eldest sister. Fastest way to kiss a merman like him goodbye. The Sharkriders were wild and did not bow to the king...the equivalent of human pirates...but for the right price, their services could be bought in times of war.

My mind seized for answers. I glanced around the bar, desperate for a reply, landing on the bartender. "Barmaid," I said the first thing that came to mind, and sipped on my drink, wincing at the fire raging down my throat.

He brushed hair from my eyes. "You're too pretty for that. But you've got the tits for it."

Excuse me? Sure, I snuck out of the kingdom to drink and party with my friends, but I still appreciated respect and loathed mermen who did nothing but leer at my body.

7

"Sorry, Sugarfins," he said, flashing that smile that hooked me like a fish. "I speak my mind. And I like what I see."

Shellfish. I decided to give him another chance. Blame it on that sexy voice of his.

He ran his long, calloused fingers along my wrist and up my forearm, and I trembled with excitement.

The swinging door burst open, and the music suddenly stopped.

I glanced over, and my heart practically exploded out of my chest. *Shellfish.* What was my younger sister Nimian doing here? How'd she find me? She was going to hold this over me for life. She'd threaten to tell Papa unless I did as she said.

Taura and Gellian disappeared behind the crowd at the back of the bar. Cowards. Leaving me behind. Taura didn't suffer fools well. She considered Nimian to be self-obsessed and a right royal pain in the tail. Best if I kept those two apart to avoid arguments.

Nimian's eye makeup was smeared from her workout. Normally, she wouldn't be caught dead swimming around like that. She ran her disapproving gaze over the bar and its patrons. Her nose wrinkled with disgust. As she trailed deeper into the bar, she made sure to avoid contact with anything. But the couple dancing bumped into her, and she jumped backward, dusting her skin as if she thought they had the black rust plague.

If I weren't so shocked at her entry, I might have laughed at her. My younger sister wasn't adventurous like I was. She preferred the luxuries my father's palace had to offer.

Everyone in the bar stared at her. The scales winding along her temples and down behind her ears had turned a shade of dark blue from anxiety. Royals like my sister and I possessed different markings from the regular merfolk, who had green and aqua scales. My grandmother always said it had something to do with our blood. Whenever I journeyed to Shark Bait bar, I colored my scales in green with coral pastel to conceal my true identity.

Adding to the mystery of my sister's arrival was her hair, all curled and pinned to her head with pearl-shell combs. Coral ink stained her small lips and her rounded cheeks red. She was wearing her favorite golden bodice decorated with aqua beads. The one she reserved for special occasions like balls and feasts. My suspicion peaked. Was she going to try to drag me on a double date? If that was the case, the answer was a resounding *no*. The last merman she'd set me up with had been more interested in talking about himself. I couldn't get a word in. No, thanks.

My sister's eyes, like those of an orca determined to catch a seal, landed on me. "Nyssa, I've been looking for you everywhere."

Her breathless voice pounded in my skull.

The Sharkrider put a protective arm over me. "The princess came to play. Shall we ask her to have a drink with us?"

"No." The word rushed out of my head.

I had to get my sister out of there as fast as possible.

"Nimian, what are you doing here?" I said, fighting the panic drumming through my body. "How…? How'd you find me?"

Shark Bait bar was located on the outskirts of the Tritonian kingdom. Nobles rarely ventured to this part of town except for business or royal matters. It was considered dirty and where the low-lives hung out. Certainly not the kind of establishment Nimian would frequent. I wagered she was probably bursting to tell me the latest scandal and court gossip, such as which handsome noble she was necking with behind Father's back. What merman she wished to date next. Or which rich mergeek one of her friends had hooked up with. Her news must have been major for her to venture all the way out here, looking a little disheveled from the exercise, her eye makeup smeared.

"Faraall told me you were here," said Nimian.

My stomach lurched. How did the commander of the merarmy know that? Was he keeping tabs on me? On several occasions, he'd exhibited behavior suggesting he might have a crush on me. But I was totally not interested in that creep. If he was following me, then I'd have to be even more discreet.

"Sugarfins, you two know each other?" The Sharkrider smirked as he twirled a lose curl around his fingers. "How 'bout some double action, princess? Cause I'm totally up for it."

Poseidon. I'd forgotten all about him and his dirty mind.

Nimian's scales flashed red. She slapped him across the face, and I flinched.

"Take it easy, Sugarfins."

"Touch me or my sister again, and I'll have my father harpoon you."

I bit my lip and hugged my arms over my waist.

It took a few seconds to dawn on the Sharkrider. His gaze skimmed her crown of starfish, the silver-and-blue scales on her neck and tail.

"You're royal?" He glanced between Nimian and me.

Flipping hell. The fish was out of the net now.

CHAPTER 2

"*Y*es, you creep." Nimian waved her hands, shooing the Sharkrider away.

My mouth gaped. I didn't know what to say. It felt like a magic bomb had exploded in my stomach. *Shellfish.* Talk about blowing my cover big time.

He steered away from us faster than a school of herring fleeing a dolphin.

"Thanks a lot," I snapped at Nimian, shrinking in my seat as the rest of the patrons stared in our direction.

Thanks to her, I'd probably never be able to show my face in the bar again. My stomach pinched with regret. I liked coming to Shark Bait bar, where no one recognized me. Until now.

But on the bright side, at least I could take comfort knowing it wasn't my fault this time—at least *I* hadn't scared the merman away.

My sister crossed her arms. "You're late."

"For what?" I sent the message to Nimian.

My response earned me a reproachful look from my

younger sister. "Don't tell me you've forgotten again? I swear, Nyssa. If your head wasn't screwed on, you'd lose it."

Whatever was she on about? I remembered everything. Except the things I wasn't interested in. My brain needed precious space, and I wasn't wasting it on all of her latest court gossip.

"You probably forgot your medical assessment yesterday, too."

What was she? My day-planner servant? "Please. I'm as fit as a sea lion! And just as fast."

Nimian glared at me, but the nasty look disappeared quickly because she started bouncing—a sign I understood as her bursting to tell me news.

"Papa has called an announcement of a royal decree," she twittered, glowing with enthusiasm. No doubt, she was excited at the prospect of the all the mermen there'd be, all gathered together in one place.

My heart sank faster than a pirate ship's anchor.

Royal decrees were an important announcement like a change in law, funding for some project, more taxes, or something else as equally horrible. They were as boring as watching the tide wear down a sand grain. When the king issued a royal decree, every member of the household had to attend. I'd have to dress up and look my finest. But I hated the way all the mermaids at court gawked at me. How they whispered in each other's ears, judging me, spreading lies about me and scheming to set me up with their brothers, all to get themselves into the royal line via marriage. No, thanks.

"I can't make it. I have a prior engagement," I said. "But I shall have the pleasure of you telling me all about the afternoon once it's over."

Nimian grabbed my wrist and tugged, as if she were desperate to leave this place and never think of it again. I felt the same way; her surprise visit had ruined everything.

"No, you're not," she said. "Father is well aware of your little disappearing acts. He ordered me to ensure your attendance."

I yanked free of my sister's grasp. Now it made sense. Nimian had traveled all this way, working up a sweat and smearing her painted face, because our father had sent her to find me and bring me back.

On the odd occasion, Father let it slide when I skipped a few events here and there. I may have played on his soft spot for me. But if he'd asked for me personally, then attending the decree was mandatory. I had no other choice, save sailing away from Nimian and hiding somewhere. Jellyfish Cove might be an option. She hated their sticky, toxic stingers dangling over her and wouldn't dare venture there. Or I could take shelter in the Sea Witch's lands to the north. There, the air was thick with sulfur and hard to breathe, and I wasn't even sure *I* wanted to go there. I rubbed my forehead, thinking over my options.

Escaping my father's orders for the third function in a row was bound to leave me in his bad graces, and I was too old for a scolding. At twenty-two years of age, I knew my place…even if I didn't like it. The role of princess to the people of Tritonia came with certain duties. I was expected to attend certain affairs. An angry King Triton was a force to be reckoned with. I didn't care for being grounded in my quarters for another week, as I'd been the last time I'd missed a mandatory royal function. It was set. I was going. Whether I approved or not.

"Fine," I said to Nimian. "Let me get my things."

She cast her disgusted gaze across the bar. "I'll wait for you outside."

While she darted out faster than a school of fish spooked by a shark, I collected my purse from our original table.

Taura blocked my path out of the bar. "What did she want? Where are you going?"

Her face paled as I explained everything to her and Gellian.

"Shellfish," Taura mumbled. "I'll be expected to attend, too."

All royalty, extended family and the court nobles included, would assemble for word from the king, after which, we'd snack on food and seagrass wine.

"I had a lovely afternoon." I kissed Gellian on the cheek.

"Enjoy the boring decree." My friend smiled. Lucky wench didn't have to go because she was the royal cook's daughter.

Gellian glided toward a table full of Sharkriders. "I'm going to try my luck with one or more of these handsome fellows."

My cheeks blazed. She had no shame. But that was what I loved about her. I just didn't think I could ever be that brave...or forward.

Outside, Nimian darted across the bright-neon coral shelf in a furious flap of fins, spooking the sea anemones back into their cavities. Fish darted out of her way in all directions. Wow. Her tail pounded like her life depended on it. I'd never seen her catch such speed.

A stingray cut across her path. Bubbles blasted from her open mouth. Her scream echoed in my head. She ducked and held her forehead, waiting for the magnificent creature to drift into the gloomy depths beyond. Then she sprang up, breathing hard, batting at her head as if she thought a sea crab crawled across her.

Taura's mocking laugh echoed in my head. "I'll leave you with the princess," she said, giving me a wave and veering off in another direction.

Part of me was tempted to leave Nimian, as well, and

continue on to the palace alone, to punish her for inter-rupting my good afternoon. But I didn't have the heart and put my arm around her waist.

"Stop that," I said, giving Nimian's back a comforting rub. "It was just a stingray. It's gone now."

Hands clenched into fists, Nimian pulled away and glared at me with her fierce blue eyes as if I'd sprouted a new bone protrusion akin to those worn by the hammerhead sharks. "It accosted me!"

What a precious princess. But I still loved her. Even if what Taura said was true about my sister being a right royal pain in the ass.

"I know. Dreadful creature," I lied, rubbing my thumbs under her eyes to clean the smeared makeup. "How dare it get in the way of merfolk?"

Nimian buried her head against my shoulder. "Oh, it was awful. I thought I was going to die."

I stroked her now-messy golden hair. "There. There."

A swim around the kingdom's gardens was the extent of adventure my sister preferred. Unlike Nimian, I enjoyed the wonders of the sea. Exploring uncharted territory beyond my father's realm and investigating hidden sea caves. The previous week, my friends and I had discovered a sunken ship, but that trip had ended when a wooden beam had collapsed and almost killed me.

"Hurry up," I said, taking her hand and dragging her through the water. "We're never going to get to the palace at this rate."

****

"POSEIDON, LOOK AT YOU!" Nimian barked, running a brush

inlaid with mother of pearl—a gift from my mother, which I never used—through the tangled knots in my silvery hair.

"Ouch," I cried, wriggling to get free of the dressing chair in my quarters.

"Sit still, would you?" My sister was like a whirlwind, turning my messy tresses to silk then twisting them into a layer of curls within minutes.

I slouched, knowing I wasn't getting out of this even if I wanted to.

Nimian set my curls. She plucked a pearl comb like hers —but with dark-purple pearls to contrast with her baby pink ones—and pinned them in my locks.

My fingers traced the ringlets with awe. I had to admit I'd be lost without her. Even though I resented being dragged to this event, I flashed her an appreciative smile for her efforts.

"You're going to look amazing," my sister cooed as she dabbed a brush in a compact of crushed coral makeup.

I sighed as she poked and prodded me with a cream to smooth my skin tone and cover the bags under my eyes. My reflection in the mirror transformed into a strange beauty I didn't recognize. The smoky gray with which she lined my lids complemented my violet eyes and broad eyelids. The plum blush highlighted my rounded cheekbones. An application of rouge brought out my pouty lips. Cream on my nose took away the pink tone caused by all the exercise I got from swimming around the kingdom on a daily basis. Even I couldn't deny that I looked like a real merprincess instead of the tomboy I usually resembled.

She was right. I looked beautiful, and I couldn't stop twisting my head to examine myself. "Thank you, Nimian."

For a brief moment, my sister glowed beneath my praise. Then she turned all wild-eyed and crazy again, yanking me to my feet, cutting short my self-admiration.

"Take that off, and lift your arms," she said.

I did as she instructed, removing my plain green corset, and she wrapped my torso in a jeweled purple version to match the pearls in the combs and bring out the silver in my scales and hair. If my sister was good at one thing, it was accessorizing. I was hopeless at it. Couldn't get clothes to match…but I did have a knack for complementing colors thanks to my artistic flair.

I grunted as Nimian pulled my corset tight and fastened it at my back.

"Poseidon, I wish I had your waist and hips," my sister groaned. "The mermen go wild for them. I'm never going to get a merchild out of these hips."

Unfortunately for Nimian, she'd inherited our grand-mother's long, thin waist and tiny hips. Me, I'd inherited my paternal aunt's curvy figure, which only she and I shared in the family. And yes, the mermen did go wild over my body. But being leered at for my hair, my eyes, my hips, and my chest made me feel shy and uncomfortable. Especially when all the mermaids in court turned catty out of jealousy because I attracted all the attention.

While Nimian reset her smudged makeup, I remembered what my aunt, Taura's mother, had taught me when I was five: most mermen were only after a beautiful princess so they could hang on her arm. Over and over, she'd drilled into me that I was worth more than that. A strong-willed, smart, resourceful, and adventurous princess like me was any merman's equal. A bright jewel of the sea. Something to be treasured. She was right. Without my aunt's mentoring, I don't know how I would have survived navigating the royal court—or sneaking away from it. For that, I owed her the world.

"Time to leave," Nimian squealed, clasping her hands and twirling in the water.

In her excitement, she accidentally knocked over a

mosaic I'd been working on for my father's upcoming birthday: a collection of shells, pearls, and corals on a bed of crushed coral glue, all arranged into a portrait of my father.

I set it back on its stand and asked, "Do you think Papa will love his birthday present?"

My sister huffed as she examined my artwork. The slightest hint of pink flushed in the scales around her eyes—a sign of anger or jealousy. Merfolk couldn't hide their emotions very well under water.

"You're the favorite daughter," she said. "Can't do any wrong in Papa's eyes. I'm sure he'll love it."

Over the years, I had learned to brush off Nimian's sour seaweed reactions. It was no different with the rest of my sisters. Collectively, they all moaned behind my back—or so the palace servants told me. Apparently, my sisters never understood why I was Father's favorite. To this day, I didn't know why, either. I never got invited to play the harp in the kingdom's orchestra like my eldest sister, and heir to the throne, Aquina. And Nimian's crab chowder had won three medals at the last Under the Sea Bake Off Competition.

My art certainly wasn't the award-winning kind. The pieces I glued on always shifted. I had a strange habit of making people look as if they had googly fish eyes. I'd always thought my father merely felt sorry for me, since I wasn't as gifted as my sisters. He always insisted on displaying my artwork next to the official portraits of his family. It annoyed the pompous court painters to no end, having their royal portraits associated with my imperfect paintings. Whenever a visitor came to the palace, my father showed them my new pieces. I didn't have the heart to tell him to stop boring everyone to death when he beamed with pride.

A horn sounded in the distance—the warning signal that the event was about to commence. The shell the guards used was one of the few instruments capable of making high-pitched sounds beneath the density of the water.

"Hurry," Nimian said, dragging me out of my quarters and down the corridor.

Nerves swelled in the pit of my stomach. Instead of brushing my skin, the water felt like little crab claws, dragging me down.

Sea flowers hung from the columns holding up the palace's roof. Silk banners decorated the walls. Seaweed in pots danced in the stream flowing through the palace. Extra crystal lamps hung from the beams. My father and his team had really gone to extra lengths to decorate for this occasion.

Soldiers positioned next to tall, thin shells stood to attention and nodded as we passed. I smiled nervously and nodded back. It seemed everyone was on duty this afternoon.

I bumped into someone and stumbled forward. "Oh, my. I'm terribly sorry." I grabbed a muscled arm to steady myself.

"That's perfectly fine, princess." Strong hands clamped on my arms and straightened me.

My heart slammed into my sternum. I knew that voice. And I did not like the owner. My gaze drifted from the bands protecting the merman's wrists and forearms, up to the metallic scales of the soldier's armor. I looked up farther, right into his cold, mud-brown eyes. Faraall, the commander of my father's army. Armed with his usual smug smile, he shifted the trident under his arm to his hand, holding it tightly to his side. Scars along his cheek and shoulders proved his might in battles. His crooked nose was a reminder he'd gotten into one too many fist fights as a teen.

What did he want? He was always stalking me around the palace!

19

CHAPTER 3

"My beautiful princesses," the commander said with all the charm of a stingray barb.

Chills coiled in my stomach whenever I was in his presence.

As per merfolk custom, he kissed my sister's cheek, and she leaned away and tensed.

"Sweet sister," he said to her.

Yuck. I hated it when he referred to us as his sisters. We weren't related and never would be. Poseidon did not bless my father with sons. Triton had taken the orphan Faraall under his wing, mentoring and grooming him. Under my father, Faraall had learned the ways of fighting and defense and had exceeded my father's expectations in all areas. Triton adored the boy, and a deep bond had formed between them. But in spoiling the rotten, little brat, Triton had given Faraall an enormous ego and a temper to match.

Neither my sisters nor I liked the slimy slug. Faraall had been cruel and merciless growing up, torturing my sisters and me, sticking snails under our tops, putting dead jellyfish in our pillows—he'd even killed my sister's pet dugong. Each time my sisters and I had complained to Father, he'd refused to listen to us, as if Faraall were his perfect child, and we were all his whining girls. On Faraall's eighteenth cycle, my father had appointed the jerk second-in-command of his army. Faraall had worked his way to the top, and now my father's army was at his disposal. A dreaded fate for Tritonia's army.

Unlike our father, my sisters and I weren't fooled by Faraall's false charm. But he had everybody else in court, including my father, under his spell.

As the commander turned to me, Nimian put a finger in her mouth, pretending to vomit.

Faraall offered me a kiss with lips like sand. "Enjoy your trip to Shark Bait bar, my beautiful princess?"

I almost choked on his horrible, sulfurous scent mixed with death. Time to find another place to hang out. The idea of his creepy eyes—or those of his soldier spies—watching my every movement made my stomach spin.

The commander pinched my cheek so hard, it stung. "Why so rigid, princess?"

I wanted to wipe that smug smile off his face and yank the shell necklace he kept playing with off his neck and clonk him on the head with it.

"King Triton is about to share wonderful news concerning your future," Faraall added.

More chills scraped along my spine. What the heck did that mean? Why had my father confided in Faraall, rather than speaking to me first? Didn't I deserve to know about my future?

"I hope to share a celebratory goblet of seagrass wine with you after the announcement." Faraall kissed my hand.

Disgust had my stomach roiling. I tried to yank away, but his fingers dug into me. Pain flared in my hands. His strong grip would leave a bruise. His horrible laugh grated along my scales.

"Everything all right?"

I jumped at the sound of the unexpected voice, twirling to face the speaker—a merman. One of the noble's sons—I forgot which one, but Nimian would know. Whoever he was, he smiled at Nimian and me, his gaze drifting across our bodies. Lecherous looks like those were why I didn't like most of the aristocrats in the kingdom. They were always treating the princesses like pieces of meat, born simply for their leering pleasure.

Horrid creep. Now I wasn't sure who was worse: the noble or Faraall.

The seedy appreciation didn't go to waste on Nimian. She fawned like a seahorse trying to impress a mate.

The water between Faraall and me sizzled. Muscles in the commander's arms and chest tightened, curling his back and shoulders forward.

Sweet Poseidon.

I recognized that position. Faraall was about to blow. I'd seen it twice before. One time, he'd beaten up a cocky noble for calling me "sugar." He'd left the poor merman with a broken nose and finger as a reminder. Another time, a soldier under Faraall's command had gotten three days in a cell for saying *hello* to his princess on a royal visit to a barrack. Of course, my father had taken Faraall's side, believing his lies, claiming he'd defended the king's daughters against insults from insolents.

For some reason, the commander thought he owned me. I didn't know why. Not once had I encouraged his behavior or given him the impression I was interested. Far from it. The creep repulsed me...even more so now that I knew he followed and spied on me. Maybe I should blame it on my father. When I reached eighteen moon cycles and came of age to marry, Papa had begun dropping hints about me dating Faraall. How happy it would make him to see his favorite daughter align with his adopted son, he'd said. Several refusals and a few cross words had cleared that idea from my father's plans.

Still, to avoid anyone getting injured, I had to put a stop to the commander's temper. Doing the first thing that came to mind, I put my hands on his chest, stroking it. Using my best feminine wiles, I batted my eyelids, pouted my lips, and stared into Faraall's mud-brown eyes.

"Everything's fine," I told the noble, my gaze locked on the commander's eyes.

Something switched behind Faraall's expression. Was it desire? Approval of my affections? Another scheme? I hoped it wasn't a promise to hurt the noble later.

Bubbles popping beside me told me the merman had continued on his way into the hall.

"Who was that?" the royal army commander growled, staring after the noble, his eyes spitting daggers.

I dropped my hands from Faraall's chest. "Who cares?" My response came out a little quicker than I'd hoped, ruining my attempt to diffuse the tension. "Let him be, brother."

"That's Charm," said my sister, either unaware of the jealousy raging inside Faraall, or purposefully stoking his fires.

Whatever the case, I wished she wouldn't encourage him.

"He has three older brothers, all just as handsome as he is."

Sea god! Shut up, Nimian, you fool.

Faraall's pale features blazed red. "Where does he live?"

"Down by the Tritonian Rim," replied Nimian.

By now, I wanted to knock her on the back of the head. Was she really stupid enough to fall into his trap and divulge those details?

Faraall's eyes sparkled with the promise of pain. "Tell him to stay away from Nyssa, or I'll squash him like a crab."

With that he streaked away in a furious haze of bubbles.

A silent terror squeezed my lungs. Faraall's jealousy and possessiveness worsened by the day. Taura's mother, my aunt, had counseled me to discourage the commander's affections. But that wasn't working. I was at a loss as to how to control the situation. Faraall was a very large and dangerous predator. Even worse than a shark. His unpredictability and rage frightened me to the core.

"Slimy slug," my sister hissed, her gaze on the retreating commander. "He makes my scales crawl!"

Mine, too. The tension Faraall had left behind tightened around me like an octopus's tentacles.

I grabbed my sister by the arm. "Why'd you tell Faraall where the noble lives?"

Nimian let out a mocking laugh and rubbed my arm gently. "Oh, don't worry, big sister. I sent that sniveling Dugong on a wild seaweed chase."

Thank Poseidon.

The water cleared of Faraall's nasty energy, and my body relaxed.

My sister swept a loose strand of hair from my eyes. Any interaction with Faraall left me drained and jittery. Irritating sand grains scratched inside my stomach. My tongue felt numb, and I was unable to string two words together.

"Let's not be late for Father's announcement."

Nimian linked arms with me, tugging me forward, and we flowed into the main hall.

Father's announcement. I'd forgotten all about it. The dread in my stomach thickened at Faraall's smug warning of the wonderful news concerning my future. Whatever pleased the commander was bound to do the opposite for me. Father had best not be planning to put me on duty supervising sniveling, snotty young nobles for a charity initiative. I'd rather do all the work alone than deal with their whining.

A crowd of important merfolk—government officials, top soldiers in the king's army, and all the other noble ranks of court, both male and female—were assembled in the declaration hall. The kingdom of Tritonia respected both sexes equally…unlike some of our human counterparts.

Per mercustom, my sister nodded at the nobles we passed.

Me? I grabbed two pouches full of seagrass wine from a passing servant and downed them both. This earned me condemning glares from the nobles. Screw them. When they leaned in toward each other, nodding, I knew the judgments flowed between them. So, I snatched a few crabsticks, stuffed them in my mouth, and chewed with it wide open. Offended by my mortal sins, the nobles huffed and slithered off.

Good. I didn't care for formality and couldn't tolerate snobs.

Many of the guests floated around the long rows of pews. Servants skittered about, carrying platters of oysters, caviar, seaweed rolls, and more, offering them to the assembled guests. Crystals glowed from the ceiling, casting soft light upon the room. Big bouquets of sea blooms brightened the room. A band played soft orchestra music and drums in the background. Curtains of sea vines draped between the columns.

Janial, one of the servants, held out a platter of caviar for me. "An appetizer, Princess?"

At events like this, my mouth usually watered. But the incident with Faraall had left me hollow and scratchy, like sand had deposited in my gut. I'd only eaten the last starter to piss off the nobles.

"No thank you, Janial," I replied.

The servant smiled and went about her duties. I'd always

had a soft spot in my heart for Janial. She'd been in my father's service for fifteen years. Worked harder than a sea lion trying to score its next meal. Always going above and beyond her duties. When I was a child, Janial had always served me less seaweed because she'd known I hated it, but my mother had insisted I eat it.

"Hurry," said Nimian, eagerly tugging me forward.

The sand in my stomach turned to rocks at finding Faraall waiting by a column, his eyes locked on me, like a predator stalking its prey. He played with the shell on his necklace and grinned.

"Ignore him," said my sister, picking a sea flower from the wall and jamming it into my hair.

I straightened and held my head high, the way my mother had taught me.

Faraall gave me a smug laugh and sailed off, targeting my father by his throne at the head of the room.

Triton, a hulking merman with a long, silver beard and mustache, bushy eyebrows, and an age- and battle-wearied face, greeted his protégé with an arm around his shoulder. Golden wristbands reflected the crystal light as he shifted. He, too, wore the scaled armor, but his were gold, signifying his status as king. A crown of gold adorned with shells, pearls, and starfish sat atop his head. The trident of the merfolk never left his grasp. He always told me he couldn't let it fall into the wrong hands.

I had inherited most of his qualities: blazing violet eyes, strong cheekbones and nose, a fierce will, and stubbornness. From my mother, I had gained empathy and tenderness. Neither encouraged my rebelliousness, but I had my adored aunt to thank for that.

Faraall, like Nimian had done with the nobleman earlier, fawned under the attention from the king. Amazing, how fast the commander's mood changed in the presence of the merking. All smiles and teeth. Relaxed and friendly posture. Nodding at everything my father said. What a barnacle. Sucking the generosity out of my father. Taking advantage of his kindness and compassion.

I wished my father could see Faraall for the vicious shark he was. My sisters and I had tried to tell Papa countless times. Even Mama had put in a few bad words to support us. But Father would not hear of it. Faraall was the glowing son Triton had always dreamed of. My sisters and I were just Faraall's jealous, snitching step-sisters. Nothing we did was going to change that.

Four giant statues of Poseidon watched over the throne room. One, a representation of the sea god with a fish head and a crown, held out a trident in a manner that suggested he was attacking a foe.

I sent out a silent prayer to Poseidon, asking for his help in bringing my papa to see the truth about Faraall. Then I thanked the sea god and glanced back at my father.

"Nyssa," someone called.

I scanned the room and found the sender.

In the corner of the room, away from all the activity, floated Taura and my aunt. Both sipped some of the seagrass wine from sea cucumber pouches. Everyone avoided them like the dark algae plague. Let's just say they were considered the Black Groupers of the family. Like me, they didn't subscribe to all the politics of court. All the fake flattery, arrogance, pretension, backstabbing, and betrayal. That got up more than a few noses. But they were my heroes, and I modeled myself after them. Why should I be like everyone else when they all thought I was a rebellious loser?

"Catch up with you in a moment," I said to Nimian, leaving her side for the comfort of my aunt and cousin's presence.

Aunt Ariel was dressed in a flame-colored corset to

27

match her hair. She always wore bright clothes and makeup to attract attention. Taura, on the other hand, had changed into a softer silver number.

"Nyssa!" My aunt threw one arm around my back and kissed me on the cheek. "Heard you chased away another Sharkrider."

Unlike me, my aunt never concealed her character, and the message she broadcast went out to everyone within a few feet of our vicinity. A few nobles passing by gasped and scurried away at the shocking news.

A thrill chased through me at challenging their prim merworld view.

"Aunt Ariel, you should have seen how fast the Sharkrider swam away," I replied, squeezing her back.

Whenever my cousin, my aunt, and I got together in her chambers, we always laughed about our crazy antics. They and Gellian were the only ones I was comfortable confiding in. Despite going along with my aunt's outburst just then, I really didn't like the nobles knowing my business.

Aunt Ariel let out a big hoot that drew more attention.

Taura's lips twitched with the hint of a smile.

My aunt's finger grazed my chin. "Don't worry, my dear. You'll find the right merman one day. Experiment with as many as you can. Delve into the delights their magnificent bodies offer. Until you find that one that makes your heart sing."

More nobles stared at us. Talk like this was generally shunned in a court environment. But Aunt Ariel never paid them heed or cared who we offended. That was what I loved about her. One day, I wished to be as bold as she was.

"Watch where you're going, would you?" someone snapped close to us, capturing my attention because it sounded remarkably like my sister Aquina.

Yes. I was right. Oysters stained my sister's corset.

Aquina's face was twisted with disgust. A servant furiously brushed at the mess.

Aquina batted away the servant's hands. "Don't touch me." Her tone rose into the petulant territory.

"I'm so...so...sorry, Princess," the poor servant squawked, clearly terrified out of her wits.

My sister made them all nervous. They couldn't look her in the eye or touch her, and they certainly couldn't speak to her without being spoken to first.

"Sea god," Taura said, scowling. "Spoiled brat."

Aunt Ariel swept over to my sister. "Aquina, dear. Decency and civility are the virtues of a great queen."

The servant's gaze flew between both princesses.

This was a tactic my aunt used to calm a situation and take the heat off the servants. Then Aquina would be angrier at Ariel. My aunt always fought on the servant's behalf when it came to the outlandish behavior of some of the nobles and royals.

Aunt Ariel dismissed the servant with a nod and a pat on the elbow. The poor girl scurried away. Aquina glared after the servant as if promising retribution.

"How dare you talk down to me in front of the servants?" Rage inflamed my sister's words.

My aunt leveled the stare from her niece. "I wouldn't have to if you weren't such a merbitch."

My sister recoiled as if she'd been slapped in the face. Previously, my aunt had resorted to such a maneuver when she needed to put my sister in her place. Sea god it was heaven to watch!

I squeezed Taura's arm, waiting for Aquina to explode. Not because I was scared of her, but because I had no doubt she would inflict pain on the servants afterward. I was surprised Father had not tried to set her up with Faraall. They'd be the perfect nasty couple together.

Aquina's lips peeled back, revealing her snarl. "Just wait until I'm queen."

Aunt Ariel smirked. "I will put you in your place then, as I did now, and find amusement in your childish, little tantrums."

A few of the nobles snickered.

"Get out of my way." Aquina shoved past my aunt.

Taura and I giggled as the precious heir of the merrealm stalked through the crowd.

Before I got the chance to congratulate my aunt for teaching my sister a lesson in humility, my father's voice boomed in my mind. "Nyssa. Please join me."

Sea god. The big announcement was about to be declared.

CHAPTER 4

"*B*etter go," I said, giving Taura and Aunt Ariel a quick hug.

"Good luck," said my aunt. "You'll need it."

I didn't want to dwell on what she meant. My stomach was already curling with dread.

A few strokes carried me to my papa's side, where he reclined in his clam-shaped coral throne.

"Hello, Papa." I kissed him on the cheek.

Father didn't return the gesture like he normally did. Usually, he would greet me with a warm embrace and a kiss. Tell me about his day. Ask about mine. Share a laugh with me. Something about him was off. His stiff posture and tight jaw. Normally, his eyes were filled with love, but they were distant and dark.

"Ah, Nyssa," he said, his voice brittle. "There'll be no more flitting off to bars whenever you like."

Shellfish. Faraall had told my father what I'd been up to.

His violet eyes flashed green for an instant. They sometimes did that, depending on the light emitted by the crystal lamps.

"From now on, you will have plenty of new duties," said Father.

Duties? What was he talking about?

"But, Father," I said.

He waved away my protest with a flick of his hand. "Soon, you shall have little ones to care for. Then you cannot just go running off whenever you like."

Merbabies? I wasn't planning on having those for at least another five cycles when I'd settled down. Why was my father being so cold and stony? This wasn't like him at all.

"Father, what are you talking about?" I glanced at my mother.

She shrugged, as if she had no idea, either.

"I don't even have a mate," I said. "Haven't even been looking. Merbabies are a long way off."

This was one of the reasons everyone said I wasn't princess material. Because I spoke back to my father. Why should I be like everyone else? I respected everyone's right to conduct themselves as they saw fit.

The king gave a hand command, and another horn sounded, cutting off any further protest I wished to make.

Shellfish.

That was the signal for everyone to take their places because the announcement was about to commence. Bubbles swarmed as everyone scattered to the row of pews. Tension rippled through the water, stirring my nerves over what my father was about to declare.

Royal procedure dictated the heir to stand beside him. Then me, as the next youngest, followed by Nimian and Lativa. For some reason, Faraall joined us, smiling at me like a whale about to catch a school of fish.

Sea god, he makes me sick.

"Thank you, everyone, for coming on such short notice."

My father's message cast out across the room, and as it

reached all the nobles, they nodded their acknowledgement to the king.

When my father's gaze flicked to me, I knew I was in trouble. He'd looked at me the same way when I'd accidentally broken a rare shell from his collection. But what was he mad about? Because I'd ventured out to the coral reef? Gosh, what a crime.

"Today is a very special day for me," he said, a glimmer of green registering in his eyes. "It is not often I get to announce an engagement."

The crowd erupted into applause that echoed in my head.

I spluttered and almost choked. *What?* But my father hadn't said a word about it. Usually, rumors of these types of announcements spread like wildfire. Nothing was sacred in this kingdom. Especially when Nimian was such a nosey, little eavesdropper.

My father made a wide, sweeping motion. "Lativa, my youngest, will be marrying her school sweetheart, Gandry."

Warmth spread through my chest. What wonderful news. Lativa and Gandry had dated since they'd been fifteen. They still couldn't take their eyes off each other. They were always together—practically joined at the hip. It made me a little sick, to be honest. But I was still thrilled by this announcement because they truly were perfect for each other.

Gandry sailed up to his fiancée. Lativa squealed and kissed him.

The crowd went wild with applause. I did, too, throwing in a whistle, and a few nobles stared at me as if I'd grown sharp teeth or something. But I just ignored them as usual. It wasn't every day I got to celebrate such wonderful news, and I wasn't going to let them spoil it for me.

Triton motioned for everyone to calm down, and a quiet fell on the assembly. "I am a proud father today, not once, but twice, as I also announce the engagement of my second eldest daughter Nyssa."

What the heck? Was this a joke? I wasn't engaged.

The king pressed his massive hands together. "For years, I have desired a union between my adopted son and dear general, Faraall, with one of my children. Today I am proud to announce this one."

Shock stole the warmth from my blood. *Shellfish no*. Not Faraall. He was six years older than I was and one of the most horrid people in Tritonia. Of all the merfolk—not him. I'd rather be digested in the belly of a whale.

An uneasy silence fell on the hall. Confused glances jumped between the members of the gathering, especially between my mother, Nimian, and Lativa. Aquina's cackle scratched in my mind.

A drowning sensation captured my gut. This couldn't be happening. I didn't want to marry anyone. My father knew that.

"But, Father," I protested. "Under merfolk law, I am entitled to choose a mate. Why am I not being allowed the same consideration as my sisters?"

For the third time, my father's eyes flickered green. "You have come of age," he replied, his voice stained with impatience, as if I were a little child again refusing to go to bed. "I have chosen for you."

My mother's eyes were round with shock. "Husband," she said, touching the king's arm.

Triton held up his hand to silence her, too. When the king had made up his mind, his wife did not argue further; she supported her husband.

Nimian's gaze met mine. Her face was a mask of revulsion and helplessness. Probably the exact same expression I carried. She reached out for me and clasped my hands. I squeezed her fingers for dear life.

The commander pranced up to the throne. He snatched my wrist from my sister and crushed it. My limbs felt heavy as he dragged me beside him. A wicked grin of success plastered Faraall's face as he dug his fingers into my skin.

I yelped and pulled back. Didn't my father love me enough to speak with me about it before handing me over to some horrid brute? The pain of betrayal stung deep.

"Father." My voice cracked as I sent only my father this message. "This isn't right. I won't marry this pig." I dared not think about how enraged such a comment would make the commander.

"Nyssa." My father's hand clamped down on my wrist. "I wish for you to take my place after I'm gone. Rule with Faraall by your side. Together, you will be a force to be reckoned with."

"But, Father?" Aquina intervened. "I am the heir."

"Succession is not always a birthright in the merrealm." My father reminded her of how he acquired the throne.

Upon announcing his heir, my grandfather had skipped his eldest son and had appointed my father the crown. After my grandfather's death, a two-year war had raged between his sons for control of the merrealm. To end the bloodshed and destruction, my father had divided the kingdom into two realms. He ruled Tritonia and gave Fable, another ocean away, to his brother. Growing up and witnessing the horrors of war on my father's kingdom, I did not want to be starting another between my sister and me.

I shook my hand free. "I cannot accept. Aquina is the rightful heir."

My father waved his great, big hand through the water between us. "You're not ready, Aquina. If you cannot show kindness and consideration to our servants, how will you rule a realm? Putting you on the throne would be like appointing my brother all over again."

I didn't disagree with my father's words. My uncle was a cruel merman. Treated his subjects terribly, and destroyed the beautiful reefs and caverns of his kingdom. Many had defected from his realm, finding refuge in ours.

"Father?" Aquina pleaded. "Don't do this."

"Hush, child," said my father. "It is decided."

Aquina shot Papa a look icier than mountains in White-peaks. She pushed forward in a hasty swim, her head high and elbows tucked closer to her body. When she passed a servant carrying a tray, she swept the items off it, and they floated to the ground.

Even with all this in mind, the idea of raising a family with Faraall made me want to vomit. Was my father going senile? He knew I disliked the commander as much as I hated eating sea spinach.

My father's brows relaxed. His palms found my shoulders. "The merfolk want a leader who loves and protects them. Aquina is incapable of that."

Now, I suddenly understood why my father favored me. He'd been grooming me. All those talks on politics. Determining my position on the other realms of Haven. Testing me on what projects within the kingdom needed the most attention. Sending me to the hospitals to read and entertain the sick merchildren. It had all been a test. To see if I was worthy of being queen.

Poseidon. How could I have been so blind? Damn me for being the level-headed one. While I might have one day considered taking over my father's role, I refused to marry Faraall.

Speaking of the slimy slug, his hand found the curve of my back and yanked me to his chest. Horror rattled up my spine as his lips attacked mine, and he thrust his tongue deep into my throat, choking me. I tried yanking free, but he was much bigger and stronger, and he crushed me to him even more.

My father held his arms out, palms upward. "Well. Cheer."

The crowd clapped with the enthusiasm of a tuna cornered by an orca.

Queasiness buried into me. I had to get away from him. The kiss, his touch, being near him—it all repulsed me to the core. Acting on instinct, I dug my nails into the commander's gills. He roared and pushed me away. The menacing curl of Faraall's lip had my stomach seizing. His hand hovered beside my face, as if he was about to slap me. But I flung out my tail and caught him in the sea pouch, where his dick and balls tucked inside his tail. He keeled over, hugging his stomach.

"I will not marry this pig," I spat at my father, not caring if my outburst alarmed the nobles. "Look at the way he degrades me in front of your court."

Green captured my father's scales and eyes. He leaped to a vertical position and snared my wrist. "You will do as I say."

"My king," my mother tried again to appeal to my father.

"Silence, woman," my father roared.

My mother fell back onto her throne.

Everybody gaped. My father had never raised his voice to his wife in all his years of ruling. Especially not at a ceremony.

No. I shook my head. This couldn't be real. It had to be a nightmare. I rubbed my eyes, hoping to wake from it. But when I pulled my hands away, everything was still the same. The frozen, uncomfortable stares of the nobles and my sisters. Faraall's snarl, flashing his teeth.

My whole world twisted out of control, and I struggled to breathe. What was wrong with my father? Faraall had tried to strike me. An insult in front of the merfolk. Hitting a female was forbidden in our culture. Punishable by a jail sentence. Striking a member of the royal family meant death. Why hadn't my father ordered his guards to chain up the commander for his impertinent crime? What was wrong with my papa's scales and eyes? Was he ill? Normally, when he was angry, his scales flushed bright red.

Wait a moment. Something on Faraall's chest caught my attention. The shell on his necklace glowed green. The exact same color displayed in my father's eyes. What was that? It looked like magic.

Then it hit me like a powerful surf wave, bowling me over.

Only one person possessed that kind of power, and the green remnants gave me a clue as to who that might be. The Sea Witch. More evidence supported my theory. The sulfurous stench on Faraall, which I'd noticed outside of the hall when he'd leaned in to kiss me. The entirety of the Sea Witch's lands and her cave in particular reeked of it.

My stupid sister Nimian had once confessed to me that she'd made a pact with the Sea Witch to gain the heart of a merman she fancied. It had cost her five years off her life cycle. The deal hadn't been worth it because the spell had only lasted for three moon cycles. Stupid fool! But the merman she'd put the spell on had had the greenish luminescence in his eyes throughout the spell's duration.

Yes. This was definitely the Sea Witch's doing. I felt it in my heart. Faraall's betrayal pierced deeper than the witch's treason. But why hadn't the spell bewitched everyone else in the room, including me?

I glared at the commander. He'd always sought control. First of the army. Then by winning my father's favor and ear. I was willing to bet my life he aimed for the crown, too. In marrying me, he would be one step closer if that was his goal.

Oh, my poor papa! His life and the safety of the sea realm

were in danger. Many of the nobles and army generals would die before seeing Faraall on the throne. I couldn't let that happen. It was high time for me to leave, find the Sea Witch, and either destroy the spell Faraall had used on my father, or make a new deal. I just had to wait for the right opportunity.

Faraall kept a tight grip on my waist as the nobles came up to the platform to pay their respects. His touch made my skin crawl.

"Such wondrous news, Princess Nyssa," someone said.

I didn't even bother to look in the speaker's direction. Instead, I stared across the room, hatching a scheme to sneak away from my repulsive fiancé and leave the palace.

"You certainly kept that secret locked tight," the well-wisher joked.

The commander's laugh scratched down each bone in my spine and made me shiver.

"Thank you for your kind words." He thumped his chest with his fist in the merfolk's customary greeting.

If anyone had any knowledge of these plans, it was Nimian. She eavesdropped and spied on everyone for the latest court gossip.

I sent a message to her. "Did you know of this?"

She furiously shook her head. "Not a word."

My head spun. I wasn't sure if the dizziness had been caused by the two pouches of wine, or by my world slipping from my grasp. Either way, I needed to get out of the room for some fresh air.

"Excuse me," I said to my fiancé.

He grabbed my arm and dug his fingers in. "Where do you think you're going? This party is in honor of our engagement."

"I need to go to the ladies' room," I blurted.

"Oh, Nyssa," complained my father. "That's no way for a princess to talk."

Faraall's hand clamped down on my behind, and I yelped at his filthy touch. "Do not worry, Father. I'll make a woman of her."

Was everyone here going mad? Could they not see I was being forced into this union and denied my right to choose my mate?

The commander's lips grazed my cheek, and I closed my eyes and swallowed hard, wishing for this torture to end.

"Come straight back, my sweet princess." He slapped my behind.

I was out of there before he could change his mind.

My heart clenched as I glanced at my parents. There was a possibility I might not return from the Sea Witch's cave. Many rumors spoke of merfolk never coming home after visiting her. No one knew what happened to those merfolk. My father never sent anyone to investigate, either. He said that if the merfolk were foolish enough to bargain with the witch, then that was that. I accepted my fate, whatever it might be; I had to try to save my father and the kingdom.

Before Faraall could change his mind, I propelled myself out of the room, not looking back. My tail pounded with fury, casting me through the corridors of the palace with such speed that I bumped into one of the nobles and even knocked over a servant.

"Sorry," I shouted in my mind, but I did not stop.

I didn't return to my room to grab any of my belongings. Time didn't permit such luxuries. If I wanted to make it to the Sea Witch in time, I had to get as much distance between Faraall—and those soldiers within the army who were loyal to him—as I could before they came after me. No one was forcing me to marry a man I detested. Nor were they getting in my way of saving my father and my kingdom.

CHAPTER 5

*M*y vision adjusted to the water turned murky. The witch's realm was a wasteland. Decaying plants rippled in the current. Skeletons of fish and sea creatures scattered about the cave's entrance. Sulfur hung strong in the water, clogging up my gills, and I could hardly breathe. It was as if death had sucked all the oxygen from the water. Red eyes blinked from all around. Sea eels. The witch's spies.

Ice hardened in my chest.

Keep going, Nyssa. You have to save your father.

Up ahead, the witch's cave awaited—an opening like the mouth of a shark with sharp teeth and jagged edges, enough to scare anyone away. But many had ventured here to make deals with her.

Expulsions of yellowed water blasted me, and I yelped, clutching my chest. This place gave me the creeps. It was safe to say that it probably frightened and deterred most creatures from visiting.

Something hissed in my ear, and I spun to face two eels. They darted forward, winding around me, and I gasped and shot upward and away from them. I glanced over my

41

shoulder as I shot away. Their mouths curled up into smiles, and they entwined their bodies.

In no time, I reached the jagged cave entrance. My shaky hands gripped the edge. The rock was so sharp, it almost cut my skin, so I pulled away.

"Hello, Sea Witch," I shouted over the lump of what felt like sand wedged in my throat. "Are you home?"

A sinister laugh boomed in my head.

"Come in, Princess," said a voice more slippery than a mollusk. "I've been waiting for you."

How had she known I was coming? Did she have some magic crystal ball or something? Or was she just psychic?

My mind begged me not to go. But my heart said otherwise. And I never followed my head.

Entering the cave, I wrapped my arms tighter around my waist. My muscles tensed in anticipation of a nasty surprise. Every nerve in me was on high alert.

More eyes watched me as I passed. Dead seaweed dangled from the ceiling, grazing my skin, and I yelped.

Poseidon. I had to get a grip, or I'd run back home screaming. A failure. Doomed to marry Faraall. Destined for a painful, torturous existence.

A magical green flame sat in a hearth, boiling the contents of a pot. All sorts of treasures rested in grooves along one wall. Jewelry, combs, daggers, sashes—even locks of hair tied with a bow. I recalled Nimian saying she'd had to trade locks of her hair for her spell.

The Sea Witch sat on a chair made of whalebones. "Welcome, Princess." She smiled, revealing long, sharp teeth like those of a dragon fish.

Suddenly, I understood why all the bones were scattered about the place. Perhaps she killed all the fools who offered her silly deals.

She lunged off her chair to circle me, fluttering her necklace of sharks' teeth. The witch's movements were graceful and slow, intended to frighten me. Slender, with long arms and a long neck and octopus tentacles instead of a fish tail, she stood a good foot taller than I did. Her dark-red hair was shaped like a conical shell and held in place by three horns on her headdress. Unlike mermaids, she didn't wear anything to cover her breasts, and her immodesty had me blushing, shying away with discomfort.

Breathing was close to impossible. Terror had my lungs seizing. Yet, they were bursting for air.

The two eels from outside the cave slithered around the Sea Witch, and she stroked them as if they were pets.

"What can I help you with, dear princess?"

My voice stuck in my throat. *Shellfish*. This wasn't the time to be losing my ability to speak.

"What did you do to my father?" I stuttered.

She smiled, unveiling a mouthful of shiny, spiky teeth. But this was no ordinary smile. It was the creepy kind—one that would have scared the stripes off a leopard shark. This was a game to her.

"A little bewitching spell," she said, admiring her claws. "That handsome commander of yours paid the highest price for it."

I moved forward a few inches. "What price?"

"A dark spell of this nature requires something valuable, a sacrifice, like a soul or your life." The words slammed into my mind.

Faraall was still alive, so he must have traded his soul. Shellfish. Did that mean I'd have to pay an even higher price to remove the spell on my father?

"Why my father?" I asked. "Why not bewitch the whole kingdom? The merfolk could rise up against the king."

"True." The witch ran a finger along one of the bones forming her great seat. "Dark magic is a trade. One for one.

43

For the commander to control a whole kingdom...well, he'd have to sacrifice many. Such a thing would not have gone unnoticed."

That idea sent shivers streaming through me.

"What will it take for me to get my father's freedom back?" I said, holding my chin high.

The witch's busty chest heaved from laughter.

What was so funny? She had just put a spell on the king. Under merfolk law, that was an act of treason. But something told me this witch did not follow the laws of the sea. She was like me. A lone fish. Operating under her own rules. Getting her to agree to my request was going to take a big sacrifice on my part. I felt it like a hollow pit in my stomach.

"Why would I ever do that?" Her mocking voice pounded in my brain. "Many moon cycles ago, your ancestors stole the source of my power and banished me to this wasteland. For centuries, I fed on the slugs to survive."

As if outraged for their master, her two eels hissed and snapped at me.

I backed away, hitting a wall hard, knocking the wind out of me. Pain sliced down my back. I rubbed what I could reach.

When the pain subsided a little, allowing me to talk, I muttered, "How did you get your magic back?"

She gestured with wide arms. "By the grace of Poseidon."

The eels opened their mouths, as if they shared a laugh with her.

Yeah, right. Pull my other fin. Why would the god of the sea do that? Legend had it the witch stole the souls of innocent merfolk who bargained with her and fed off the energy, increasing her power.

The witch squirmed over to her brewing potion. She grabbed a jar from a shelf carved out of coral, from which she plucked out the dried eyeballs of some poor creature. The potion sparked as she tossed them into it.

It felt like thousands of mollusks crawled along my skin, and I shivered. The sulfur in the water was beginning to burn my lungs and gills.

Green flashed in the witch's eyes as she turned to me. "I would consider removing the spell on your father in exchange for the pearl of Aluria."

I gasped, and my hands flew to my mouth. The pearl was a gift from the sea god himself. It was the heart of the ocean. It powered my father's magical trident—granted the merfolk the ability to control the water. Without it, we were power-less. Taking the pearl was akin to condemning all my people. I didn't want that on my conscience. But how else would I save my father?

"There must be another way," I said, my head starting to spin and my eyes burning from all the sulfur.

"Afraid not, my princess." The sea witch turned her back on me and threw dried clams in her bubbling pot.

Well, if I was going to give it to her, first, I wanted to know what she planned to do with it. "Why do you want it?"

She collected a skewer of shrimps from a shelf and shoved it over her fire. It cooked in an instant, and my eyes widened.

"To restore my power," she said before taking a bite of her meal.

What a predicament I found myself in. Wed Faraall and leave my father and people as his hostages. Or hand over the sea realm's ultimate source of power to the evil Sea Witch and free my father, while condemning my people. Dooming all the sea creatures and the entire ocean to a life of despair and pain. Both options were just as depressing, and neither appealed to me.

The sea witch stared at me, waiting for my decision.

"Very well," I lied, steadying myself on a rock because the sulfur made me feel lightheaded.

Part of me had agreed to the deal just to escape her cave. *Poseidon.* I could hardly breathe. My eyes, gills, and throat itched and burned.

The witch held out her hand. Against my better judgment, I shook it. Green magic swirled around our wrists, sealing the deal, branding me with a tattoo of my promise.

But I had no intention of delivering the pearl. This witch was not going to steal my people's treasure. Somehow, I would find another way to save my father and my people... before it was too late. Even if it meant having to make another pact with a witch on land.

"Goodbye, sweet princess." The witch waved her hideous hands. "I look forward to our next meeting."

I bet you do, I thought. Pity our next meeting was going to be bittersweet, ending in me piercing her through the heart with my father's trident.

Red eyes blinked as I sped out of the cave. Shadows shifted in the murk. Slimy things grazed my skin, and I jerked away from their touch.

My tail carried me away as fast as it could. The instant I exited the dense and sulfurous water, my head cleared of the fog that had settled over it. With it came a torrent of guilt. What had I done? The witch's contracts were binding. The only way to get out of one was for her or me to die. I was fin deep in some serious seaweed. To get out of this mess I needed some help, and I didn't have a clue who to turn to.

The skin on my back pinched as if someone watched me. I scanned the area but could barely see a thing in the murk, despite my highly attuned mervision. It was probably one of Faraall's spies, come to bring me back to the engagement celebration. Well, I wasn't going back there.

Rubbing my arms, I sped away, heading for my little rock

by the shore. Whenever my mind spun with confusion, I'd go there to think. Something about the salty breeze and the lapping water cleared my mind, allowing me to analyze my thoughts.

Sometime later, I emerged from the depths, taking a deep breath of fresh air. Whenever merfolk surfaced from the water, our gills deactivated, and our nose and mouth took over. I really needed the break, too. My gills stung from the sulfur in the Sea Witch's cave. I cleansed them with water and rubbed my fingers along the slits to remove any gunk stuck to them. Shellfish, it hurt. But I didn't want any part of that evil witch remaining on me. She'd made me feel dirty and contaminated. When I was finished, I leaned against the rock, inhaling deeply, letting the clean air invigorate and refresh my lungs.

Right now, I didn't want to think about the deal I'd just made with the witch. I just needed to clear my head. Too much had just happened in such a short space of time. My mind tumbled with the weight of it all. The betrothal to a man I detested. My future stolen from me. The spell holding my father's mind captive. A new threat to the sea kingdom.

Crustaceans plastered to my rock grazed my scales as I pulled myself onto its edge. It didn't hurt one bit because merfolk's skin was thicker and far tougher than humans. Thank the sea god for that.

Sunlight warmed my skin and made my silver scales tinge with orange. I stretched my arms behind me and leaned back, absorbing the warmth from the heated rock. It stripped away the coldness the witch had filled me with. The end of my tail dangled in the water.

I rolled onto my belly and watched some sea lions on a rock thirty feet from me. They dived into the water, spun around, and climbed back up, having the time of their lives.

Their antics made me smile. Such a simple and happy life. Not complicated by pressures like mine was.

Poseidon. For one moment, couldn't I just forget about everything? Didn't seem like it. I guessed I had to face the inevitable sometime.

How the heck was I going to beat Faraall and the witch? The commander had the merfolk army by his side. With the Sea Witch's magic, he also controlled my father and the kingdom. I had no one. The odds were seriously stacked against me. An invisible hand tightened around my throat.

Say I did steal my father's pearl and used it as bait for the witch. Going back to the palace was risky. Guards were posted all over the place. My father never left his trident alone. Somehow, I'd have to distract him long enough for me to remove the pearl from it…or steal the weapon itself. But I wouldn't have long before Papa realized it was missing. Alarms would be sounded. The palace scoured for the thief. If I was found with it, then what?

Imprisonment? That would give Faraall the chance to move on to my next sister. I couldn't do that to Nimian. There had to be another way.

All of a sudden, my fin prickled with the subtle detection of a shift in the currents around me. This was one of the many gifts the sea god had blessed the merfolk with. I sat up and slipped back into the water.

I made a few clicks, sending out my sonar to find out what was approaching. Then I moved to three more positions along the rock and discharged more clicks. In a few moments, my first echo returned to me. A picture formed in my mind. Two mermen armed with tridents headed for my rock pool. But why? Then the rest of my echoes hit me in quick succession. Another two soldiers from the east. Two more to the west.

My pulse drummed in my head. *Shellfish*. They were coming from every direction.

My gut tightened. This wasn't a friendly visit. My itching scales told me Faraall was behind this. Surrounding the rock in all directions was a classic merfolk attack strategy. My father had taught me about many such things. All bets pointed to the commander's men having tracked me down to return me to the palace. But how'd they find me? After I'd left the cave, I'd felt something watching me. Had they followed me?

A slimy sensation licked my back as I played over scenarios in my head to escape. There was nowhere for me to hide. Going into the water left me vulnerable. I wasn't getting off this rock without a fight. Against trained soldiers. My stomach locked tight, I crawled all the way onto the rock. They couldn't detect me above water. Technically, I had the vantage point. But they had the weapons.

Most merfolk, given enough time to respond, were able to escape a predator by manipulating the water around them…unless they were caught in a surprise attack, which occasionally happened. For some reason, Poseidon had granted royalty with stronger powers than the average merfolk. I didn't know why. Neither did my father. But every day, I thanked the sea god for the gifts he'd blessed us with.

My stomach dropped as Faraall and the five soldiers surfaced at different locations around my rock. Several of the mersoldiers sneered at me. One growled as if he were an animal. Another smiled like an orca about to devour a seal. Traitors.

CHAPTER 6

The commander lifted himself onto the platform beside me, and I shifted backward, ready to dive into the sea if need be.

At first, he tried the doting fiancé act. "My sweet princess, you left without saying goodbye."

Although he tried to project heartbreak in his voice, I didn't believe a word. He touched his chest where his heart should be but wasn't—because he didn't have one.

"Your father's heart grieves, along with mine, at the fact that you ruined the celebration he spent weeks planning."

My father had known about this for weeks? Exactly how long had Faraall been planning this? My stomach boiled at how conniving this merman apparently could be.

Faraall held out his hand. "Come with me at once, my sweet. All the guests are waiting for you back at our engagement party." With his other hand, he toyed with his flickering green necklace.

"I will never marry you." My words came out harsher than I'd expected. Something about Faraall just stirred up a fierce riptide in me.

Faraall's eyes and face darkened. "Yes, you will." He lashed out with incredible speed and seized my upper arm.

I kicked with my fin, but he grabbed the end of it.

The commander glanced at each of his men. "Do not fight me, my sweet. You will not win."

I wrestled with all my might, but he was much bigger and stronger, and he pinned me by the neck. Pain blazed down my throat as he squeezed it, demonstrating his power.

"Mersoldiers," I spat out. "Arrest him at once for threatening your princess."

They laughed in my face. One spat on the rock.

"We don't take orders from you, Princess," said one, sealing my fate.

Traitors!

Faraall's grip tightened, and I clawed at him.

"I know you went to the Sea Witch. Making deals behind my back. How could you betray me?"

He was one to talk!

"What did you expect?" I snarled at him. "You put a spell on my father to force me to marry you."

Angry heat surged in me, and I grabbed the shell around his neck. I screamed as it burned me, and blisters formed on my hands.

Faraall and his creeps snickered at me.

My lungs burned for air, my throat for release. The magical shell had rendered my hands useless. If I didn't do something and fast, the commander was going to kill me. The only way I was getting free was with a distraction. So, I called upon the sea to rise up and strike him down. Every part of my body buzzed with magic. I felt the waves crash in my blood, the tide rolling in and out, the destruction of stormy seas, the deeper and powerful currents warming and cooling the ocean, all of it flowing through me. Raw power at my disposal.

Shadows danced above me as a wave curled overhead. It crashed down on Faraall with such force that his grip on me released. It carried him away, allowing me to dive into the ocean and make a run for it.

My plan? Go ashore in search of a powerful witch. One who could erase the spell on my father.

The last words I heard as I got a head start were, "Get back here, you bitch, or I'll kill you."

I'd never moved so fast in my life. My heart was practically exploding out of my chest from how furiously I pushed my body. Staying close to the surface, I skirted around a school of hawkfish, choking back the pain in my burned hands.

Five hundred feet separated my rock from the shore. Thanks to the wave I rode, I might just be able to make it to land and hide. First, I had to check how far away my pursuers were. This required emitting a few aquablasts. This was a technique merfolk and dolphins used to detect objects in the murky depths of the ocean. A pressure built in my mind as I spun around. Sacs in my nose spat out three clicks, each one reverberating through me. The returning echo tingled in my jaw some moments later. It formed a picture in my mind of my seven pursuers, some fifty leagues behind me, all spread out in a fan.

Shellfish. Merman like Faraall and his soldiers were much faster than I was. Speed increased with size in merfolk.

The sea called to me, offering her rescue, and I accepted, using my powers to push me even faster through the water. I'd made it a few hundred feet when a suction slowed me down and dragged me backward. A glance behind revealed a whirlpool had captured hold of me. Faraall's handiwork, no doubt. With all my might. I twisted to get free, but the eddy held me firmly in its grip.

Faraall's menacing voice diced through my thoughts. "Got

you now, you little bitch."

His words turned my stomach to mush. Once again, I summoned the sea to free me from his grasp. A vortex circled in front of me, small at first, then expanding, and I launched it at the commander. The force propelled him and his men backward twenty feet.

Even from far away, I could see Faraall's eyes burning like fire.

A small explosion from his hands rocketed me into a spin. I tumbled, as if caught in a powerful wave, hitting the ground, scraping, dragging, spinning. Air expelled from my lungs from one nasty crack on a rock.

The commander's cruel laugh echoed in my mind.

Over and over, he blasted with his merpowers, rendering it impossible for me to escape. The waves spat me out onto the sand face-first. Pain cracked down my back and neck. Dazed, I fought to clear black dots from my vision. Despite this, I summoned my aquanium, a transformation from mermaid into human form. Water poured in my cells to keep them moisturized. Tingles swept across me as the change took hold of me. Scales vanished on my tail. My fin reshaped into feet, stripping away the last of my ocean body. Aching and tired from using my powers, I crawled along the sand.

Water splashed behind me as the mermen emerged from the sea.

"Get her," barked Faraall.

Moments later, a trident jabbed me in the back.

Fire boiled in the pit of my stomach. I wasn't even close to being finished, and I kicked him backward. His angered cries raged in my mind as I staggered away.

I didn't get far. The commander's soldiers surrounded me.

"Stop, Princess," said one. "There's nowhere left to run."

I refused to give in. My legs wobbled, carrying me up the

beach. Being on land was so different from swimming in water. It felt much heavier, almost as if my body were being dragged into the earth itself. During previous times I'd visited land, it often took a while for me to find my balance.

Everywhere ached like hell, making walking difficult. Black dots peppered my vision. Using my sea gifts had weakened me. I needed to rest. But I'd be damned if I let Faraall beat me so easily.

I heard the soldiers' slurping footsteps on the sand behind me.

"Bring her to me," said Faraall.

My hobble turned into a run. I disappeared into the beach shrubs along the dunes. But I stumbled, and one of the soldiers caught me, grabbing me in a headlock and dragging me back to the sand.

I didn't have any fight left in me. The pain in my back blinded me. My power drained. I'd die before I married the commander...kill him before I saw him on the throne.

"One more chance, Princess," said Faraall, his naked body dripping with water. "Marry me, or I'll kill your father."

The air was ripped from my lungs. I couldn't get a word out even if I wanted to.

"Tie her up." The commander's tone carried venom, the kind promising repercussions.

Two of the soldiers removed the shark leather belts they wore. One bound my hands behind my back. The other fastened me to a tree, and I kicked at him with all my might. He smashed my head against the tree. Everything rocked before me. Sand flicked up into my face. The bastard had kicked it at me. I spat it out and snarled.

Shadows danced over me as the commander stood over me, his small dick twitching...probably with glee. Teeth bared, I lashed out with my leg, but that only made him laugh.

He grabbed my cheeks between his thumb and fingers and squeezed. "Your feistiness excites me, my sweet princess. I should take you here."

He grabbed his stirring, sardine-sized cock, licked my cheek, and I shivered.

"Rather than wait for our wedding night," he added.

Pig. I yanked my face free. How dare he speak to me like that? If he touched me inappropriately, I'd kill him in his sleep. I wriggled as he ran his fingers down my chest, circling my nipples beneath my corset. The nerve of him touching me in such a fashion. Behavior like his was against Tritonian law. Mermaids were to be respected.

"Perhaps I'll even share you with my men."

Ice ran down my spine as he traced my jaw.

"Let them fuck you up the ass until you bleed." He sneered, his face inches from mine.

Disgusting pig. This was the man my father had chosen as the commander of the sea army. I spat in Faraall's face again in response to his degrading words.

He slapped me hard across the cheek, and I whimpered.

Tears stung my eyes, but I wasn't going to let him see how he'd hurt and offended me. I bit back my pain and fear, glaring at the soldiers. What worms they were for daring to follow this slimy slug. *Poseidon help their souls.* They'd be damned for eternity for this...along with their leader.

Faraall's words made me even more determined to save my father. I imagined the slimy slug in prison, rotting away for his crimes, and me smiling as I swam away from him.

The commander stroked my face with the back of his hand. "For years, I've desired you," he said. "And the Sea Witch has promised I'll have you forever once the king is dead. But I cannot have you interfere or ruin my plans in the meantime."

What did that mean? He was going to leave me here to shrivel up and die?

"Get the pirates," he barked.

Pirates? What business did he have with them?

***

BY THE TIME the sun commenced its decent below the horizon, three pirates had arrived by ship, and Faraall stood, still stark naked, negotiating with them.

Word in Tritonia had spread about how these barbarians of the oceans sold merfolk and other creatures to the highest bidder, including the Sultan of Utaara, who had purchased tiger shifters for his menagerie.

"I need you to confine the princess for me until I send word," Faraall snarled as if the pirates took orders from him.

The pirate with the long beard and dark eyes held his palms up. "I don't want no war with the king of Tritonia."

Gold filled the spots in his mouth where his teeth were missing. Jewels twinkled in the oversized buckle on his belt. A triangular-shaped hat sat atop his head. Long boots crept up his legs beneath his pants.

Faraall touched the shell on his necklace, and it glimmered green. "The sea king is under my command now." A vicious edge scored his words. "Take her, or start a war with me."

I wriggled against my restraints. "What in the name of the sea god is happening here?"

The head pirate turned to me. Uncertainty flashed in his eyes. He glanced at his associates, and they nodded.

"Very well." Their leader gestured with a flick of his flingers. "Load her in da' cart with the rest of 'em."

Two pirates started for me.

My breaths raced faster than Sharkriders competing at a race. Every part of me trembled. Where were they taking me? Who were they selling me to? Serving another was not the fate life had in store for me. Had the sea god abandoned me because I'd rejected my royal duties?

I narrowed my eyes at the commander, even more determined to destroy him for his cruelty.

"No," I shouted, digging grooves in the sand as I kicked my feet. "I am the second daughter of the sea king. What you're about to do is against the laws of Tritonia!"

The wind picked up, as if raging along with my blood. Sand lashed at the pirates, soldiers, and Faraall as if sent by the sea god himself. They shielded their eyes with their forearms.

"We don't abide by no laws, love," said one of the pirates, stomping over to me and cutting at my bindings with a knife. He reeked of rum and urine. Unlike the head pirate, his teeth were blackened and rotting.

"You might want to gag her," said Faraall. "She's very mouthy. Not an attractive quality in a bride."

"Don't worry," said the pirate. "We'll knock 'at out of her."

Oh, yeah? Over my dead body!

Faraall seized the man's wrist and twisted it back, producing a loud snap. "Do not lay a hand on her. She is mine. If anyone touches he sea pearl, I will flay them and dine on their innards. You hear me?"

The pirate whimpered and nodded.

Faraall shoved him aside.

Two pirates went to the aid of their comrade.

Another one came for me. My foot shot out and cracked him in the shoulder. The pirate stumbled back and fell onto his behind.

"Bitch," he said, scrambling across the sand with his

dagger raised. He grabbed the back of my neck and ran the filthy tip of the knife along my cheek. Hadn't he learned from his friend's mistake?

My entire body vibrated from the drumming of my heartbeat. I closed my eyes, praying to the sea king for mercy.

Three tritons aimed at the pirate's throat.

"Knock her out," growled Faraall, "and she'll be less trouble for you."

My eyes snapped open. What did that mean?

A pirate pulled out a long flute from where he'd had it tucked into his sash. He put his thin lips to it and blew. Something shot out of the end of the device. The sharp dart jabbed me in the neck. Hot fluid coursed through my veins.

"What was that?" I demanded.

Faraall leaned down beside me and grabbed the sides of my head. "Goodbye for now, sweet princess. I look forward to our wedding night. To fucking you every night until your sweet seal pearl is bruised and sore."

I wanted to say *Shellfish off, you creep*, but my vision blurred. Dizziness hit me, and I moaned, leaning my head against the tree. His spinning figure crouched beside me. Nausea struck, and I retched, but nothing came up.

"Let go of me," I moaned, swaying to one side and sagging against the tree.

"Shhh, Princess, don't fight it," whispered the commander, stroking my hair. "Soon, we will reunite. Then I will be your new master."

My insides rolled at his disgusting words and plans. "When my father finds, out he'll…" My throat was so dry, I could barely get a word out.

That was all I remembered before I passed out.

CHAPTER 7

*S*omeone stroked my hair, humming a tune, calling me back from slumber. I didn't recognize the voice. A male. Perhaps a merangel. Sea god, I hoped so.

Panic hit my throat. Where was I? In a cell somewhere? A prisoner of the pirates? I tried to kick and scratch, but my limbs wouldn't move. Probably a residual effect of the drug the pirates had injected me with. My head ached, and I could barely pull a thought together. Heavy eyelids weighed down on me, but I pried them open. A hazy cloud hung over my vision.

One figure huddled beside me. Another two sat opposite me. Darkness filled the space beyond them.

All of us lay on some sort of rocking platform. The pungent smell of piss and shit affronted me, and I gagged. Cool air filled with the distant call of the sea grazed my skin. I knew this because merfolk bodies were sensitive to water and air currents, and were able to guide us back to the sea, or to water where required.

"Captain, she's awake," whispered the figure closest to me.

His warm, deep, happy voice reminded me of my father's…when he wasn't under a spell.

The person moved his hand from my hair to brush my face, setting my flesh ablaze against the cool of the night.

I squeezed his hand, holding him tight.

"Great," snapped another man. "Now the princess can order us around."

He knew I was a princess? That meant he knew about the color of my scales. The men surrounding me must be well educated.

"That's enough, soldier," said a third man, with a firmer and more commanding voice that stirred something inside me. "Show your princess the respect she deserves."

Your princess? They were soldiers? Merfolk? My heart soared. Thank the sea god! Being with my kind brought me some comfort.

The grumpy merman huffed and shifted in his position.

Shivers racked my body, but not from the cold. Merfolks' bodies were acclimatized to cooler temperatures. The shaking must have been caused by the drug wearing off. Similar symptoms took hold of me when I had a really bad hangover.

"Oh, my sweet princess. How do you fare?" The merman leaning over me cupped my cheek.

Energy danced along my skin, the sweetest sensation I'd ever experienced. A merman had not touched me like that before, and I quivered.

His concern moved me. Back in the kingdom, I'd fought for my independence and freedom from the strict confines of royal protocol. So, when I really needed an ear or a shoulder to cry on, few were ever there for me, not even my sisters. But for once, I desired to bask in such attention like my pet flounder fish did when I stroked his sides.

"Water," I said, my throat dry and burning.

My scales, buried beneath my human flesh, called out for the touch of the sweet liquid.

"I'm afraid we're several hours away from water," he said, sending my hopes floating to the surface like a dead fish.

The merman lifted my head, resting it on his thigh. Poseidon, he was so warm. The heat leached into me, spreading all the way to my toes. He continued to caress my hair, soothing me, helping me relax. His flesh against mine created an electric current, and my skin blazed. It sparked my hand to twitch, and when I tried to flex my fingers, they moved.

Thank the sea god!

I groped around with my hand, finding something curved and hard, then exploring, poking it. Continuing, my fingers traced what felt like a merman's chest, up his neck, then along his strong jaw.

"Having fun, Princess?" The merman's voice was full of jest and made me feel at ease, despite the circumstances I found myself in.

I liked him immediately...whoever he was.

"Sorry," I said, pulling my hand away and pressing it to my stomach.

Heat scaled across my cheeks. I hadn't meant to do that. But it had felt incredible, and my fingers itched to do it again...only when my vision cleared. Sea god. Why did I always say and do inappropriate things with mermen?

"Touch me anytime you want." He brushed hair from my face.

"Stop getting familiar with the princess, Nemo," barked the one who'd sounded like a leader.

"She's not well and needs attention, Captain," said Nemo.

My own heart spun in circles at having someone care for me. I hadn't realized I'd wanted that before. Sure, I was a princess, pampered with food, clothes, and all the finest things the sea kingdom could offer. But I never acted spoiled like my sisters. Never bossed the servants around with my demands. That must have been why my father respected me more than he did my siblings. I didn't rely on my privileges. To be tended to by this merman was like nothing I'd ever felt before—exhilarating, uplifting, and frightening at the same time… After all, I didn't know him, nor he me.

We stayed like that for some time. My vision cleared slower than a turtle crawling along the beach. But as it did, it allowed me a better view of my surroundings. Bars lined either side of our enclosure—a cage of some sort. Not very big, either. Just large enough to fit us all. Horses drew the cage in a black box on wheels. I believed the humans called it a "wagon." The iron lock on the door rattled with each step.

More wagons trailed behind us, carrying other creatures, such as fae, wolves, tigers, and bear shifters. My heart tightened for all of them. Then a blazing heat consumed me. How could those pirates do this? They had no heart!

Somehow, we were going to get out of there. I didn't know how or when, but I was determined we'd make our escape. The survivor in me crouched, waiting for the right moment.

I rubbed my temples, and it helped eliminate more of the cloudiness from my eyes. Head leaned back, I lay there, drinking the merman above me all in. A giant, with a great, big chest, and thighs as thick as a dolphin's body. His skin was tanned but clammy, as if he was sick. With eyes slanted slightly, he reminded me of the islander merfolk who lived between my father's kingdom and my uncle's. Nemo, or Nemes, his comrades called him, greeted me with a dazzling smile that scorched me to the core. On his left shoulder, he wore the tattoo of the mersoldiers: a trident with waves along the middle. His dark hair was cropped, and stubble lined his chin.

I tried to sit up, but my head pounded, so he lifted me and

positioned me beside him. *Sea god*. I loved the way he looked after me. Next to him, I felt safe, as if my worries had vanished.

I rested my head against the bars, scoping out the other two mermen. One of them, a brooding and dark merman with cinnamon-colored skin, stood in the corner. He had eyes like amber, and a body like the sea god himself, and he also brandished a mersoldier's tattoo. He too looked sweaty and a little pale, and he shivered. My eyes dipped to his nakedness. Dark curls decorated the top of his manhood. But I didn't dwell there long with them all staring at me. I didn't want to seem like a creepy pervert.

Had they all been given the drug, too?

"Nemes," said the grouchy one, not looking at me, "I think we've all had enough of your little crush."

Heat claimed my cheeks. Nemo had a crush on me? Well, he was sweet. Built like the Sharkriders, but he didn't talk degradingly to me like those rough mermen usually did. Nemo had a face like a smiling, happy god—exactly the kind of guy I could fall for.

"Give it a rest, Gill," the leader said. "You're being a guppy."

I giggled into my hand. "Guppy" was the word merfolk used when someone was immature or acting like a jerk.

"Fuck off, Fin," Gill growled.

Ahh. The leader's name was Fin. Suited him. Golden like the sun, his hair and skin contrasted with his rich blue eyes, reminiscent of crystal waters in the bay. Blond stubble lined his chin. His hair was cropped to his shoulders but gelled back with sticky extract, most likely from a dead sea snail. His shoulder bore the mark of a captain in the merarmy.

Gill glared at Fin. Then he pretended to bow to me, but it was more a mockery of a bow than anything.

"Guppy," I murmured.

His gaze trailed up my legs, over my hips, grazed over my breasts, then dipped back to the jewel between my legs.

Suddenly, the realization of my nakedness below hit me, and I curled my legs up to my chest. *Poseidon.* My father would kill these three for looking upon me naked. Exactly how long had I been cooped up with them? Had they been leering at me this whole time? Obviously, they didn't have the decency to avert their gaze from a helpless princess.

"Don't worry, Princess. We've all seen each other nude," he said.

But his tone did nothing to console me; in fact, he sounded as if he were trying to rub it in.

Jerk. The ashamed and irritated fire burning through my insides could ignite the entire forest our wagon passed through.

"Gill," Fin barked.

Gill closed his eyes. "Why should I be nice to the family that forced me into the military for life?"

Ah. So he had a grudge against my family. Why had he been forced into life-long service? My father always let the mermen choose. Something about this story didn't sit right with me. But now wasn't the time to delve into that topic. Maybe when he'd calmed down or we'd gotten to know each other a little better.

Nemo rubbed my back, but it didn't help relax me. I felt raw, like a pearl commencing its journey inside a clam, being polished by grains of sand. Still, I leaned into him for comfort, hugging my legs to my chest.

Well, if I was nude, it was only fair I enjoyed the view. After all, they were delicious, well-built, and tall. Just my type.

Gill let out an exquisite, gruff laugh as my gaze dipped to his member. "Like what you see, Princess?"

"As a matter of fact, I do." Sea god. There I went again. Not thinking before I spoke.

Gill huffed and looked away. Hah! He liked to challenge people, but couldn't handle a serve in return.

Nemo gave me a *hand slap* to say well done.

By now, my head had cleared of the ache, and I could think clearly. "Where are the pirates taking us?"

"Princess," Fin said, "we're being taken to the black market in the Darkwoods, where they intend to trade us."

The words scraped my throat raw. Farrall hadn't wanted me traded. He'd demanded the pirates contain me until he'd finished his plans. Had the pirates betrayed him as he had done my father?

I had to do something about this. There was no way my men, or the rest of the shifters were being traded.

Holding on to the bars, I pulled myself to my feet. "You there. Pirate," I called out to the man steering the wagon.

"Yes, my love," he growled, not even turning to look at me.

"I'm the second daughter of King Triton," I declared. "You will release me and all the creatures held captive this instant. My father will reward you handsomely for your efforts."

The pirate cackled—it was a horrible sound that grated on my every nerve and set fire to my insides.

"King Triton ain't himself these days," the man said. "The commander rules the sea throne. I answer to him, not you."

I slumped to the wooden floor of the wagon. What I needed was to figure out how Faraall fit into this whole scheme.

"Don't waste your time, my sweet princess," said Fin, warming my hands in his. "They're paid soldiers of fortune. They care not for our plight. Or the plight of the other shifters."

He had an air of aristocracy about him. The way he

addressed me told me he was well-educated. Of high birth, perhaps. Possibly a member of one of the noble families. But what was a noble doing with soldiers? Normally, they only took strategic and elevated positions like that of general, not lower ranks such as captain, which would force them to mingle with the everyday soldiers.

"Shadow, the panther in the next wagon." Fin was treated to a growl as he said the man's name. "He was kidnapped from his tea plantation days ago, along with all his workers. An attempt to earn their freedom by offering to pay off the pirates failed. Sadly, he discovered, these pirates don't bargain. They want power and control, and to expand their empire."

My chest did a one-two punch at Shadow's courage and love for his workers. But then it sagged at our plight. *Shellfish.* We had to get out of here before we were split up and traded to sick slugs who kept us in cages like dogs.

"They will pay for this." My voice came out hoarse.

Fin shuffled to my side, and little fireworks popped in my chest as his leg grazed mine. "Princess, did you get caught in the pirates' net, too?"

"No." I said, biting my lip to hold back the anger and hurt of Faraall's betrayal. "Is that how you ended up here?"

Fin stared at his hands and nodded. "We were searching for Gill's missing sister. We tracked down clues that led to the bay in Shell Cove. The pirates were moored there, unloading creatures from their ships."

News that the pirates were trafficking shifters hit like a hammer blow to the chest. How many merfolk and shifters had they kidnapped? Their poor families must have been worried sick.

"We snuck aboard, searching for her." A dismayed tone crept into Fin's voice. "We found her trapped in a cage. But when we tried to free her, we were apprehended."

I glanced at Gill. Shadows crept across his expression.

"We lost her when they unloaded us," Fin said, "and three separate caravans departed Shell Cove. One headed north into Utaara. Ours headed northeast, toward the Darkwoods. A final caravan headed west into Tritonia and into the voodoo witch territory."

How horrible. *Poor Gill.* "I'm so sorry," I whispered, reaching out to squeeze his hand, but he yanked it away.

Fin hung his head. "I let my men down."

Nemo stretched his arm over my shoulder, and clamped his huge hand on Fin's shoulder. "Don't say that. It was an accident."

My heart twisted with anger at those filthy pirates setting traps for my people. One day, I would seek vengeance on the no-good bandits. Feed them to the sharks, along with Faraall, until there was no more of them left to scourge my father's kingdom or the other realms of Haven.

I fiddled with my fingers, unsure whether to admit how I'd ended up in the wagon. These three mermen were soldiers. Would they believe their leader had given me to the pirates?

"Princess?" pressed Fin, refusing to give up.

"I was kidnapped by the commander." My voice was tiny, like that of a child. "But he insisted the pirates keep me until he finished his business."

Nemo both squeezed and rocked me at the same time. "No way. He would never do that."

White-hot heat coursed through my veins. Not at what Nemo had said or over the fact that he seemed to only see the good in people. But because this morning my whole world had been turned upside down. I'd been betrothed to a man I loathed, a man who held my father under his spell like a puppet. Then that same man had tossed me to the pirates. Sea god knew what the slimy slug was doing to Nimian. The ache in my chest threatened to split me in two. I held back tears on the verge of spilling.

Gill glared at Nemo. "Nemes, you see way too much good in merfolk, especially the ones who don't deserve it."

Fin grabbed my hand and stroked it. "I want to hear your story."

Even Gill stared at me, suddenly interested in what I had to say.

My hands clenched into fists, and my nails dug into my palms as I recounted everything that had happened. By the end of my tale, I couldn't control my emotions. All the fear, hatred, anger, and betrayal stung like the cut of a knife and rushed out in hot, bitter tears.

Nemo pulled me onto his lap and cuddled me. I held him tightly, sobbing. Terrified to let go. Terrified over what was going to happen with the pirates and beyond that. Terrified to think about what would happen to my father the merfolk, and Tritonia.

"I never liked that guppy," said Gill.

I glanced at him.

"I saw him beat soldiers," Gill went on. "Bully them into silence. Torture enemies. Wouldn't put it past him to do all this."

Fin supported Gill's story with a nod.

I put a hand to my mouth. Torture was against my father's rules. Triton and my grandfather both believed in upholding the rights of prisoners by giving them fair trials and storing them in reasonable accommodations, not dirty, dark, rank prison cells. We were a peaceful race, not savages like some of the human and shifter clans. But I wasn't surprised by Gill's admission. The sting of the commander's betrayal dug even deeper into my heart, as if it had been pierced by a swordfish's upper jaw.

Gill shrugged and returned to watching the forest pass by.

"When I told the generals, they accused me of making up lies about a senior-ranked official and put me on cleaning duties."

"You never told us that," Nemo said.

Again, Gill shrugged.

No wonder he didn't like merfolk of authority. The nerve of them to punish him for telling the truth. This was why I hated politics and snotty nobles. They thought they were better than everyone else. Once I saved my father from Faraall's evil grasp, I was going to attend the next war council, where I'd have a word with them about how Gill had been treated. If I heard any more stories like his, so help me sea god, there'd be hell to pay.

"I'm sorry the generals treated you like that," I mumbled.

He stared at me as if my words surprised him. His hard countenance softened a little. The disdain behind his eyes vanished. Hopefully, he would begin to see me and the royals in a new light, and not as the guppies he'd believed we were.

Nemo ruffled Gill's dark hair and gave him a big hug.

"Princess," said Fin.

Sea god! A delicious shiver trickled through me every time he called me by my title. I could lie there beside him, listening to him say my name all day long.

"What can we do to help our great king?" he asked.

For a moment there, I was lost in his crystal-blue eyes. I sat up straight, snapping out of a daze. But even then, I found it hard to look away from his beautiful gaze. His eyes were mesmerizing...they reminded me of home and filled me with a deep longing for the ocean.

"The Sea witch will remove the spell from my father if I give her the pearl of Aluria," I replied, staring at my hands, lost as to how I was even going to steal it from my father, and unsure if I wanted to.

What was worse? My father under a spell? Or all the

powers the sea god had granted my father—and all the merkings before him—in the hands of an evil witch? That kind of power in her possession would be deadly. What might she do to the merfolk? Turn our waters into a barren wasteland? Use us as slaves? Right now, my father kept her somewhat in check, but without his full powers, he would be defenseless.

Fin squeezed my hands. "We must not let that happen, Princess."

I nodded, on the brink of tears again. Shellfish, I was such a baby!

"Don't cry, Princess." Nemo gave me one of his warm, uplifting cuddles again, and I snuggled into him. "There's always a way. In fact—"

His voice was so cheerful I wondered if anything ever got him down.

"I know one," he finished.

"What?" I shifted to face him.

"There are two pearls," he said.

"I've never heard that," I said, seriously doubting this was true.

"The gods say there must always be balance in Haven," Nemo explained. "Light and dark. Good and evil. Everything has an opposite."

This was all news to me. Still, it made sense. I grabbed his arm. "Where can we find this other pearl?"

I almost got lost in the dark-brown eyes surveying me.

"My grandmother used to be the keeper of the dark pearl, until it was stolen by a collector of magical items."

I felt the blood drain from my face. Shellfish. Why did my day keep getting worse? We had to find that pearl. My father must not die. I would not survive if I ended up as Faraall's property, available for him to rape every night.

Gill gave Nemo a friendly kick in his meaty leg. "Your grandma isn't much of a keeper."

"Leave my grandma out of it." Nemo nudged Gill with his shoulder.

"Do I have to separate you two children?" Fin joked along with them.

I giggled at their frivolity. Their humor took my mind off my worries. Their company was a stark contrast to the palace, where everything was always serious and boring... except for Taura and my aunt's sense of humor.

The gaiety didn't last long. Fin turned to me and grabbed my hands again. "Wherever the pearl may be, I pledge my allegiance to help you find it."

My heart raced with joy. What a relief to know I wouldn't be alone in my search. To be honest, I didn't even know where to begin to look. But Nemo's information was invaluable.

He wriggled closer and squeezed me. "Count me in, too."

Fin and Nemo both looked to Gill for his vow.

Gill shifted as if put on the spot. "What about my sister?"

"We must help the king first," Fin said to his soldier. "Then he can help hunt down every last one of the pirates."

"If Kaya's traded before then, we'll never find her," snapped Gill.

The rawness of his statement scratched in my gut. I couldn't imagine his pain. I didn't know what I'd do if one of my sisters had been kidnapped. Go insane with worry probably. We couldn't leave his kin to be traded.

I crawled over to him and held his hand. "We'll find her. I promise."

For some reason, my words pushed him away as if he didn't like showing emotions, or he felt abandoned by his men. Either way, I refused to move.

A shiver tore through Gill, and he clutched his stomach, wincing as if he suffered cramps. Right now, he was in no state to save his sister. By the paleness of all three of the mermen's scales, I knew they'd been out of water for at least two days. Merfolk had a limited ability to change into human form, but we couldn't go without contact with water for longer than three days. Anything beyond that would kill us. Didn't the pirates know that?

"You're sick," I said, stroking the dark blemishes under his eyes with my thumbs. "You need water."

He moaned at my touch. I put the front of my wrist to his forehead, and it burned as if he had a fever. His lips were cracked and dry like the other two mersoldiers' were. His tender scales were hard to the touch. All signs of severe dehydration. Gill didn't answer me. I got the impression he was in too much pain. Over the years, I'd visited the merhospital many times, telling stories to the sick children, feeding them, singing to them. I knew the signs of illness well.

"Soon, Princess," Nemo said. "Don't you worry."

Wow. How could he stay so positive in a time like this? Nothing seemed to bother him. But if the mersoldiers didn't get water soon, they'd perish.

Nemo put his thick, hulking arm around my shoulder and pressed me to his side. Poseidon, it felt good being in his embrace. My mind soared like the eagles floating above us. So far, I hadn't embarrassed myself... Well, besides feeling him up...and you couldn't blame a girl for doing that, could you?

"How do we get out of here?" I asked.

"Princess." The way Gill snarled at me made me wonder what had I done to him to deserve his malice. "We aren't getting out of here."

His words slapped me in the face and I recoiled. Why was he always so bleak?

"We're going to be sold to the highest bidder," Gill said. "To some rich, fat fucker who will use us for his pleasure and make us do tricks, like catch a gold coin from the bottom of his pool. Considering how exquisite you are, he'll probably rape you."

I gasped, and my elbows banged into the iron bars. Would my father send a rescue party out to find me and return me to the kingdom? If he was under Faraall's control, would Triton even notice me missing? My worst fears hit me with the force of a dolphin's body slam.

"Way to go, you guppy," said Nemo, punching Gill hard in the thigh.

"The princess needed a reality check," said Gill. "We're not embarking on a shopping trip for corsets."

Both of Nemo's arms surrounded me. This time, it did little to bring solace to my mind. Gill was right. We were in deep shellfish.

CHAPTER 8

The wagon stopped all of a sudden, and I sat up, along with the mermen. My heart froze. Had we arrived at our final destination?

I glanced around. It was pitch black under the canopy of the forest. My eyes were accustomed to the murkiness underwater, not out of it. But I made out all the trees rustling in the breeze and the furry animals scurrying on branches. A bird with big, round eyes blinked at me and hooted from atop its perch.

"What's the fuckin' hold up?" grumbled the pirate in the wagon behind us.

The horse towing our wagon took advantage of the break to take a big dump, and the smell of it hit me, causing me to gag.

"Pipe the fuck down," growled the head pirate, the one who'd negotiated with Faraall. "I'm takin' a piss."

More groans flew through the train of wagons.

One of the pirates, a fat, bald one, his belly bursting out of the cloth covering his hairy chest, grunted at me. "You're quite beautiful. Look at that silver hair and violet eyes. Bet you'll fetch a handsome price." He poked me through the bars and laughed, showing off his rotting teeth.

Fin grabbed his finger and cracked it. "You will address the crown princess of the sea kingdom with the reverence a mermaid of her rank commands."

My heart fluttered at him standing up for me. This was all new to me. Back in the palace, no one had dared to address me in such a deriding fashion. If one of the nobles tried to belittle me for my behavior, I shone the honesty torch back at them. That usually shut them up or drove them away.

The pirate huffed, untied his pants, pulled out his shriveled dick, and urinated on the wheel of our wagon. "I ain't gotta do nothing, Your Highness." His laugh was just as horrid as the head pirate's was.

What a guppy. Few people ever disrespected me to my face. Was that how humans treated each other? If so, I was glad I didn't live on land.

Nemo scratched the air, trying to snare the pirate. "You'll apologize for addressing my princess like that and for degrading her with your filth."

"Try your best," the pirate taunted, snorting.

Nemo slammed against the bars, rocking the whole cart, and I squeezed the bars just in case it tipped over.

"If I ever get out of here, I'll…" Nemo began.

"You'll what?" the pirate goaded. "Think we'll sell you for meat. You're not worth trading for labor."

Before Nemo exploded again and rocked the cart onto its side, injuring one of us, I took his hand.

"Thank you for defending my honor," I said softly. "But this is a fight you can't win."

Nemo backed away. I'd wounded his pride. I shouldn't have. I didn't dismiss Fin. Guilt flooded through me. But as a princess, I had to ensure the safety of my people. No one had ever stood up for me. They hadn't needed to. My chest warmed with appreciation for his efforts.

He spat at the pirate's feet. "One day, I'll kill you."

The pirate took a big tree branch out from beneath the seat at the front of the wagon, and he jabbed Nemo in the gut with it. The hulking merman didn't even flinch, so the pirate took out his dagger and slashed the merman's leg. Nemo hobbled backward, clutching his wound.

Fin dragged Nemo to the back of the cage and pushed him to his knees.

My whole body iced over. I hated the sight of blood. Even after all the hospital visits, I still couldn't stomach it. Fighting the nausea, I pressed a hand to my mouth.

Sea god, give me strength.

I tried to think of anything but Nemo's wound, while Fin tended to it, tearing some material off the pirate's flag soaring above us. The leader secured it around Nemo's leg and tied it up.

Already, I had a strong impression of the mermen. Fin, the calm, reasonable diplomat who cared for his men and their safety. Nemo, the happy-go-lucky spirit who would defend my honor and tend to me. Gill, the strong, silent type who had some serious coral to grind and whose eyes never missed a beat.

"This should stop the bleeding for now," Fin said, hauling me from my thoughts. "But you'll need water to heal."

Because merfolk had the ability to shift between legs and fins, we also possessed the ability of advanced healing, but only in the presence of water. If we could find a way to escape and get to a river or other body of water, then Nemo's cut would stand a good chance of healing.

"Princess." Nemo took my hand.

My mother always said I had to be strong for the ill children. That I could never show them my fear, pity, or sadness.

She'd said that if I did, I'd be delivering the kiss of death to them. So, I always kept my smile bright, letting my joy and my love shine on them and keep them in good spirits. I decided to do the same for Nemo.

"Yes?" I asked.

"We're going to get you home safely, okay?"

Nemo's promise kept rolling around inside my skull. I held on to it with all my hope. Ending up as some rich merchant's slave was not going to be my fate. I had more to give to the world. If Poseidon chose to save me, I swore this very day, I'd take my duties as a princess more seriously.

Out of the stillness of the night, a loud noise, like a siren, blared. The first time, the sound caught the pirates' attention. The second time, their expressions tightened with fear.

Poseidon had heard my prayer!

"What the fuck is that?" shouted the head pirate.

"Dunno," replied the one who had slashed Nemo. "But my whiskers are twanging with danger. We better clear out real quick."

The horn blasted again, and this time, the timbre was deeper and lasted a bit longer. All the shifters in the other wagons growled or moaned. Those in their animal form stalked along the edges of their cage, suddenly alert and on edge. Even the horses whinnied nervously, fidgeting and pawing at the ground.

Tension coiled around my lungs like one of the Sea witch 's eels. What in Haven was going on?

The head pirate climbed back onto the cart, sat in his seat, and whipped the reins. Tossing their heads back and chewing at their bits, the horses stomped forward. The wagon creaked as it jolted forward, rolling across the well-worn path in the forest. I braced myself, holding on to the bars.

Something shrieked in the canopy above, startling me,

and I jumped. Nemo wrapped one arm around me, crushing me to him, but not even his warmth could chase away my mounting concern.

The shifters' complaints grew louder. Tigers chewed at the bars and scratched at the wood. Wolves howled, as if calling to someone. Panthers kicked at the bars, as if trying to bust them down.

"Shut them up, would ya?" barked the head pirate.

The other pirates took out long sticks and beat at the cages, trying to scare the shifters into submission, but this only made them go crazier.

My heart pounded from all the commotion. Something was setting them off, but I couldn't see or hear a thing. Merfolk's hearing wasn't the best. I sent out a sonar blast into the forest. The echo returned, telling me we were surrounded by a band of humans and shifters were coming at us from every angle.

Then I heard it. Hooves. Footsteps. Giant wings flapping. To my left, fire exploded, setting a pirate alight. He screamed and fell backward off his wagon.

Fin and Gill leaped to their feet on weak, shaky legs, searching the canopy, no doubt looking for the source of the flames. Gill's stance was wide and ready for attack. Both had clearly seen war before. Instinct must have told them another was on its way.

My muscles tensed. Something was about to happen.

A shrill scream cut through all the commotion, silencing everything. Something heavy thudded on the ground thirty feet into the forest ahead. Leaves rustled as something moved through trees.

The wagon suddenly swerved, and we all lost our balance, rolling onto each other. Shrieks flew from the horses. They bucked, trying to get free from their restraints. My heart constricted for them. I hated seeing animals in peril. Our cabin jolted all over the place, sending me crashing into Fin. He wrapped a muscled arm around my shoulder to hold me steady. My whole body buzzed from the connection.

My gaze flew to the source of the horses' terror.

Shellfish.

A dragon.

Despite its frightening appearance, it was one of the most beautiful creatures I'd ever beheld—covered in green and aqua scales like the merfolk. Two horns protruded from its skull. It opened its mouth and shrieked, revealing bone-crushing teeth. A man in a dark cape rode atop the beasts back.

Shifters whined. The pirates cursed.

The merman holding me pushed me behind him. Fin. I held on to his arm. His pulse raced beneath my touch.

"Get him," ordered the man in the cape, pointing at the head pirate.

The dragon stomped forward, snatched the pirate in his teeth, and crunched on his body before swallowing it in one gulp.

Nemo raised a fist. "Damn, you stole my glory, Fire Breath. But I'm so happy."

"Are you crazy?" I snapped. "We're next."

"If we are," said Nemo, taking my hand in his, "this was the perfect vengeance. And the best way to go out."

Why was he so happy that we were about to die? That was just twisted. There was nothing pleasant about being crushed to death in a dragon's jaws.

Panic clawed at my throat. I held on to Fin for dear life.

More caped men poured out of the trees. Some jumped onto the backs of wagons, picking at the locks with little bits of metal. Others surrounded the pirates, who plucked their swords from their scabbards. Metal clashed as swords beat together, spitting sparks that illuminated the night. Pirates shrieked and groaned as swords plunged into their bellies. Bodies slumped to the ground.

"Don't let them get away," shouted the dragon rider.

The beast responded, chasing the fleeing pirates through the forest.

I flinched at every bone-snapping sound that emanated from its great jaws.

"Oh, thank you," said a released elf, grabbing one of the caped men in a hug.

"Don't thank me," he growled. "Just get out."

The caped crusaders were freeing us. But why? Who were they?

Another of them approached our wagon with his sword raised. He smashed the hilt on the lock on the door, and it broke into pieces and thumped to the ground. The iron door creaked as he yanked it open for us.

"Gill," said the caped man in a husky voice. "That you?"

The man took off his hood, revealing a face and neck scarred from too many battles. I supposed he was handsome in a rough way. His dark-brown eyes were the color of the soil of the forest. He had a square face framed by heavy, brooding brows. Slightly crooked lips lifted in a smirk. Dark stubble coated his chin and jaw. The more I examined him, the more I came to admire him.

"Blade," said Gill, grabbing the man's offered hand. "Shit. You're the last person I'd expect to run into here."

Blade? What kind of name was that? Who was this mysterious stranger who had come to our rescue?

Gill sat on the edge of the wagon and slid off. When he hit the ground, he groaned, the sound telling me his joints were sore and weak, a side effect of his scales drying out. No doubt he was probably experiencing a headache, dizziness, and aching muscles, too. Humans suffered the same symptoms when dehydrated, but merfolk felt them ten times as hard because we lived in water.

"Getting a bit old, are you, my friend?" Blade nicked Gill on the shoulder with a fist. "Bit too slow? That how you got caught?"

"They took my sister." Gill's words were coated with enough venom to kill the collector. "We were investigating her disappearance."

Blade frowned and put his hand on Gill's shoulder. "Sorry to hear that, my friend."

Fin climbed down slowly, clearly weak and shaky. "Come, Princess," he said, ever the gentleman, offering me a hand.

"No, you're exhausted," I said, climbing down myself.

No one ever helped me navigate anything back home, and that wasn't about to change now. I wasn't a baby anymore. Nor was I a helpless princess. I could take care of myself. Even though the thought of being lost in this strange world both excited and terrified me at the same time.

"Wait," Fin said to Nemo. "Let me help you."

He took one of the giant's hand, and I took the other, and we worked together, gently easing him onto the ground.

Nemo had lost a bit of blood. The combination of that and the dehydration seemed to have zapped him of most of his energy, and he leaned against the cage for support.

My gaze panned to the handsome rescuer. "Who do I have to thank for saving us?"

"Apologies, Your Highness," said Gill.

His sarcastic tone earned him a slap on the back of the head from Nemo.

"This is Blade," Gill went on. "Trust me. You don't want to know him. shadow assassins aren't known for their integrity."

A shadow assassin? What the hell was someone who killed for a living doing freeing us? Did he do it out of the goodness of his heart? Or was someone paying him to free us? Either was I was grateful.

"Hey!" Blade pressed his hands to his breast. "Are you still pissed that I beat you at poker?"

Gilled nudged Blade with his elbow. "You stole my boat."

Gill had a boat? Wow. I loved sailing. That elevated him one bar in the sexy contest. But he had a long way to go after the way he'd treated me.

"I won it fairly and squarely." Blade traced his finger along my collarbone. "In fact, I win a lot of boats. The sale of them affords me a lifestyle filled with delicious women."

His gaze dipped to my nakedness, and I crossed my legs, shifting to stand behind Nemo.

"Eyes up here," Nemo told the assassin, pointing his finger at his eye level, then at Blade's.

Gill laughed. The deep, rich sound reached to the core of me, stroking something buried within me, and I stepped backward, a little alarmed at my reaction. I didn't like this guppy, yet, he did something to me, called to a hidden darkness inside me.

"Highness? As in a merprincess?" Blade's eyes glimmered with flirtation as he shifted around Nemo to take my hand and lift it to his lips. "I eat beauties like you for breakfast."

A blaze spread across my cheeks from his backhanded compliment. He reminded me of the forward Sharkrider from Shark Bait bar. Such intensity made me even more nervous in his company.

"That's enough of that," Nemo said, brushing away Blade's hand as if he were jealous.

Cute. Sweet. I giggled, loving all the attention. "So many males fighting over me."

They all stared at me as if surprised by my statement.

Shellfish. Fin in the mouth disease. Fin in the mouth! I

cringed, thinking how arrogant I must have sounded. *Just let me crawl under a sea rock and hide. Forever!*

"I've got a bad habit of doing that," I mumbled. "So." I tried changing the topic. "Why would someone who kills for a living save us from pirates?"

Blade examined me as if imagining which sex position he wanted to take me in. "I'm part of the resistance. Fighting back the scourge consuming Haven. The pirates are kidnapping creatures from every realm and delivering them to the collector."

"Not the same collector who stole Nemo's granny's dark pearl?" Gill asked.

Blade rubbed his stubble. "Probably. The collector gathers magical artifacts and talismans and trades them to the highest bidder." He gestured at me. "Including beauties like you and ogres like these."

He ruffled Gill's hair, and the merman punched the assassin in his arm.

This collector had to be stopped. Countless more shifters might be taken if she wasn't. How many families and lives would she destroy? No more! Not if I had anything to say about it. Though sea god knew I didn't need anything else on my shoulders to worry about.

Again, Blade's gaze trailed down the length of my legs.

Fin placed a hand on Blade's shoulder. "Please, treat the princess with the respect she deserves."

Thank you! It was nice to know that Fin and Nemo both had my back.

"Shall I get the lady some clothes?" Blade said.

"Yes, please," I squeaked, burning with so much humiliation, I swore I lost half the water in my cells.

Blade's gaze devoured me one final time before he left to scavenge among the chests atop the pirates' wagons.

His associates, whom I assumed might also be assassins,

handed out blankets to the shifters they'd removed from their cages. One man was rummaging through a chest and pulled out some goblets, which he filled with what I assumed was wine or rum, and then he passed them around.

Some moments later, Blade returned with a bundle of clothes and boots piled in his arms. "Put these on, my friends." He smiled, wagged his eyebrows, and glanced at the pile.

I noticed all the men's clothes, including jerkins, long-sleeved blouses, leather pants, and boots, were on top. That left my dress on the bottom. I wagered he'd arranged them that way on purpose so he could examine me while the others collected their clothes. My suspicions were confirmed when he smirked at me the whole time the mersoldiers picked through the pile.

Nemo caught Blade staring at my breasts and grabbed Blade's arm and growled, "Eyes up here."

Blade laughed him off. What a rogue. I supposed I should have liked him. He reminded me of the kind of characters haunting Shark Bait bar. But then again, I'd never been in this position before today, vulnerable and oh-so-naked. The sight of a nude mermaid was probably a real turn-on.

"Lucky last," said Blade, beckoning me with a little wave of his fingers.

I rolled my eyes. He was definitely too brazen for my liking.

When I stepped forward to collect my clothes, I accidentally tripped on something and fell to my knees. My hands flew out to cushion my fall. But instead of hitting the ground, they found Blade's thighs.

Damn. Well, this is awkward.

There I was, crouched between his legs, my face in his crotch, looking like a two-bit floozy.

He chuckled and said, "We can get acquainted later tonight if you'd like."

Mortified, I burned hotter than the sea witch's cauldron.

Poseidon, I was making myself look like such an idiot today! Gill, Fin, and Nemo must have thought I was such a spoiled fool. Cooped up in the palace, having my hair and nails done, my skin exfoliated with coral, servants waiting on me all day. It wasn't like that at all. Maybe for my sisters. Not me. I never wanted to be pampered brats like they were.

Nemo rescued me, and he wobbled as he lifted me to my feet.

"Thanks," I said, flicking hair from my face and snatching the clothes from Blade's waiting arms, then stalking behind the wagon to put them on.

Shellfish. Trust me to do something embarrassing in front of another handsome male. What was wrong with me? Why did they always turn me to mush?

Blade had selected a plum silk bodice with leather braids, a white chemise with long sleeves, and a mustard-colored skirt. To my surprise, each item fit perfectly. I huffed. Clearly, he wasn't lying when he said he ate beauties like me. No doubt, he had stripped many a dress off a young woman. Either that, or he'd memorized my measurements while leering at me.

When I returned to the group, their conversation ceased, and they all panned me up and down. Even Gill, who normally ignored me, gaped at me.

Fin smiled. "You look beautiful, Princess."

Nemo thumped him in the chest.

Fin groaned. Normally, a blow like that probably wouldn't hurt. But when his skin and scales were tender, it would have hurt like a mother fish.

"As your commanding officer," Fin said, gritting his teeth, "I order you not to do that again."

Nemo smiled like a pleased shark.

"Listen," said Blade. "I'd love to stick around and share a rum with you all. Maybe get the princess drunk. But I've got a date."

Scoundrel! Checking me out and flirting with me, all the while knowing he had plans with another female later.

"Can I get you a few horses to carry you back to the sea?" Blade asked.

I doubted my merfolk would get far in their current state...not without some kind of transportation. I met the assassin's questioning gaze. He may be a womanizer, but at least he had some manners, and that redeemed him one bar in my eyes. But he still hovered on the same level as grumpy Gill.

"Please," I replied. "My men need water. They won't get far without a horse."

"Let me get you a wagon and horses, Highness," he said with a wink before he disappeared amid the train of wagons.

"And our weapons," Gill called after the assassin. "And a little rum, too."

Blade glanced back, and he and Gill shared a knowing smile. I wondered what it meant. A joke between them, perhaps.

"How far is the ocean?" I asked my mermen.

"A day's ride at best," said Fin.

Damn. That was too long. We needed to search out a body of water for them to lift their energy levels to make the journey back to the sea.

Blade soon returned atop a wagon drawn by two horses, stopping it nearby.

"Your Highness," he said, jumping down and taking my hand, leading me to the cart.

Sea god. Normally I was used to doing things myself, but

I dared any woman to not accompany this handsome scoundrel.

"Thank you for saving us," I said, staring into his eyes, noting the honey flecks in them. "All of us."

"You're welcome, pretty little lady." He was so bold as to press his face forward, apparently assuming I'd reward him with a kiss.

I twisted his face and pecked him on the cheek.

The hollowness of his laugh and the way he rubbed the spot my lips had touched told me it was as rare day when a woman knocked him back.

Someone's knuckles cracked behind me. I assumed it was Nemo, given his little jealousy act from earlier.

One of the horses snorted, and I flinched. With a shaky hand, I approached it and stroked its furry neck, marveling at the silky hair, which felt a little dirty, as if grit clung to its coat. Still, it felt smooth and nice to my touch. Surely beat a gooey and slippery seahorse any day.

Blade pointed to a step between the ground and the top of the cart's wheel. "Put your foot on the mounting step here."

When I lifted my leg, I wobbled. My skirt was quite heavy, and it was going to take a bit of getting used to.

"Here." Blade grasped my waist in one hand and my butt in the other and boosted me onto the step as if I weighed nothing. Then he gave me another little tap and winked when I'd settled. "That's a fine royal ass."

My, he was a cheeky one.

Nemo's knuckles cracked again.

Fin and Gill were around the back of the wagon, rearranging a few barrels of rum, their tridents, and two chests.

Blade jumped up after me and put the horse's reins in my hand. He squeezed my fingers before climbing down.

Nemo sighed. "I'm not getting into that cage again." He jumped into the seat beside me and smiled.

It was nice to see that even with his optimistic outlook, he was flawed with a jealous streak. Now, he didn't seem too perfect.

"Guess we're riding in the back, Captain," Gill said to Fin.

"Thanks, brother." Gill wrapped his arms around Blade and patted him hard on the back.

"You owe me." Blade's wicked grin promised Gill trouble in the future.

"No more boats," said Gill as he eased into the wagon like an old man.

Blade laughed and raised a hand as he strode off into the night.

"Wait," I called out after him. "Where are you going?"

"Taking these clowns back for questioning," he said.

"But I don't know how this works." I glanced down at the reins in my hands. During my brief captivity, I hadn't exactly studied the pirates when they'd driven the wagons. If I couldn't figure it out, we weren't getting very far. *Damn Blade for leaving us stranded.*

I turned to Nemo. "What do I do with these?"

The giant merman shrugged. "I think you wriggle the straps."

I tried that, but the horses just snorted, as if laughing at me.

"Give it a bit more oomph, Princess," Nemo encouraged.

I shook the reins harder, and the horses grunted. I tried one more time, cracking the leather straps, and the horses jolted forward.

"Watch out," shouted Nemo, pointing to the other wagon directly ahead of us.

CHAPTER 9

I screamed and yanked the reins, and the horses ground to a halt. My heart lodged in my throat and refused to settle back down.

Laughter echoed through the clearing, and Blade reappeared. "Merfolk," he said, shaking his head as he leaped onto the carriage with ease.

The assassin nuzzled up next to me, taking a few extra wiggles of his behind to get comfortable, given Nemo's hulking frame consumed most of the room on the seat. The mersoldier grunted as Blade put the reins in my hand and held on to my wrists.

"Pull like this to make them back up."

The assassin demonstrated, and the horses responded by clomping backward.

Wow. That was too easy. Heat flushed to my cheeks and neck. Sea god. When would I stop making a fool of myself in front of hot males? *They must think me stupid.*

Some shifters standing around drinking rum moved out of the way of the cart. Most of them still stuck around to

89

stretch their bodies after being cramped in the tiny cells with four other shifters.

"If you want to turn in a certain direction," said Blade, tickling my wrist with a finger and making Nemo tighten beside me, "just pull the corresponding rein in that direction."

He tugged the right strap, and the horses jerked the wagon forward and toward the right.

Amazing, and so easy!

"You know, you can whip me with the reins any time," Blade teased.

Kinky. Definitely not my style. Not that I had one. My sea pearl hadn't been deflowered yet. But when it was, I was sure that whipping someone with leather wouldn't be my thing. I bet my friend Gellian would have been up for it though. *Maybe I should invite Blade to the kingdom one day and introduce them.*

"That's enough." Nemo stood up, glaring at Blade like an enraged walrus.

"Okay, big fella." Blade climbed down. "Don't want to cut in on your territory. Adios." He went to the back of the wagon and gave Gill his leather water pouch.

"Thanks, buddy." Gill clapped Blade on the shoulder. "Owe you again."

"I'll remember that, don't you worry." Blade pinched the pouch of a caped crusader stalking past and tossed it at Nemo.

The hunky assassin saluted me and then wandered away once more.

Gill and Fin chuckled from the back.

I swear I went even redder. This crush thing was getting a little awkward. Nemo was sweet and all, fun-loving and flipping gorgeous. The kind of guy I'd love to date. But my father would never allow it. Not with someone far below my rank. If my father were in his right mind, he'd never have agreed to a marriage with Faraall. Guilt weaved through my chest. Was I leading Nemo on? Maybe I shouldn't be so friendly and encourage his affections. But something inside me wanted to do just that. I loved the way he made me feel. All protected and cared for. His attention made my insides dance around like an elegant seahorse.

I glanced at Nemo. "Where do I go?"

He pointed into the sky. "Follow that star. It will guide us back to the sea."

Why didn't I think about that before? When we breached the surface, we used the stars for navigation.

Before I set off, I examined all the mermen. Fin and Gill had turned a shade of gray. Dark circles clung to their eyes. Sweat pasted their skin. They wouldn't last much longer. Beside me, Nemo fared a little better, but his skin was developing that sick-looking hue. I estimated they would start to throw up in a few hours. Then the cramps would become so painful, they wouldn't be able to move.

Follow the star. The words kept banging in my head. Our survival depended on this. I had no doubt I could get the mermen back to the ocean. But then what? When we arrived back at the palace, I'd love to report the kidnappings to my father so he could stop the collector. Except Triton was still under Faraall's control. Until I stole the pearl and gave it to the sea witch, freedom would not be granted to my father. That task would prove no easy feat when Faraall was practically glued to my father's hip. The moment I put a fin in the palace, I would be apprehended. I couldn't let that happen. I was *not* going to be returned to the pirates.

"Let's get home," Nemo cheered, slamming his palm on the side of the cart. "I'm dying for a crab."

But I couldn't move. The pressure of everything weighed too heavily on me. That sandy feeling in my gut returned.

What if I went in the wrong direction? What if it took longer than a day? If horses were anything like the dolphins that drew my father's chariot, then they'd tire out. That meant we'd probably have to camp out. Our cart was packed with some supplies—namely rum and some dried foods. That should tide us over for a night.

Get a grip, Nyssa. You can do this.

I copied the actions Blade had shown me, and the horses slowly pulled away from the destroyed camp. But they drifted toward the tree up ahead. *Remind me why I decided to drive again?*

My pulse pounded in my ear. "Flipping hell. Why are they walking into objects?"

Nemo took my left hand. "Steady, Princess." With his free hand, he guided them back onto the path.

Steering the wagon was starting to stress me out a little. "Do you want to navigate these horses?"

"Believe me." His voice was turning croaky and parched. "I'd love to. But my vision is starting to blur."

Oh, no. This was bad. My freak-out factor raised one hundred bars. I had to hurry. My mantra from earlier repeated in my head. *Get a grip, Nyssa. You can do this. You have to save your people. Then they can help save your father and the kingdom.*

With this in mind, I cracked the reins on the horses' backs, and they climbed to a trot, carrying us away from the remains of the pirates' ambushed caravan.

Darkness swallowed us.

Fin and Nemo groaned as if they were about to vomit.

Bile rose in my throat, too. "Sorry. Want me to slow down?"

"No, Princess." Fin's voice was calm, soothing, hypnotic.

The way he'd said "princess" sent goosebumps skittering all over my flesh. I wanted to listen to him whisper it all day.

Have his breath tickle my ear. His lips graze my lobe. Have him deliver soft kisses to set my skin on fire...

I jolted the straps, and the horses kicked into a run.

"Go, Princess!"

Nemo's raised voice startled me. Even though my effort so far was terrible, I loved the way he complimented me. For some reason, his opinion mattered and made me feel special and warm inside.

Thankfully, no one else traveled down the road, which eased my twisting gut. Guiding this thing left me totally out of my element. But the longer I did it, the more I started getting the hang of it.

"How are you faring?" I asked Nemo when I felt steadier.

"Just happy to be going home," he said, slumped against a barrel of rum behind him.

He started to hum a tune. Pretty soon he broke into a song. The other two joined him. I didn't recognize it. Something about mersoldiers and warriors. It was nice to list to and lifted the morale.

After that song, they fell quiet, and the gentle rocking motion of the carriage put them all to sleep. Their snores stroked my ears. It wasn't the honking, snorting type emitted by some of the pirates, but more of a heavy breathing noise. The noise was strange and foreign yet somewhat comforting. Back in Tritonia, the water distorted most sounds, so we didn't hear it. But I could always tell whenever someone dozed off during one of my father's strategic meetings by the way their gills fluttered from their relaxed breathing. It annoyed my father to no end, and he would poke the snoozer with his trident.

I laughed at the fond memory.

An overwhelming urge to be with my father hit me. I missed his firm and bellowing voice. Our private conversations over breakfast. Hugging him before I went to bed.

Fine. I may be a daddy's girl. I didn't care. My dad was the center of my world. Knowing he was helpless against Faraall made me mad as hellfire and had me longing for justice.

A little sparrow landed on the long bit connecting the wagon to the horse. It twittered, wagging its tailfeathers, and hopped along the length of the strap. I was grateful for its presence. Anything to distract me from thinking of home.

"Hello," I said.

The bird cheeped at me, before flying off.

"Don't go!" I called.

But it didn't return, and I slumped in my seat.

The woods were quite beautiful. Smaller ferns nestled among the thick and tall trees. Patches of moss hugged the trunks. Mushrooms sprouted at the base. Fallen leaves turned brown on the forest floor and along the trail. In a way, it reminded me of home. I inhaled all the different smells that invited me deeper into my surroundings—dried leaves, earthy floor, clean and crisp air, citrus and wood. Branches swayed in the breeze, like a symphony of wind. This place was heaven.

****

SOMETIME LATER, my senses tugged me to the west, and I cocked my head. Merfolk had an amazing ability to track water when we were on land. Don't ask me how it worked because I didn't know. My father just told me it was how we survived in an amphibious state.

Nemo snorted himself awake beside me. "Water," he groaned.

"Do you sense it, too?" I asked.

"Sense what?" He rubbed his forehead. "My head is killing me."

"Mine, too," Fin chimed in from behind us.

I hadn't even known he was awake. "How'd you sleep?" I asked them.

"Like a merbaby," said Nemo.

Sea god. How was he always so chipper? Whenever I got my moon cramps, I curled up in bed, wanting to die from the pain. For the first two days, I was as grouchy and prickly as a stonefish.

"Been better, Princess," replied Fin, rubbing his neck.

"Don't worry," I said. "I've detected water to the west."

Up ahead, the road split at a fork, one route going in the direction where my senses called me. Perfect! Surely, we could spare a bit of time for a dip. As we approached the intersection, I jerked the horses' reins, and they shifted right, following my guidance.

I glanced at Nemo's wound. His bandage was soaked with blood. It needed changing, and the cut needed cleaned.

"How's your leg?" I asked him, clasping his hand and squeezing it.

"Better now."

The way his eyes lingered on me sent a tingle up my spine. His smile was like the rising sun, bursting with light and beauty, and I couldn't pull away.

He laughed and ended my little trance.

I snapped out of it and tried to concentrate on the path. But that was a little hard. In his presence, I felt strange. A little out of control. The sensation was exhilarating and daunting at the same time. But I didn't want it any other way.

A few leagues down the next road the desire for water became stronger, telling me we were on the right path.

My instincts told me to take the next two rights, and we passed a little town with a well in the center, but that wasn't what I sensed. This was a large body of water. My chest wouldn't throb over something so small.

Four brick huts with straw roofs lined either side of the lane. Judging by the size of them, they were reasonably spacious like the apartments at the palace. Horses were tied up to wooden poles outside. Smoke curled out of the chimney of each structure. The smell of something delicious wafted from one of the buildings, making my stomach groan.

"Give me some of that." Nemo rubbed his flat stomach. "Gill, we'll sell your trident for some of that grub."

"More like we'll sell you," said Gill.

I raised a brow, surprised to learn he actually had a sense of humor.

We all laughed at that one.

A couple of children who were playing kickball and jumping on strange ropes in the courtyard stopped to run up to the horses. Watching their delighted faces warmed my heart. One day, I wanted three little ones of my own. I'd picked out names for two of them. Ariel after my aunt. Neptune for a boy. The third…well, I wasn't sure what I'd call him or her yet.

When I turned the next corner, and the wagon headed along a massive field, the internal barometer inside me was practically exploding. Strange animals with hulking bodies and tiny legs that didn't look strong enough to hold them up grazed on the grasses in the field along the road. They kind of reminded me of dugongs, but with longer legs.

A couple of leagues down, I spotted a huge lake bordered by forest on one side and grass on the other.

"Poseidon," I whispered.

Oh, my. I had cursed too much today to the sea god. He'd already passed me to the pirates. What next? Strike me down with a tsunami?

"What?" Nemo swung his head. "I still can't see."

"Me neither," Fin said.

As usual, Gill didn't say anything, but that was probably a good thing when he was such a grouch.

"A big, beautiful lake," I said.

"Water," Nemo groaned.

"Thank Poseidon," Fin muttered.

The fields were surrounded by fences made of vertical timber batons. For the life of me, I couldn't locate a track leading to the lake.

"We might have to climb the fence to get into the field," I told the mermen. "Do you feel well enough to do that?"

"Anything for water," mumbled Nemo.

"Agreed," said Fin.

Gill grunted, and I took it as his way of saying *yes*.

I yanked on the reins, pulling the horses to a stop. "Wait here," I told Nemo as I climbed down to investigate.

A few of the funny-looking animals approached as I walked the length of fence.

"Hello," I sent out the greeting as a telepathic message to them.

They stared at me, one chewing some grass.

Not the friendliest beasts in Haven. But I wasn't there to make friends. I needed water to heal my men, especially Nemo with his injury.

Half a league down the fence, I found a gate and unlatched it. Luckily, the animals on the opposite side of the fence didn't exit. Instead, they followed me back to the wagon, keeping to their side of the fence line. I was puffing by the time I climbed back onboard. Using my legs was even more tiring than swimming. As a human, I had to force two legs to move, not one fin. In my seat, I cracked the reins, and the horses charged forward. I didn't stop until we were inside the fence.I climbed back down and locked the gate again, and then we were off once more, my heart pounding with excitement the closer we got to the lake.

The horses came to a skittering halt as I pulled up beside the lake.

I helped Nemo navigate the step down, taking some of his weight, and almost falling over myself.

"Thank you, Princess." He gave me a kiss on the cheek for my effort.

The intoxicating scent of his muskiness engulfed me. The heat he left on me spread across my whole body. I touched my cheek, standing there like a real dope, unable to move.

"Princess," he said, wrapping an arm around me.

I shook off the lethargy and helped him hobble to the back of the cart.

Nemo weighed a ton. His body was stocky and very athletic. One of his arms was easily twice the size of mine.

"Come on, you mergrandmas," he said to his companions.

Fin clasped Nemo's hand and slid off the back of the wagon.

Gill climbed down by himself and grabbed Nemo in a headlock, messing up his hair. "Who you calling grandma?"

The mermen's laughter was like music to my ears. I admired the joint respect and friendship between them. This must have been what it was like to be in the company of a brother I actually admired and enjoyed. All jokes and shenanigans.

"Quick," I said, sounding a little like an impatient mother. "Put your arms around my shoulders, and we'll go together."

"Come on, you guppies." Fin put an arm around my shoulder.

"Yes, Captain." Nemo claimed the other side before Gill had a chance.

Not that Gill would have leaned on me for support. He hooked on to Nemo. The broody mersoldier seemed very reserved and standoffish. I still couldn't tell if it was because I was royal. Either way, I had this deep desire to understand his motives. Something drew me to him even though he wasn't very nice to me.

Sea god! I hoped I wasn't becoming attracted to someone who would treat me poorly and keep me hanging. Three mermen had done that to Nimian and broken her heart. No one was going to treat me that way, especially not Gill.

The mersoldiers leaned on me for support as we slowly crossed the field to the lake. My shoulders and back ached from their weight. I wasn't sure how much longer I could bear it. But I'd be damned if I was stopping for anything. My mermen were getting water.

Little white flowers exploded with life in a ring surrounding the banks. Beautiful plants. They reminded me of the sea ferns growing along the bridge of the palace.

"Sweet water," said Fin as it lapped at his feet.

Nemo was a little more dramatic, slumping to the dirt and crawling into the lake. Scales came to life on his wrists and down one side of his face. They glimmered for a second then faded. They'd need a good soaking before they revived completely. But so far, their response to the water was a good sign.

Gill scooped up a handful and splashed it over his face. Then he waddled in deeper and dove into the water.

Merfolk scales and skin were accustomed to saltwater rather than the fresh water found in lakes, ponds, and rivers. But right now, we'd take anything we could get.

Fin stood on the edge with me, took off his boots, and let his feet sink in the water and mud.

"You're not going in with them?" I asked.

"No," Fin replied, his gaze full of longing for the water. "It's my duty to protect you and my men."

My heart fluttered at his loyalty. Sure, the guards back at

the palace did the same thing. But they weren't nearly as handsome or considerate as Fin. As soon as the change of guard arrived, they were down at the bar, grabbing a beer. Something about Fin told me he would never abandon me.

Nemo floated on his back, singing again, this time about how sweet the water was, and it made me smile.

Within a few moments, the color of the other mermen's skin revived, Gill's turning a deep olive, and Nemo's changing to a golden tan. Fin was pale, like me. From my position, I admired them all. Nemo, for his height and breadth, as well as his fun-loving nature. Gill, for his dark features and broodiness. Fin, for his manners, his respectfulness, and a smile that could knock me off my feet. All traits I found very attractive. At that moment, I felt a little crush blossoming for each merman.

Gosh. If anyone had ever taken a serious fancy to me, Faraall might have killed them and dumped their body at the wastelands. I shivered at the thought. What would he do once he found out I was attracted to three mermen under his command? Faraall already hated me for my rejection and for discovering his secret. If he was capable of giving me to the enemy, there were no limits to his wrath. I knew deep in my heart he would never let me have any happiness if I was alive, would never let me live if I was a threat to his endgame. There'd be no piece of coral left unturned. I'd never be able to hide from him. As much as I hated to admit it, I had to destroy Faraall before he eliminated me. How I was going to take him down, I didn't know.

CHAPTER 10

"*How* long have you been in my father's service?" I asked Fin, taking off my skirt and leaving them on the grass by the banks. What the hell? The mersoldiers had already seen half of me naked. I still kept a bit of my dignity, leaving my corset on to cover my breasts, and then I sat on the edge of the lapping water, dipping my feet in it.

"Three years serving as a captain," Fin said, taking a seat beside me. "My father made it hell for me to sign up. Threatened to disown me if I joined. Had words with the merarmy, and they refused my application three times."

Odd. Joining the merarmy was considered an honor. Mersoldiers were held in very high regard in the kingdom, and many joined fresh out of school. Bagging a man in uniform was a popular goal among all the females. That was possibly why no one had said anything when my father had announced my engagement to Faraall.

"When the recruitment officer realized I was determined to come back every day, they registered me as an officer. That pissed off my father to no end."

Fin's bravery at standing up to his father touched me. "I'd

never have the guts to confess my little visits to Shark Bait bar to my father," I told Fin. "Sea god! The lectures I'd be in for. Tarnishing our image, blah blah, blah. Spare me, please."

I stretched my hands behind me and leaned into them.

Fin did the same, and his fingers brushed mine. A spark shot up my arm.

"My apologies, Princess," he said, shifting his position.

My fingers tingled for his touch again.

"Don't treat me like a delicate little sea flower," I said, half-joking, half-serious.

He shrugged. "You're a royal. I don't want your dad piercing me in the chest with his trident. Honorable as it would be to die that way."

Fin's honesty was refreshing. All the servants were nice to me because I was the princess. They were frightened I'd fly into a rage like my sister Aquina always did. But I wasn't a hothead like she was. And the nobles, well, they just kissed my scaly behind for favors and because I was the princes. The only real people I had in my life were my aunt and cousin.

Fin's intoxicating, salty, sandy scent drove my pulse into a frenzy. If I wasn't careful, I was going to say something silly and embarrass myself in front of him, just like I had with every other guy. Maybe I should just keep my distance, and play it cool. But something inside me wanted to flirt with him. Discover more about him. Have him touch me again. Listen to his voice. Sea god, it tickled my insides.

"My father's not here." I flicked water on him to show him I was normal and could have fun, too.

He splashed me back, and we laughed. It felt nice just to sit here with him and let loose. He scooped up water and dribbled it on my head. I let out a squeal and shifted aside. Well, two could play at that game. I pushed my hand through the water to splatter him, but instead, I got him with mud—and right in the eye.

"Sea god, I'm so sorry," I said, scraping some of it away.

"It's all right, Princess." He flicked the rest away then leaned on his knees, washing the rest away with water.

Heat crept up my neck again. Now I was definitely convinced I was cursed with bad luck around guys. Every time, this happened. Every time! Like the time I'd accidentally bit one guy's tongue when we'd been kissing. Or last moon cycle when a Sharkrider had been feeding me calamari and dip and it fell down my corset between my boobs. Of course, he'd loved it, and Gellian had been cheering for him to lick it off before it washed away, but I hadn't wanted to do that in front of the whole bar. Ugh, and I didn't want to be reminded of the previous year when some guy had been chatting me up at a party, and a shark had chased us. Me saying or doing stupid things scared most guys away or ended things before they had a chance to blossom.

I buried my face in my hands. "I'm so sorry. I'm terrible around cute guys. I always do this."

"Flick mud in their faces?"

Amusement weaved beneath his words, but it only served to deepen the heat burning across me.

"No," I said. "Bite their tongues, have two guys fist fight over me, get drunk and fall asleep on a guy, fall in their crotches. You know."

Fin laughed so hard, he clutched his stomach. When he finished, he said, "Remind me not to kiss you."

"You don't want to kiss me?" *Shellfish*. Did I just say that? I really had to slow my brain down and think before I spoke.

"Of course, I do," he replied.

I eyed him in surprise.

"But that would be inappropriate of a man of my rank," he added.

A traditionalist? Damn him and his manners. I guessed I'd just have to make the first move. Before I could stop myself, I crawled across to him and kissed him. My lips sizzled on his. A strange sensation engulfed me; a powerful magnetism that wouldn't let go blended with a hunger for more. He parted his mouth and brushed his lips across mine, but I pulled away before I could ruin the perfect moment.

"See?" I said, sitting back down. "Nothing bad happened."

He stared at me, his eyes a mix of disappointment and yearning. I wanted more, too. But I was terrified to move, to wreck the moment. His fingers locked with mine and squeezed. For now, I was content with that.

"So, let me get this straight, princess," he said, and I hung on his every word. "You're royal by blood, but not in your heart?"

I nodded and smiled, even though guilt stabbed me in the chest for admitting it. All I wanted was for freedom from the strict confines of my life. Relief from the pressure put upon me. Pressure I did not ask for or want.

"I'm the same," Fin admitted. "Well, not royal…noble."

"I know what you meant." *Wow.* Fin's admission caught me by surprise. Most nobles dreaded a fall from grace. A life without their luxuries was a life not worth living. Neither Fin nor I cared about those things. Finding someone who thought like I did was rarer than discovering a passel of whale teeth. "What brought you to that conclusion?"

"I recognize the same qualities in you," he answered. "You don't care for power, prestige, or position."

How could he tell that about me?

"My aunt's the Black Grouper of the family," I said. "She speaks her mind, whether it garners her enemies or not. So do my cousin and I. It doesn't win us favor with the nobles. In fact, our attitudes and behavior often earns us whispers behind our backs."

Fin hugged his stomach as he laughed. "Pretension: one of the things I loathed about court."

Me, too. I nudged him with my elbow. "I couldn't imagine you saying an ill word about anyone. You're too nice."

"You'd be surprised."

I challenged him with a look to divulge more information.

"My mother died at childbirth," he said.

I squeezed his hand.

"My father was never there for me," he went on. "Cheldra, my nanny, raised me. She taught me to be kind, honorable, respectful. Traits my father and his associates did not possess."

Nannies were typical in some noble families, and were popular even in my father's brother's kingdom across the sea. A far cry from the way Triton had raised his brood of wild girls.

"Believe it or not, my father was very involved in his daughters' lives," I told Fin. "From picking tutors, overseeing our studies, spending every meal with us, even playing with us...and he always made time to read to us at bedtime."

Only after we'd hit our teenage years—when our hormones raged and my sisters' conversations turned to handsome mermen—did my father realize it was time to back off. But not when it came to me. He and I still remained close.

My heart wept for Fin and children like him. I couldn't imagine not having my parents in my life. They were my rocks. My world. They'd supported me in everything I had done. Even my terrible art. They'd never criticized me for a bad grade. Recalling all these things only strengthened my desire and resolve to free my father from Faraall's wicked grasp.

"I'm glad you're close with your father," said Fin, staring

out at the lake. "He's a merciful king with integrity and compassion."

I put my hand over Fin's, and that feeling returned again. This time, he didn't pull away, and my chest was popping like crystal fireworks.

"Why didn't your father want you to join the merarmy when it's an honor to serve the king?" I asked, unable to stop with the questions because I wanted to know everything about Fin.

He gave me a rueful smile that made my heart splinter. "My father, the Earl of the Western Coral Shelf, considers a position within the merarmy below his son."

Oh, my. So that's who his father was. A god-awful merman. Known for his ruthlessness in trade. Claiming the lands of adjoining nobles. Running through mistresses after his wife died. The type to stare down his nose at the common merfolk as if they were a grain of sand on his shoe. But Fin didn't seem a thing like his father. He was polite and respectful, and he cared for his men. Honor meant more to him than wealth, title, and privilege. I admired our similar values and rebelliousness. Any man who defied tradition was very appealing to me. Especially since many of the merfolk customs were millennia old. They needed changing to reflect the current age.

He kicked at a reed floating on the water. "After my mother died, my father's heart turned black. I didn't want to travel that path with him." The bobbing of the apple in his throat conveyed his pain from speaking on the matter. "Now, I'm nothing to my father. I don't exist."

My chest wrenched for the choices Fin had made. He'd done what his heart compelled him to do. He'd wanted to be a better man than his father. For those decisions, he'd been disowned and disinherited. That wasn't fair. But nothing in life was. Especially not for a noble or royal. We didn't really get a say in our own lives, and if we tried to break free of the constraints, we suffered the consequences.

This insight propelled me to assess my own situation. What if I couldn't save my father? Would I be banished from the kingdom for refusing to wed Faraall? A fate I'd gladly accept. But I couldn't float around and do nothing, leaving my family and people to suffer. Unlike my sisters, I didn't just drift on the current all day, doing my hair, makeup, and nails.

Tears trickled down my cheeks as I squeezed Fin's wrist. "Your strength inspires me. All I ever wanted was to be free of the expectations put upon me. To be me, not what others demanded of me. Not be tied down by royal duties, like speaking five different dialects, learning politics, understanding the history of Haven. It's too much responsibility. I crave freedom."

Poseidon, listen to me blabber. I probably sounded ungrateful for everything the sea god had blessed me with. But I wasn't. I thanked him every day.

I smiled and stared at my feet. No one had ever called me *inspiring* before. Beside my father, who seemed to have a serious case of rose-colored fins when it came to me and Faraall, everyone always thought I was the silly, rebellious dreamer, good for nothing.

"We're not that different, Princess," he said.

I cocked my head, curious at what he meant.

"We're all running from something," he added.

The rawness of his words hit me deep like a blow from a wave crashing on top of me. Fin had escaped the expectations of his rank. I tried to in my own way by sneaking off to bars, sunken ships, secret parties in underwater caves, and hanging out with my aunt and cousin. But I wasn't brave enough to completely say goodbye. I drowned under the pressure and guilt.

"Don't worry, Princess." He patted my hand, leaving the spot sizzling and aching for more. "I have no regrets. It was the best decision of my life."

I was glad to hear this. It eased the ache in my chest.

"I just wish I was free of my father," he said. "Of his shadow that hangs over me. One day, I'd like to prove to him that I'm something better than he ever was."

What a noble goal. I'd love to be free of the shadow of my expectations and obligations.

My mind wandered to Gill and Nemo. They were floating in the middle of the lake, currently out of earshot. I was sick of thinking about my problems, and curious to know more about the other two mersoldiers, too.

"Why did Gill and Nemo join the army?" I asked Fin.

"It's a family tradition for Nemes," Fin said. "Every male in his family has been a mersoldier for the last five hundred years. He'd wanted to be one since he was little."

Poseidon! There I was, whining about my royal duties and expectations, when Nemo was in the same boat, and he embraced it. I tucked my head and fiddled with my fingers.

"Gill, well, he's more complicated," Fin said. "He got into trouble in his teens for stealing and vandalism. The judges didn't know what to do with him. So the case was presented to Triton. The king felt the military would straighten Gill out, teach him a code of respect, loyalty, and honor."

"Has it?" I asked, watching Gill float on his back beside Nemo.

"To an extent." Fin shook his head and laughed. "I don't think anyone can tame him. Gill's as wild as they come. Gave me cheek when I first joined the unit as captain. A few fist fights sorted him out. I won the first one. He came out on top the next. The last time we tussled, we tied and called a truce."

My hands flew to my cheeks. This news made me see Fin

in a new light. "You punched an officer under your command?"

"It was the only way to get through to him," Fin explained. "I had to earn his respect and loyalty. Don't think less of him, Princess. He comes from a rough home, a bit like mine, but we each come out of these things in different ways. His home life left Gill a little jaded and angry."

Fin's assessment explained a lot about Gill and his attitude toward me. My father had tried to help lift Gill out of a life of crime, but the blind merman had mistaken his military assigment for punishment.

A noise behind me sliced through my thoughts, and I spun around to face it. The strange animals with their skinny legs crowded behind us. About ten more than before had wandered down from the fields. They made a strange call that sounded like a *moo*.

"Hello, again," I sent them as a telepathic message.

A bunch of them returned the communication with the word, "Food."

"There's plenty of grass in the field," I told them.

"Grain," they kept pressing.

"I don't have any."

One nudged me. Then another.

"Food."

Shellfish. They were big, pushy things.

One licked my ear with a long, slimy tongue. Another lathered Fin, as well, and he pulled me to my feet to escape the onslaught.

"What's going on?" asked Nemo, sloshing water as he climbed out of the lake onto the banks. His muscles rippled with each step. A scar remained where the pirate had slashed his leg. His skin still appeared a little dry and pale, but the water had worked its magic on him.

Gill emerged beside him, and I lost my breath as he brushed his dark hair back.

Sea god, they were hot.

Out of all three of the mermen, Fin had the largest package. It kind of seemed appropriate, given he was the leader and thus, supposedly, the more virile of the bunch. Nemo was next, but I wasn't surprised, given his overall size. Then Gill. I wondered what they would all feel like inside my sea pearl.

Gill caught me admiring his privates, and he squeezed them. "You know what they say about a long fin." The smile and wink he gave me nearly knocked me over.

Damn it. He was just as bad as Blade. Now I saw why they were friends. But there was something about Gill that drew me to him.

Nemo cracked up and thumped Gill on the back.

Fin was a bit more respectful. "Not in front of the princess."

"What?" Gill held his arms out wide. "She was checking me out."

Flames curled over my body. That would teach me. Next time, I should practice the art of subtlety.

Luckily, the beasts crowding around us and squashing Fin and me, distracted me from my mortification.

One of the animals clopped into the water and nudged Nemo.

"I don't have any food." He laughed, giving the beast a pat, and it nibbled his wrist.

With a snort, the animal turned around, knocked him over, and walked away.

"Hey!" Nemo cried.

Gill laughed and said, "Don't think she's that into you, Nemes."

"All the mergals love me," Nemo bragged.

He grabbed Gill in a headlock, and the two began to play-wrestle, tossing each other into the water, climbing on each other's backs, and rolling around.

The more I witnessed of Gill's fun side, the more I grew to like him, despite his misgivings for me.

Poseidon! Was it wrong of me to be attracted to all three of them? Normally, I didn't crush on guys for long. My embarrassing antics usually chased them away before things could get serious.

I didn't get to finish my thoughts because a beast bumped me in the back, and I stumbled forward.

Fin defended me, pushing the beasts' noses away. "Time to go, soldiers," he ordered.

Nemo and Gill ceased their games, rinsed off the mud, and collected their belongings.

Fin's forehead pinched as he gathered my clothing. "Sorry, Princess," he said, handing me the muddy clothes, which the beasts had trod all over.

I didn't mind. All the mermen's garments were the same. "Thank you."

We all tried to dress in our dirty clothes, but the beasts mooed at us and prodded us, and we kept tripping. I was totally enjoying the change in pace. Things at the palace never got this exciting.

A few of the animals lifted their skinny tails and left sticky greenish-brown messes before they wandered away.

Nemo cupped his nose. "Oh, that's just rotten." Those were the first negative words to come out of his mouth.

"Even worse than an orca!" Fin's gray pallor turned green.

"Let's get out of here," said Gill, wrestling an animal for his pants as it chewed them.

Nemo hopped after another to get his boot back.

Arms bundled with clothes and shoes, we all took off into the field, laughing our heads off. *Sea god.* We must have looked a sight—four naked merfolk, dressing on the run, pursued by a bunch of hungry, moaning beasts. But I loved adventures like this one. They always stood out in my mind. And I knew I'd never forget this day...not ever.

Back at the wagon, we were able to dress without disruption, as the animals circled us. But they all congregated by the fence, mooing, begging me in my head for some grain. I had to use all my concentration to block them out.

"Who wants to ride upfront?" asked Fin.

"Me and the princess," Nemo said, claiming the right to sit beside me. "But I'm steering this time."

Fine with me.

Fin gave us a mock frown, curled his arm around Gill, and climbed into the back.

"Ladies first." Nemo gestured for me to lead the way.

Manners—so charming in a guy. Especially a soldier who was also a little rough around the edges like Nemo was. Made him even more attractive. Being in his presence made me a little giddy and love-struck.

"Thank you." I grabbed on to the side of the wagon and put my foot on the step.

Nemo cupped my butt in his hand and hoisted me up.

Had the mersoldier done that on purpose? Used the opportunity to assist me as an excuse to grab my behind? Either way, I liked him touching me and wanted him to do it again, longer next time, and maybe put one hand on each of my cheeks.

He chuckled. "Sorry for touching the royal ass."

Geez, it seemed Blade's nickname was contagious...

"The perfect royal ass."

I glanced over my shoulder. Oh, now Gill had decided to include his opinion, too?

"We don't mean to offend you, Princess," Fin said.

I braced myself, sensing he was about to say more.

"You and your cute, little royal ass," he added.

I cringed inwardly. Sometimes, I felt like the odd one out. A girl in a boys' club.

"Shut up about the royal ass," I said, burning hot thanks to everyone teasing me about my butt.

Nemo grabbed me in a bear cuddle. "Oh, Princess…"

His kindness made me loosen up a little, and I snuggled into the big merman's side as if I belonged there.

"Nyssa," I corrected him. "Please, call me 'Nyssa. 'Princess' is too formal."

"Oh, pardon me, Nyssa," Nemo said in a posh voice.

Okay. I had to admit, his silly accent got to me, and I laughed along with the men. To show them I wasn't a stuffy royal, I stood on the seat, turned, and shook my behind, just for them.

Fin clapped. Gill whistled. Nemo hugged his belly.

I basked in the attention. *Sea god*. I was becoming like Nimian, and I loved it! I finally understood why she acted the way she did sometimes.

"Come on," said Fin, after the laughter died down. "Let's get going."

"Yes, Your Highness." Nemo bowed, long and deep.

As he settled into his chair beside me, I had the urge to grab his face and run my hands through his hair. Of course, I resisted. For too long, I'd been taught to act like a lady. But I wasn't one. I wanted to be my own woman, not what everyone assumed me to be because of my title.

Nemo's biceps flexed as he grabbed the reins. An image of him holding me with those arms and me wrapping mine around his neck flashed in my mind.

Poseidon. Sitting beside him was driving me crazy. I wasn't sure I could get the thought of being in his embrace out of my mind. Nor did I want to.

The horses and wagon kicked up dust as we took off down the path.

"Captain," Gill said from behind me. "When we get to town, I want to trade the rum for a horse, and go find my sister."

"I cannot allow that," Fin replied. "You didn't fully recharge at the lake. We need to get back to the sea. Then we can figure out our next move."

Nemo and I exchanged a glance.

Judging by the darkness storming across Gill's face, I sensed an argument brewing. "So, even after all the times I saved your ass, her father trumps my sister."

"Gill, we need the merarmy behind us to rescue all the other creatures and destroy the pirates."

"I'm not leaving her behind. She's all I have left."

Believe me, I didn't want to leave his sister or the other merfolk behind, either. But we didn't know how many pirates we were up against. My men were weak from dehydration. The brief soak in the water was not enough. We had to stick together and work as a team. One rogue and rash merman was not going to free merfolk from the grasp of ruthless pirates working for an evil collector. Together, we were stronger and had more chance of success.

Fin stood firm. "As your commanding officer, I order you to stay with your unit."

Conflict flashed behind Gill's eyes. His forehead pinched, and his jaw tightened. I knew that look. The look of defiance. I recognized it because I'd seen it in myself—the guilt between staying and going when I'd objected to attending courtly functions and acting on my parents' demands.

Fin placed his hand on Gill's shoulder. "Sleep on it, Gill. Okay?"

Gill grunted. I wasn't sure if it was his agreement or refusal.

Obviously, he thought Fin and Nemo had taken my side because I was a princess. But Gill's heart ruled him, and he wasn't thinking straight.

"Don't think of disobeying an order, mersoldier." The words, aimed at Gill, spilled out before I could control them.

"Wouldn't be the first time," Gill said. "And probably wouldn't be the last, sweetheart."

Sweetheart? Why, I ought to punch him for that. How had this merman remained in the merarmy with an attitude like that? Who would want to fight beside someone who wouldn't have their back? No, thanks. Perhaps it was best to let him leave now. He was crazy and had a death wish.

I hated to admit it, but there was the deeper, selfish, and ashamed part of me that didn't want Gill to go. I wanted to break through the thick wall that separated us. But after the way he'd treated me, maybe it was time to give up on that idea, and admit it was a one-way crush. I knew when to stop wasting my time.

Another league down the road, we came to a tavern where we disembarked the wagon and gave it to the stable boy to lead the horses away. Tonight, we'd rest here, think on things, and leave at first light.

CHAPTER 11

"*W*anna play a game of clam, seaweed, rock?" Nemo asked.

He, Fin, and I stood beside the wagon, waiting for the servant of the tavern we'd slept in the previous night to retrieve our horses.

Nimian and I used to play that game all the time as children. We'd loved it. Our mother always told us to stop it at the dinner table. Apparently, playing hand games under the table wasn't becoming of two princesses.

"I warn you," I said, clenching one hand into a fist, trying to shake off my earlier disappointment. "I'm the merworld champion."

Nemo laughed. "Challenge accepted, Princess."

"Call me Nyssa, okay?" I said. "No more *princess*. I'm as much a princess as you three are merdancers."

Both Nemo and Fin belly laughed at the comparison.

"You're hilarious, Prin…" Nemo began.

Fin thumped Nemo's chest.

"Sorry…" Nemo gave me a sheepish smile. "I mean, *Nyssa*."

I grinned like a clam about to seize a fish for dinner. Nemo was about to be destroyed by the best.

Nemo held out his fist, prepared for the game. "Get ready to be beaten, Nyssa."

Yeah, right. "On the count of three. One. Two. Three," I said and flashed a seaweed.

Nemo flashed a clam.

Damn. He'd beaten me. Annoyance flashed through me. His sweet, mocking smile only stoked my temper.

Fine. Now it was my time to beat him.

"One, two, three." This time I showed a coral.

Again, he beat me with seaweed.

Heat scaled along the back of my neck. Okay. I'd admit I was a little competitive. Okay, *a lot* competitive.

"Decider round," taunted Nemo.

Poseidon. I had to win this.

I counted, and on the last number I threw up a clam. His coral trumped me. *Damn it.*

"You win," I begrudgingly admitted as I shook his hand.

"Oh, is the champion of the merrealm a little upset?" He gave me a huge hug and tickled my arm.

His coral scent filled me, sending my senses into a frenzy. My hormones spiked. Electrical pulses ravaged my skin. My heartbeat tripled, pounding in my ear.

Poseidon. What were these three doing to me? All these new sensations drove me wild, like a dolphin in heat…and dolphins were known for their horny nature.

Fin decided to jump in on the joke. "You shouldn't tick off a princess, Nemo. She might feed you to her pet sharks."

What? Now that was ridiculous. "I don't have pet sharks."

"I bet you do," Fin teased. "Reserved for fiends like my friend, here." He wrapped his arm around Nemo's neck and patted him on the chest.

Poseidon, they were sexy. I couldn't stop admiring them.

Over the images running through my head—namely of me running my hands all over their chests—I barely remembered what we'd been talking about.

"I bet you'd be a screamer," said Nemo.

I coughed and spluttered, thumping my chest. Were they thinking along the same lines as I was?

"One nibble from a shark and you'd cry like a baby," said Nemo.

Heat flushed my cheeks. Nope. I just had a dirty mind.

"Oh, really, Nemes?" challenged Fin. "I'd wager you'd faint at the sight of a shark fin."

Both boys burst into laughter. The sound was like music to my ears. Sweet and sexy. I could listen to them all day. The camaraderie between them touched me. Complete strangers, thrown together in battle, had forged a friendship stronger than steel. Times like these really made me enjoy being in their company. It was refreshing and exciting.

Hooves clomped behind us, signaling the servants had brought our horse and wagon.

"I'm going to go get Gill," Fin said, excusing himself.

"Thank you," I told the servant.

The young man nodded then disappeared back around the corner of the tavern.

I started to climb onto the wagon, and Nemo lifted me. He climbed up behind and claimed the seat next to me. I really liked the way he made it known he wanted to be beside me all the time.

His eyebrow rose. "Another game?"

"No way." I laughed and put a hand on his chest.

His hand covered mine, holding it there. We stared into each other's eyes. Warm honey tones circled his irises.

"Gill's gone," Fin said, interrupting Nemo and me. "Left in the middle of the night."

Flipping hell! I knew it. Lava bubbled and churned in my

chest. If I saw him again, I'd punch him for disobeying an order.

"For Poseidon's sake." Fin grabbed a log from a wood pile and hurled it, and it smashed onto the ground some feet away.

Fin's outburst startled me. Nemo pressed me protectively to him.

I couldn't believe what a foolish idiot Gill was being. We hadn't submerged in the lake for very long. The mermen needed a good soaking. Half a day's worth, at least, in order to moisten their scales.

I grabbed Nemo's arm. "We have to find him. He's too weak."

"Stubbornness and recklessness are that man's vices," Fin replied, jumping aboard the front of the wagon and taking a seat beside Nemo. "You'll never change his mind. I learned that the hard way."

Something told me I shouldn't ask. Doing so would only serve to fuel my anger. But I couldn't help myself. I wanted to know more about the mysterious Gill. "How?"

Nemo chuckled. "Gill was a real, royal pain in the ass when he first joined the battalion. Talking back. Refusing orders. Disrespecting the generals. Fin felt sorry for Gill and was lenient with him because the merarmy was his last chance. One time, Fin covered up a fight between Gill and another mersoldier. When one of the generals investigated the matter, Fin was demoted for not reporting the incident."

"When he wants to be, Gill is a talented mersoldier," Fin said. "I build careers. I don't destroy them."

Part of me pitied Gill. From what I'd been told, it appeared he didn't know how to channel his anger. I related to that. Many times, I had returned to my chambers after a merrealm meeting, wanting to tear someone's head off. To blow off steam, I'd channel all my energy into my artwork, painting up a frenzy. Perhaps Gill needed a hobby so he could do the same thing. Otherwise, he might get thrown out of his battalion one day.

Hearing this made me see the mermen in a different light. Fin was a kind and supportive leader, not a harsh, intolerable one. He ruled with heart and not an iron fist. In Gill's case, that was the best thing he could hope for in a leader.

My heart was heavy. Leaving Gill to his own devices spelled trouble for him. The collector's hunters were still out there. Gill wasn't fully rejuvenated, and while we'd escaped a small band of pirates with the help of the resistance, how would we fare against an even bigger group if one ventured our way? My gut ate away at me, telling me we couldn't leave him to fend for himself. But my mind screamed at me to choose the safer option and continue to the sea.

I bit my fingernails. This was one of the hardest decisions of my life. Did I leave a one of my merfolk behind and risk him getting recaptured and dying? Or should I do everything in my power to stop him? If we could catch up to him, we could knock him out and steal him away to the sea!

Something my father had said to me when I'd been ten cycles old floated into my thoughts. Sometimes, in times of conflict, you had to make sacrifices for the greater good in order to protect the lives of the majority. During that cycle of Haven, the prevailing currents had failed to bring the nutrient-rich warm waters that fertilized Tritonia's crops. Our people had starved, and many children and elderly merfolk had died. My father had reluctantly sent three missionaries to his brother's kingdom, begging him for food, knowing this might upset the shaky peace that had existed between us. In return, my uncle had killed them and sent their heads back to my father. At the time, my father had prepared to retaliate and fight for the lives of his slain men. I'd talked my father out of seeking revenge. Hundreds of merfolk had then perished from starvation, and many more suffered under my uncle's cruel regime. Because of me, my father hadn't saved them. What a valuable lesson. I'd never make that mistake again.

Deep in my heart, I knew Gill was his own merman and could make his own choices. It was time to let him accept his fate and for me to face mine. For now, I had to focus on healing my two mermen. Then we could think about saving the other kidnapped merfolk.

Still, that didn't stop the leaded weight taking residence in my stomach.

"Go," Fin instructed Nemo/

The wagon rolled away, and that weight grew even heavier.

Fin climbed onto the wagon, taking the seat beside me, squashing me between him and Nemo. But I didn't mind one bit. Having him beside me filled me with some comfort, and I leaned my head on his shoulder for comfort.

Fin fell silent as we left Gill behind. Nemo and I respected the commander's wishes and refrained from chit-chatting, although the ever-joyful Nemo hummed a little tune, the sound reminding me of home.

***

SALTY AIR LICKED at my face and hair. From several leagues away, the sea breeze called to me. My pores responded, buzzing with urgency to return home and preparing for my merging with the ocean. I enjoyed every adventure on land—even this one, though only for the company I'd kept—but my heart belonged to the sea.

"Home," said Nemo, pushing the horses into a canter to reduce the distance separating us from the ocean.

A ball of excitement charged through me as I brushed aside the palm leaves scraping my skin.

Over the many leagues we'd traveled since leaving Gill behind, the terrain had graduated into a flat slope. Trees decreased in height, making way for the smaller dune shrubs. Wind had blown the sand this far, and it crunched under the wheels. Spindly roots and trunks sprouted up everywhere, and the wagon bumped over them. The path led us all the way to one of the two ports on the Tritonia beach.

"You two go ahead," Fin said, climbing out of the cart. "I'll tie up the horses out of sight. We'll need them if we're to return for Gill and his sister."

I didn't want to leave Fin. He was still sullen from Gill defying a direct order. I knew how much I needed company to cheer me up when I was upset.

"I'll do it," I said. "You need the water more than I do."

"I'm not leaving you alone again," Fin replied.

His response struck a chord inside me. Was it bad that I didn't want to be alone? Be away from him? Or from Nemo, for that matter? Damn it, I even missed Gill. What was it about these three mermen? I hardly knew them, but every fiber of my being wanted to know more about them. To hell with my odd attraction. I didn't care to understand it. All I wanted was for them to feel the same way about me.

Nemo and I waited for Fin to lead the horses away into the bushes. He was gone awhile, and I started to worry and bite my nails...something I'd never done before.

At last, Fin returned. "They were sure thirsty. Almost drank up an entire puddle. Now, they're grazing on the dune grass."

Thirst tightened my pores, and I longed for water. "Will the horses be safe?"

"I spotted some caves to the east," said Fin, gesturing for Nemo and me to venture down to the beach. "After a swim, we'll take them up there and camp for the night."

The idea of camping with these two—just the three of us, all alone—sent a thrill skating along my stomach and down between my legs.

"Sounds like a plan," I replied, unable to hide the excitement in my voice.

Sun-kissed sand trickled between my toes as I walked. I loved the feeling, loved *everything* about the ocean. The waves crashing in my ears. Wind dancing along the shore, carrying sand grains in little funnels.

Nemo took my hand, and we raced through the dunes. At the foreshore, he tugged off his clothes and charged into the water, leaving me to yank at the strings of my corset. Damn thing took so long to undo. In my mind, he screamed with joy, and I smiled with anticipation of joining him shortly.

Fin caught up and stood beside me, but he wasn't stripping off to join us.

"You're not coming in?" I asked, pulling off my skirt and corset, leaving my merrealm cloth on to cover my chest.

"No," he said with a smile. "I'll keep a vigil."

"Boring!" I slapped him on the shoulder.

Fin was too serious. He needed to lighten up. Let his hair down and party a little. We were free from the pirates, for Poseidon's sake! That alone was worthy of celebration. It was also a shame Gill hadn't joined us. He, like Fin, needed the rejuvenation only the sea could grant.

"Yahoo!" Nemo dove underneath the water.

I tugged on Fin's arm. "Please." He needed this more than I did.

"Once Nemo's had his turn."

"Always looking after your men."

"That's what a good leader does."

His words hit me hard. Unlike him, I wasn't a natural leader. Didn't want to be. But something about the way he'd said those words ate away at me. Reminded me of what my mother always used to say. "A princess must be a good example for her people." Did that mean I should stay with him?

I didn't get the chance to offer because something seized me around the waist and forced me off balance. I crashed into the water and kicked. My sea vision activated. The grip released me, and I spun. Strong, thick legs propelled Nemo away from me.

Why, that cheeky guppy.

I stood and twirled in circles, relishing the sand mushing between my toes, the waves crashing into my knees. Froth hissed as the bubbles popped. Salty liquid diffused through my skin. I fell to my knees and sat in the water, letting its cool touch caress and recharge me. The water called to my scales, and they flashed along my elbow and hands. I let my transformation overcome me. Magic sparkles radiated outward. Silver scales sprouted across my skin, reshaping my legs into a fin and tail. My gills inhaled the wondrous, salty air, flushing out the smoke I'd breathed earlier when we'd stayed in the little town.

I ventured deeper in the water after Nemo, wanting to bathe in the wild call of the sea. He grabbed me by the waist, and we twirled in circles, him clasping my hand. Bubbles tickled my skin as we sailed along the ocean floor. The warm water brushed my hair behind my back and slid along my skin like silk. I loved the weightless, airborne sensation the ocean gave me.

"You hungry, Princess?" Nemo said in my mind.

Now that I thought about it, yes, I was. I hadn't eaten since breakfast the previous morning. "Starving," I told him.

"Let me get you something," he offered, squeezing my waist.

Electricity charged through me. I adored the way he looked after me. His doting attention left me feeling a little giddy. In that brief moment, my attraction to him owned me, and his touch left me wanting more, so much more. I placed one hand on his arm, the other on his chest. We stared into each other's eyes. Recognition hit. An attraction flashed behind his gaze. Desire pulsed in my veins, too.

Before I knew what was happening, he kissed me and spun me in circles. It felt like butterfly fish fluttered in my stomach. His lips melted on mine, soft and passionate. I devoured the taste of him, that saltiness mixed with oyster and the rum he'd sipped earlier. His heat roared through me, and I could hardly breathe from excitement. Firm hands explored the curves of my hips, leaving my flesh buzzing and wanting him to explore more of me. I pressed myself against his hard chest, needing him, drowning in his sweet kisses. Everything in my head screamed at me to slow down. But all I wanted was to make him mine.

I shivered in his grip, both from anticipation and nerves.

"Are you cold?" Nemo asked me, holding me tighter.

I shook my head. My uneasiness got the better of me, and I pulled away. This was all so new to me. I didn't really know what I was doing. No one had ever instructed me on the ways of the flesh, and my sea pearl remained untouched. Sure, Nimian and Gellian had given me some tips, but at the moment, I couldn't recall a single word either of them had said.

"Don't you like my salty lips, Princess?" he joked.

I loved his lips on mine. That wasn't the issue. Having him close, being vulnerable, and doing something stupid played on my mind.

Nemo held me, and I leaned my head on his chest,

basking in the delicious feeling of being in his arms. He trailed his finger down the side of my arm and along the edge of my wrist.

That was one of my ticklish spots, and I moved away. "Stop that. I'm ticklish."

"Really?" he said in a cheeky way, doing it again.

This time, I jerked upward, slamming my head into his chin.

"Oh, sea god." I rubbed the impact spot.

Pain carved his expression. "Bit my tongue," he told me.

Trust me to ruin a perfect moment. Most of the time, my embraces with mermen ended like this, thanks to my habit of ruining a perfect situation. Poseidon, why did I do this every time? Me with guys spelled trouble.

Poseidon, help me get a hold of myself around these mermen.

Humiliation and frustration swept through me like a vicious storm. My heart was ready to explode from the disturbing emotions. I had to get out of there.

"I'm so sorry," I told him as I rocketed away.

Before I breached the surface, I heard his apology, "I'm sorry if I crossed the line, Princess. I'll be back soon with some food."

Guilt added into the mix of feelings flooding me. I felt so awful for running away. Now, poor Nemo thought I'd done so because of him. Maybe, when my heart stopped thrashing in my chest, scolding me, burning me, I'd talk to him about what had almost happened between us.

CHAPTER 12

My stomach scrunched as I changed back into a human and climbed up the shore.

Fin was there to greet me with a gorgeous smile. "How was the water?"

I rubbed my arms and stared at the ground as I collected my clothes. "I'll meet you at the cave."

He grabbed my arm with one hand and pushed my chin with the other so our eyes met. "Whatever is wrong?"

His heat chased away the cold settling in my stomach.

"Nothing." Right now, I just needed some time to process my emotions. I couldn't do that with Fin near. Being right next to him clouded my head further. The smell of him... Poseidon... That fresh seaweed bloom...it made my mind swirl with thoughts of kissing Fin, too. And after what had just happened with Nemo, I wasn't sure I wanted to kiss another merman ever again. If I avoided those kinds of situations, I would save myself the shame.

"Where's Nemo?" Fin splashed beside me in the water.

"Gone hunting for food," I yelled to be heard over the rising wind blowing along the shore.

"I'll go with you." He kept pace with me.

In all honesty, I just wanted to be alone. But perhaps that wasn't a good idea, given the circumstances with Faraall and the pirates. So I let Fin accompany me. He didn't say a word, which I appreciated, but the silence also annoyed me a little because my mind tortured me, going over and over what had happened with Nemo.

"Why do I always do stupid things in front of mermen?" I blurted out, and then I cringed, wanting to take back the question. I sighed. "I wish I could be normal around them."

Fin laughed, but not in a way that made me feel silly. "You think the mud incident was embarrassing?" Wind whipped at his gorgeous blonde locks.

"And Blade's crotch," I muttered, kicking the sand.

A roguish grin stretched across Fin's face. "When I first went to kiss a girl, I head-butted her."

"Done that," I replied.

"When I met her family," continued Fin, gazing out over the sea, "I asked if her sister was pregnant. Turned out, she was just voluptuous."

Now that made me laugh. Fortunately, I hadn't done that.

Fin picked up a shell and tossed it into the water. "On a date with a different mermaid, I spilled garlic prawns on her hair."

My stomach ached from laughing so hard. Yep, I'd done something similar. It felt so good to know I wasn't alone.

"It happens." He shrugged. "Don't torment yourself about it. Just laugh."

At that moment, I wanted to hug him. Instead, I touched his arm, getting that familiar zap, and a flood of warmth moved through me. "Thank you for making me feel less like a dopey dory."

"You're welcome."

We walked for several hundred feet in silence. For once, I

relished the lack of chatter. What Fin had done had calmed my angst, allowing me to enjoy the moment with him.

He glanced at me, his blue eyes restrained. "Nyssa, may I ask you something?"

"Ask away," I said.

"You remind me of me when I was younger," he said. "A little rebellious. Wanting to follow your own path. But what would you do if you weren't a princess?"

"No one's ever asked me that," I said, drawing a starfish in the sand with my toe. "Teach art or dance at the Academy." That wasn't going to happen since I wasn't very good at either of those things. But I could still dream.

"You dance?" Fin's wicked grin returned. "I better get out the way of your whirlwind."

"Ha ha." I elbowed him. "I have to. I'm a princess."

Unexpectedly, he grabbed my hands and pulled me close. "Dance with me."

Bad idea. Especially after what I'd done to Nemo. I tried pulling away, but he twisted me to the left, and I stumbled, not used to dancing on my feet. Even though the thought of being close to him was overwhelming, all consuming, I didn't want to get too close and have something go wrong.

He grabbed my hand and spun around me, forcing me to twist with him. This was the start of dances conducted at court. He repeated the same move, and I watched him, transfixed. His smile coaxed me to join him, but my nerves held me back. He lifted his arm so his elbow pointed to the sea and his fingers to the sky. Then he positioned my arm in the same way. Sparks exploded inside me, urging me to continue, to have him near. So I pressed my hand firmer to his.

"That's the spirit," he said, his delicious voice convincing me to do anything he asked. *Anything*.

We twirled in a circle and pressed our other hands

together, palm to palm. Our eyes locked as we circled each other, pass after pass. Each time I had to spin around him, I missed gazing into his eyes, even though the moment only lasted an instant. He pressed one arm in front of his chest, the other behind, and revolved around me. But then he broke the steps in the dance, falling in beside me and pressing me to his chest. My wrists tingled as he locked his fingers through mine, lifted one hand, and placed it on my shoulder, holding my other arm out in the waltzing position.

Sea god, this was romantic. Secretly, I'd always imagined doing this with my future partner. Fin matched the qualities of the man I had desired: well-mannered, educated, kind, romantic, strong, and principled. A far cry from the last creep I'd danced with, a jerk who'd insulted me, commending me on my perfect breasts and ass, which had earned him a slap across the face and me the judgmental stares from hundreds of pairs of curious eyes.

Fin led me across the sand in small, box-shaped shuffles. The weight of his stare drilled into me, and my shyness claimed me, forcing me to focus on his muscled chest instead of looking into his eyes.

"Chin up, Princess," he teased as he shifted me in another direction.

I giggled and lifted my head. This time, his gaze held me captive...a willing prisoner. I hadn't noticed the green flecks in his eyes, the color of the water in the lagoons of The Cove. My heart sprouted wings as he lifted my arm above my head and twirled me then pulled me back into position. This moment, Fin—they were both perfect in every way.

"Why are you holding your breath?" His breath brushed my skin like a soft breeze.

"I am?" I hadn't even noticed. Being this close was electrifying. All I could think about was him. I felt like I was gliding across the currents as he zigzagged me over the sand.

Then he did the unexpected, leaning me back, and I tightened in his grip. Blood rushed to my head. I didn't like the feeling of being upside down—not on land, at any rate. At least in the water, I was weightless. This felt like my whole body was being dragged to the ground by an invisible force. In a rush of fear, I scrambled to regain my footing. Instead, I accidentally kicked him.

Air rushed out of his mouth. He grunted and dropped me to the sand before hunching over, cradling his merman sack.

Poseidon! I'd kicked him there. From what I'd been told, that was excruciating, and the discomfort lasted a while. Guilt curled through me like a stomach cramp.

"Sea god, not again." I went to rub him then pulled away. My mind screamed at me not to touch him. That could only end in disaster. But my heart trumped my brain, and I stood up, reaching out to stroke his face a few times, then lower, where I'd kicked him.

"Close call, Princess," he said, gritting his teeth. "Got me on the edge. Not as bad as what I've had in battle."

Warriors kicked other soldiers in the groin in battle? Dirty tactics.

The pain cutting into his expression tugged at my guilt, and the crackling feeling in my stomach wormed up into my chest. Right then, I didn't care about my actions. How inappropriate massaging his balls might be. All I wanted was to kiss him better and wipe that look from his face. I brushed his hair aside and left a soft kiss on his forehead.

"I'm so sorry," I whispered.

"You're making it really hard to be respectful," he growled.

Shellfish. He just wanted to swear at me for what I'd done. Tell me to get lost.

"Sorry." Heat pooled in my face and neck, and I tucked

my hands between my legs, refusing to let them go anywhere near him again.

My gaze dipped to the growing hardness between us. Voices screamed inside my head to look away. But I couldn't. I admired all of him in his glory. Muscles in his arms flexed as he tried to cover his erection. My knees weakened at the sight of his chiseled stomach. An itch took residence in my fingers, and I longed to run them along his hairless chest. My lips swelled at the thought of brushing them over his skin. Of kissing his warm flesh. Sucking it. Biting it.

The sudden awkwardness of the situation struck me. By the stormy seas, I hoped he hadn't caught me ogling him. I didn't want to appear desperate and creepy like Nimian who had earned the nickname "barnacle" after following mermen around like a lovesick stonefish.

Shellfish. What had I done? I just wanted to turn into a puddle of water and drain back into the sea.

"I've tried to be respectful, but to hell with it." He grabbed my hand and wrapped it over his pulsing cock.

His admission made my breath catch in my throat. My heartbeat charged like a spooked horse. Right then, I really wanted this second chance and to not mess it up. My lips ached for him to kiss me. I longed for the courage to not become terrified and pull away. Instead, I would throw caution to the winds and sink into his arms. But then my mind seized as his penis twitched in my grasp. I didn't know what to do with it.

He cradled my neck and pulled me to him. "I don't care if I'm crossing the line anymore."

Shellfish, neither did I.

His lips pressed mine with fervor. They were soft and warm, and they tasted like sea honey, and I sucked them, eager for more.

I moved into his embrace, melting, my head spinning,

letting go of my earlier fears. His heart called to mine, and I accepted with boundless regard. Flames of desire raged through me. The sensation stirred my sea pearl, which tingled, desperate for his touch. I wanted to become one with him. Wetness pooled between my legs the longer he kissed me. Foreign thoughts and feelings coursed through me.

He eased me to the sand and placed himself atop me. Nothing else in the world mattered right then. Not the wind that picked up and tore at my hair. Not the call of the sea. Everything melted into one. My body into his. His lips opened, and his tongue slipped into my mouth. At first, it gently prodded mine, twirling, exploring, then he sucked my tongue between his lips. I could hardly breathe. My pulse beat so hard. His hands ran through my hair. I linked my hands around his strong neck for support. Heat swarmed in my mound below.

His warm, sweet kisses moved to my neck, and I moaned, enjoying the sensations he sparked inside me. I was falling. Surrendering. Lost in our desire. And I didn't care about finding my way back.

Fin explored my body with calloused fingers, grazing them along the indentation of my waist and down to the curve of my hips. Each motion sent electricity arcing through me. He grew bolder, reaching to caress my breast through my corset, and I pulled away.

"Was I too bold?" The way he rubbed my sides made it hard for me to think straight.

Yes. But I loved every second of it. He'd surprised me when he'd brushed his hand over my tingling nipple. In all honesty, I hadn't imagined anyone but my husband touching me there. Of course, my interaction with Fin threw *that* idea out the window. My whole body ached for him. As did my soul. No one had ever made me feel this way. One touch and I felt like I sailed the ocean currents on a complete high.

Smiling, I pressed his hand to my breast, as he had done to me earlier. He gave me a grin that took my breath away. I was lost in his touch as he ducked his head and sucked my nipple. I groaned and wriggled beneath him. My sea pearl begged for him.

But then a harsh reality struck. We were out there in the open. Nemo might return at any moment. After what had happened, what might he think of me?

"What if Nemo returns?" I asked.

But then I gasped, unable to resist the lure of Fin's hand snaking down my belly and between my legs. Poseidon, this felt amazing. A thrill skated down every vertebra in my spine.

"He'll be a while," Fin said, creeping lower, laying kisses along my belly.

I groaned as Fin's fingers stroked the folds between my legs. No one had ever touched me there before. It felt like heaven. His fingers moved across me like silk, teasing open my soft pink lips. Bolts of energy cascaded through me. Warmth spread from my sea pearl into my stomach.

"Poseidon," I cried, gripping his hand.

"You like that?" Fin's finger sped up, setting me on fire.

"Yes," I moaned, arching my back.

"What about this?" He buried his face in my mound, spread my legs wider, his tongue stroking my slickness up and down, working me into a frenzy.

"Poseidon, yes," I cried, my nether regions going wild from his touch.

"Good." His breath tickled me.

He plunged a finger into my waiting entrance. It hurt a little at first, stretching me, preparing me for more. My muscles tensed with nerves, and I shifted with discomfort.

"What's wrong?" he looked up, his lips slick with my wetness.

I didn't know what to say. Every second of this entire experience had been breathtaking. But a little fear had inched up and had taken hold of me, and now I couldn't relax.

"Are you a virgin?" he asked.

Shellfish. How did he know? Was it that obvious? Burning shame consumed my whole body. Everybody in the merealm was sleeping with their partners. A princess didn't have to be chaste before marriage. I know my sisters Aquina and Lativa weren't.

He sat up and brushed his hair from his eyes. "Poseidon! Your father's going to kill me!"

Sorrow burrowed under my ribcage. My father would never let me have a relationship with a merman below my station. I was going straight to hell for what I was doing. But I didn't care, and I wanted more.

"No." I sat up and grabbed him, pulling him close. "Don't go. Please. I want you to claim me."

His eyes told me he needed this as much as I did. To join with me, soak in the comfort of our entwining bodies, and take the gift I offered him.

With a shake of his head, he muttered, "Dying would be worth it for you."

Other than my father, no one had ever made me feel so worthy, so valuable and honored. The fact that Fin was willing to risk so much for me touched me deep inside.

Poseidon, don't take him from me. Never let my father find out. Let this be our little secret with your blessing.

He kissed my inner thighs and hauled my legs over his shoulders again. Shellfish, the position—the very act—was awkward but sexy as hell. One touch of his tongue on my folds had me coasting along the waves of pleasure. His lips clasped around my privates, sucking, licking, nibbling. I moaned, forgetting my shyness, and dug my fingers into the sand. Sea god, that was divine. The pressure of his tongue sent me over the edge, and I panted, rejoicing in the continued waves washing over me.

He lowered me once more and crawled over top of me. By the look in his eyes, I knew he wasn't finished with me nor I with him. His gaze promised me heaven, and I surrendered to him, knowing he'd take me there. My mind spun in a whirl of delight as he painted my neck with kisses filled with power, passion, and longing. My heart opened to him like a flower welcoming the light. I held on to his strong arms, melting in their warmth, their touch, their promise to protect me.

"Poseidon, I can't take it anymore." He shifted onto his knees, spread me wide, and lifted my hips over his thighs. "This might hurt a little," he whispered, looking at me as if asking for my permission.

How could I resist his request? I nodded furiously. Today, this little mermaid would become a merwoman. Fin was just the right merman to claim me. To hell with my father and the consequences. I was already in too deep.

For a few moments, he stroked his throbbing shaft, and a little pearl drop squeezed out of the head. My sea pearl blazed with such intensity, wanting him, begging for him. Fin ran a hand over my stomach as he eased his pulsing head into the velvety-soft petals of my slick pussy. It stung like I'd cut myself on a broken shell, and it stretched me in strange and wonderful ways. My fingers raked through the sand as he pushed harder and deeper, filling me.

A groan resonated in my throat as he tempted my body in ways I'd never experienced before. Every inch of me sizzled as he plunged deeper into me, carrying me closer to another orgasm.

He grabbed my hands and interlocked our fingers again.

The feeling of his hand in mine felt so natural. So right. Like salt in water. Air in the ocean.

Loving every moment, I screamed as a new wave crashed over me. My whole body quivered with delight. I hadn't even known such pleasure existed. I yearned to remain on this high with Fin forever, to never have to go back to the troubles that awaited me.

Fin groaned and stiffened as he exploded inside me. Then he pulled out of me and lifted me onto his lap, where we stayed, his breaths coming hard and heavy like mine were. My heart beat wildly. For those few moments, everything was perfect.

I nuzzled into his neck, smiling. I hadn't messed anything up for a change, and I'd found the courage to rub his balls. Good thing; otherwise, this might never have happened.

"That was..." I puffed.

My nipples were so hard, they jabbed into him like daggers. He teased one with his fingers, and I moaned.

"Amazing." Fin finished my sentence for me.

"Yes."

His lips on mine silenced any further words.

Soon, he climbed to his feet, with me holding on like a sea monkey. "I'm taking you to the cave to do that to you again."

My heart bounced against my ribcage. I ached to stay in his arms. For us to stay on the beach forever. Only getting up for food and a swim. Now that was my idea of heaven.

But that wasn't reality. When Nemo returned, we'd have to rest for the night then return to search for the Pearl of Aluria. And after that, we'd tackle Faraall and my father. I wish I could throw away my troubles and stay with Fin in bliss forever.

CHAPTER 13

I still felt Fin's tongue on my lips, and I couldn't stop touching them as we stood on the grassy knoll behind the cave.

"What do we need to make a fire?" I said, unable to remember what Fin had told me earlier.

"Kindling," replied Fin, picking up long, thin twigs from the scrubland. "We'll light this, and then we can add the larger logs."

My stomach twirled with excitement. I'd seen fires from afar. People on the beach had bonfires to celebrate special occasions. Merfolk lucky enough to sit beside one spoke of their intense heat and the way the burning logs spewed sparks into the air like an angry sea monster. Human culture fascinated me, and I was eager to learn new things about it.

"Then we shall use this to stoke the fire." Fin showed me a branch that had broken off a nearby tree.

I picked my way through the shrubs, hunting for twigs and grabbing as many as I could. Ahead of me in the scrubby forest, Fin collected thicker branches and a few logs. Once we had amassed a reasonable pile, we dumped them near the lagoon inside the cave. Then we returned to collect some rocks from the entrance.

A flock of seagulls flew overhead, as if they retreated to their nests for the night. The air carried the sweet song of crickets, and it enveloped me in its embrace. Cottony clouds streaked the peach sky above. It wouldn't be long before the sun disappeared below the horizon, and the stars danced above us. I loved watching them, especially shooting stars, and any time I breached the water's surface at night I would stay to watch them. We didn't have a night or day sky in the depths of the ocean. Our light was artificially made with glowing crystals and neon sea anemones.

These thoughts led me to wonder where Gill was and if he slept under the stars or if he had taken cover in accommodations somewhere. I prayed to the sea god that he found and returned with his sister safely.

"You're beautiful when you smile," Fin said, his arms full of stones.

My heart did a flip. He gave me a quick kiss and waited for me to enter the cave first.

Inside was breathtaking. Sunlight streamed through an opening in the cave's roof. Crystal blue waters within the lagoon beckoned for me to join it. The walls shimmered from the light reflecting off the water. Green mossy growth crawled up the wall. I couldn't stop looking at it all as Fin and I built the stone circle for the fire.

By the time we finished, Nemo emerged from the water, his skin flushed pink from the swim.

"Anyone hungry?" he asked, his voice full of his usual cheer, as if our earlier encounter had floated away like bubbles drifting with the tide. Nothing seemed to bother him, and I liked that about him.

A seaweed basket was strapped across his chest. Every merchild was taught to weave a basket when they were young. I hadn't made one in over ten years, but I still remembered how. Memories of my grandmother teaching me the technique flooded back. Poseidon, rest her soul. Nemo must have made his while hunting. He removed it and handed it to Fin.

"Just in time." Fin slapped a hand on Nemo's back and rummaged through the basket, removing an oyster and downing it. "I was just about to start a fire to cook the fish."

Nemo clutched his stomach. "Roast crab and salmon." He clasped his fingers and thumb together, kissing them and making an *mmm* sound.

I wasn't watching what delicious treats were on offer. My gaze trailed the beads of water rolling down Nemo's perfect barrel chest. Then my gut pinched as I thought about what had happened between us earlier—and then I'd turned into a trollop and slept with Fin right afterward. I couldn't deny that my heart had fallen for both of them. But Nemo was the jealous kind. What would he think of me if he found out about Fin and me? My heart would break if I hurt him.

Nemo took my hand. "Come. Light the fire with me, Princess."

"Watch out," Fin warned. "The princess might set your eyebrows alight."

"Hey!" I slapped Fin on the arm. "That's enough of your cheekiness."

Fin cackled as I sat beside Nemo on the rocky floor.

Nemo leaned on his knees behind me. "Hold these."

My skin electrified as he reached around my sides and placed two small rocks in my palms. His arms brushed my waist as he held my wrists. A tremble ran through me. Poseidon, I hoped he didn't notice how nervous and crazy I turned in his presence. *Please, sea god, don't let me hurt him with these rocks.*

Nemo's breath tickled my neck. My skin was on fire, being so close to him.

"Scrape the rocks together like this." He moved my arms in opposite directions.

Sparks flew off the rocks and into the wood. They flared inside me, too. It took me a few moments to gather myself. I could barely concentrate with his fresh seaweed smell clouding my mind.

"Amazing!" I'd never seen anything so magical before.

"You try it," he said, releasing my wrists.

But I didn't want to. I didn't want him to stop touching me. I wanted his hands on me. Our bodies close. For him to hold me and me to lean into him and breathe him in.

My mind spun in a whirl of uncertainty. I'd bonded with Fin. Flirting with Nemo might hurt Fin. Or vice versa. I didn't want that. If only I could have them both. Sea god! Why was I attracted to them both? Damn it. They were both my type. Fin the quiet, respectful, well-mannered rebel. Nemo, the sweet and fun, hulking giant who reminded me of the sexy Sharkriders. Fighting how I felt was useless, and I knew it.

"Sea to princess," said Nemo, shuffling around to wave in my face.

That was a saying we used when someone drifted off into watery space.

"Oops, sorry." I repeated the motion he'd taught me. Sparks glimmered and fizzled but didn't catch fire. It took me a few more attempts before the sparks caught on the twigs, and they turned red hot and smoked.

"Great job, Princess." Nemo's coaxing voice turned me into a puddle.

"Nyssa," I corrected him.

He smiled as if he'd called me by my title on purpose—possibly to get my attention—and crept around me to blow on the kindling and add more twigs to the orange glow. They quickly caught alight with flames.

I stared into the bright, flickering mass of hazy light, hypnotized by it.

Fin threw a few small branches onto the fire, and they blackened, smoke curling from them. Next, he laid two flat stones inside the fire. I wondered what he was going to use those for.

Nemo dragged the basket over to me. "Hungry?"

Uh. Yeah. For him… I meant, for both him and the food. Sea god. These two were turning me into a bumbling mess.

My eyes widened at the bountiful supply of oysters, mussels, crabs, and salmon. Sweet Poseidon. My favorites. I couldn't decide which one I wanted first. Every part of me was excited to try the fire-roasted fish, but it might be a while until the fire really got going. My stomach growled like a wild bear, as if it hadn't been fed for a week.

Back at the palace, I ate well and at regular intervals— dining on all sorts of treats: fish, clams, oysters, shellfish, crab, sea grasses, and more. But on land, I never knew when my next meal would be or if I'd even get one, so the smell of the roasting seafood gave me comfort.

I couldn't stop thinking of Gill, even though I was still pissed at him for leaving. Was he dining tonight? Was he starving? Was he feeling the effects of the dehydration again? A part of me felt terrible for eating such delicacies, knowing Gill might be going hungry.

"Princess," Nemo said with a laugh in his throat. "Hurry up. I'm starving."

"Oh, excuse me." I selected two oysters and then let him take his pick. A giant like him needed the sustenance more than I did.

He grabbed a fish and bit a chunk out of it. Unlike

humans, we merfolk didn't use knives or forks. Hands were good enough—even for royals.

My goodness, the oysters were fresh—slimy and salty. Just the way I liked them. "These are delicious. Thank you for catching them."

Fin whacked Nemo on the back three times. "Yes, thank you, Nemes." He laid two salmon on each of the flat stones.

Fish oil and juice dribbled down Nemo's chin as he grinned. *Poseidon.* That made him even sexier and raw. I had to call on all my restraint not to shuffle over to him and lick those juices off his chin. Humans might think merfolk disgusting for our barbaric eating practices, but in the water, the juices always washed away. We didn't need napkins and all that useless finery humans relied on.

"You eat like a sparrow fish, Princess." Nemo shoved the basket at me. "I don't want your royal ass to get bony."

We had a good laugh at that one.

My ass sure wasn't going to shrink from not eating for a few nights. I grabbed one of the branches from the pile and poked Nemo with it.

"Watch it, or I'll spank that royal ass." A deep, hearty laugh flew past his lips.

My knees weakened, both at the sound and the promise in his words.

"Careful, soldier," Fin warned in a lighthearted tone. "She might feed you to her sharks."

The way he sucked another oyster down made me burn down below. I imagined him pouring them on my stomach and licking them off me.

"Yes, I might," I said, giving him a seductive glance as I devoured a mussel.

He cocked an eyebrow, as if accepting my challenge.

Nemo viciously jabbed at the fish to turn them over.

Scales on his temples flashed green with envy. "Did you have a swim yet, Captain?"

"Not yet." Fin's smile faded, and he avoided my gaze.

Uneasiness sat like a boulder in my gut, putting me off my food.

"What's the plan to save the king?" Nemo tore the head off his fish, spit it out, and it hit a nearby rock, making me jolt.

Nemo's jealousy was raising its ugly head again. For some reason Nemo didn't like me flirting with Fin. Nor did he like Blade flirting with me. It was as almost as if Nemo thought I was his. His behavior reminded me a little of Faraall and made me feel sick.

"Camp the night here," replied Fin, tossing another log on the fire. "Then leave at first light, and search for the dark pearl."

The mention of the pearl made my mind wander to my father. I imagined him having a fit back at home, wondering where I was and why I had disobeyed his order to wed that slimy slug. Would he send a search party out to find me? Bring me back and force me into the marriage? These thoughts made me even more determined to find the magic pearl the sea witch had asked me to bring to her.

Fin lifted the fish off the hot stone with two small branches and rested it on the rocky cave floor. "Let this cool a little first," he told me.

I nodded. Moments earlier, my mouth had watered at the thought of tasting the cooked fish. Now, I couldn't get anything, not even a word, past the thickness in my throat. After a few moments, I pulled off a sliver and bit into it, pretending nothing was wrong. The taste of creamy and feathery fish filled my mouth.

"Delicious," I said, forcing myself to eat another mouthful, even though I couldn't stomach any more. A shame, really, because the salmon was very tasty. Even better than when eaten raw.

No one said anything. Only the crackle of the fire and shifting of the embers echoed in the cave. The painful silence struck me harder than one of Faraall's blows.

Nemo selected his fourth raw fish.

"Another one?" I managed to ask in an attempt to start a bit of friendly conversation.

He flexed one of his arms. "Got to maintain these muscles somehow."

Good. The Nemo with the golden smile had returned.

Fin let out a nervous laugh. "Remember the time Gilled dared you to eat a whole tuna, so you did?"

Tunas were huge. Some of them were up to three feet long. One that big had fed my family for two nights.

Nemo grabbed his stomach, as if recalling the pain of it. "My stomach hurt for three days after that."

We all laughed together. Fin's attempt to lighten the mood seemed to be working.

Sitting by the fire with the mersoldiers was a far cry from meals with my family, where we discussed serious topics like politics of the realm, palace matters, treaties, and alliances. Poseidon. After twenty-two years of it, I was well and truly bored. If I wanted to talk politics, I'd visit one of my father's advisors.

Spending time with these mermen reminded me of my escapes with my cousin. A real treat when compared with the stuffy and claustrophobic environment I'd grown up in.

Fin put aside the last of his fish. "I'm full. Nemes, do you mind guarding the princess while I swim?"

"Sure," Nemo said through a mouthful of crab.

Fin sprang to his feet and backed into the water. "With all my heart, I wish to kiss you." His voice echoed in my mind.

I longed for the same thing, but having Nemo there made

things a little awkward. Even more awkward since I had a crush on them both and didn't know how to deal with my feelings—or with Nemo's jealousy.

Green luminescence lit up the water as Fin's legs transformed into a merman's tail. "I won't stray far," he told me. "Don't worry about Nemes getting jealous. By the morning, it will blow over like a storm."

"Bring me back some more oysters, Captain," Nemo said with a wave right before Fin dove into the water.

Alone with Nemo, I began to dwell on the events of the last few hours—the meal that had turned sour, head-butting him and then running away from him, what had happened immediately after that, and how mad he'd probably get if I told him what Fin and I had done. My stomach felt as if it was filled with coral dust. I picked the shell off a crab but didn't eat it.

"You're quiet, Princess," said Nemo, looking at me at last, the hardness in his eyes melting away. "Something wrong?"

"No," I lied.

"You haven't eaten much of your fish."

"Not hungry."

"Want to play a game of truth or dare?"

Amazing how his dark mood had cleared now that Fin had left.

I welcomed anything to get my mind off my troubles and to get past the awkwardness of earlier. "Sure. Truth."

"What frightens you?" said Nemo, sucking the meat out of another crab.

Good question. "Not being in control or having a choice when it comes to what to do with my life."

He nodded. "Nothing frightens me. But it sucks when you disagree with an order from your superior."

It was nice to hear that we had things in common. Who'd

have thought a soldier and a princess would have anything relatable when our lives were so vastly different?

"One time," said Nemo, "the commander forced my squadron to attack an innocent village to smoke out a pirate. Whispers through the seaweed vine said the pirate owed him money. We got the bandit in the end, but loads of humans were hurt in the process."

Bile rose in my throat. The idea of being married to such a pig revolted me. I hadn't thought his crimes could get worse, but apparently, I'd been wrong.

"That's horrible," I said, snapping a twig I'd picked up. "My father would be outraged if he found out the commander abused his merarmy so."

Nemo nodded. "Yeah. Fin's butted heads with the commander over quite a few operations. If he quits the merarmy, I'm going with him. He's the only thing keeping me there."

I was glad to hear Nemo didn't hold a grudge against Fin for flirting with me. But how was Nemo going to take the news when he found out I'd lain with Fin? Given Nemo's sudden change in mood over Fin's flirtatiousness—I imagined not well. The words "gutted fish" came to mind. The coral dust cemented in my gut.

Nemo sharpened the end of his trident. "Don't get me wrong. I love the army. But the commander corrupted it. I don't like to dwell on that."

A serious edge captured his voice, and I knew better than to ask anything more about his current military life.

If only I could be more like he was. Then nothing would worry or upset me. But I had to tread carefully with his jealousy. If I didn't, we were going to have a problem. I didn't want him hurting anyone the way Faraall had.

Sea god! I should never have encouraged the mersoldiers affections. By doing so, I had inadvertently pitted two friends against each other. I didn't want to be the mermaid who came between Fin and Nemo.

"My turn," said Nemo, moving to the water to rinse his chin. "Truth."

His muscles rippled with every moment.

My eyes were glued to his amazing physique. To pull myself away, I threw another log on the fire, as the flamed had begun to dwindle. "What are your post-army plans?"

"I'm not leaving until I get a medal and make my family proud. It's a family tradition," he replied, wiping a hand across his face to brush the water off.

I liked his simple philosophy. It made me wish I was someone like him. Without the expectations and obligations I bore. Wanting to win a medal for his duty as a mersoldier was a great honor in the merealm.

"Then I'll go back to my family's farm on the seaweed plains," he added. "We harvest all the fresh seaweed for the kingdom."

My father had settled hundreds of refugees from my uncle's kingdom in the seaweed plains. After my grandfather had stepped down from his throne and given the kingdom to my father, not my uncle, and a war broke out over who was the rightful heir.

"Were you a refugee in the great war?" I scooted closer, eager to hear his story.

"Yeah."

"How old were you?"

"Ten," he replied.

Which would have made me seven years old at the time.

"Your uncle destroyed my father's crops." Nemo's voice took on a sad edge. "Brought in the whales to clear them all so he had land to fight on. My family's source of income was wiped out. We were homeless and starving."

I squeezed Nemo's arm. "I'm sorry to hear that. My uncle is a cruel and ruthless merman. I never liked him."

More and more merfolk defected to our kingdom under his strict reign. But my father forced us to visit every year on the anniversary of my grandfather's passing to commemorate his good name. Called it a way to keep the peace and to remind the family of why the kingdom had been divided in the first place.

A huge grin lit up Nemo's face, sweeping away any sorrow and brightening my heart.

"A squadron of your father's men rescued my family and relocated us. I've been loyal to your father ever since. Listen to me." Nemo slapped a large hand on his leg. "Blabbing more than a dory fish."

"It's okay," I said, wanting to know more about this incredible guy.

"Nyssa," he said, getting serious all of a sudden. "I'm sorry for being so forward before. Back in the ocean. You know. Kissing you."

Whoa! Invite the elephant fish into the room here, why don't you?

"Don't be," I said. "I liked it."

Shellfish. Me and my big mouth again. I wasn't supposed to be encouraging his affections. But part of me couldn't help it. That side of me wanted to explore my attraction to him.

"You did?" His eyes sparkled, telling me I was in trouble. "I've got to tell you something. In the spirit of truth or dare."

I leaned forward, curious to know what it was.

"Princess." He seemed breathless for some reason. "I've admired you for years."

His admission caught me off guard. *Shellfish.* Now, I really was in trouble. But the headstrong rebel in me didn't care and opened the floodgate, unleashing the torrent.

"When the king built us homes, you were there at the

ceremony," he said. "You put a wreath around my neck. I told my mother you were the girl I'd marry. She told me that was a preposterous notion. But I said I'd prove her wrong."

"Kids are so cute," I said with a laugh.

My chest swelled with joy at knowing I'd touched his heart. Discovering he had feelings for me, and for so long, had me soaring.

A war battled inside me. I craved Nemo like I did Fin. Confusion, passion, and fear whirled in my mind. Despite everything, being this close to Nemo, the way he smiled at me—as if no other mermaid existed—pushed all my doubts to the back of my mind.

He held up both palms. "I don't say that to freak you out. I'm not a creepy stalker, I swear. But the boys already let the tuna out of the net. I just wanted to explain my crush on you."

I recalled Gill mentioning Nemo's crush when I awoke in the pirate's wagon.

An image of Fin and me on the beach flashed in my mind. Then another of me piercing Nemo's heart with his trident. *Sea god.* This was going to torture me until I admitted the truth. My head told me I should be honest with him. But after his recent admission, I wasn't sure I could bring myself to break his heart…or mine.

So I said the worst and best thing possible. "I have a crush on you, too."

Little fissures splintered through my heart. I hadn't lied. But I wasn't being totally honest, either, and it killed me to hide things from him.

Nemo leaned forward and grazed my lips with his. "I knew I'd marry you," he joked, pulling me closer.

I succumbed to him, melting in his arms.

But those pesky visions persisted. They weren't setting me free until I confessed my indiscretions with Fin.

"Nemo," I said, swallowing hard.

A mask of confusion swept across his face as I pushed him away.

"What I just said is true. But there's something else I have to tell you."

"Don't tell me you're going to marry that creep Faraall?" He flexed his pecs and made them twitch. "Over this handsome beast?"

Sea god, he was making this hard for me. "No." A hiccupped laugh flew out of me. Sea god. How could I say this gently? "I…I was intimate with Fin earlier." My throat clogged up with that coral dust, preventing me from explaining further.

"What?" Nemo shuffled backward a few paces on his knees.

The distance between us made me ache for him.

"I've fallen for you both," I said, choking back tears.

"This wasn't how I planned it." He stood up and paced the floor.

"Nemo, please, sit with me."

He raised his palms in the air. "I'm sorry. I can't."

With that, he left me alone. Against his captain's orders. He might as well have stabbed me in the chest with his trident.

Curse me and my honesty. It was my best and worst quality. The reason I always put my fin in it. Why the nobles despised me. Now, I added Nemo to the list, too, and it crushed me.

I crawled into the water, hoping its loving embrace might comfort me, but it did nothing to ease the ache in my chest threatening to tear me apart. There I lay, staring at the sand, wanting to curl up and die like a sea slug that had abandoned its shell.

CHAPTER 14

*W*hen I woke from my restless slumber, neither Nemo nor Fin were present in the cave. The fire had all but died, and only dull, glowing coals remained… like what remained of my heart.

My stomach sank. Nemo had probably abandoned me. I supposed I deserved it for breaking the poor guy's heart.

But where was Fin? Was he still out swimming?

Something scraped along the cave floor.

"Nemo? Fin?" I called out. "Where are you?"

Chills crawled along my skin when no one replied. What was that? Someone was in here. My instincts were pinging with alarm.

That's when I saw the blood and the dead eel lying on the edge of the lagoon.

But that wasn't any old eel. It was the sea witch's pet. One of the ones that had tried to bite me in her cave.

Before I could go and investigate, a hand clamped down on my mouth.

My heart exploded. I screamed against my captor's fleshy palm.

Fin shuffled to my side and placed a finger over his lips. His hand fell from my mouth.

Poseidon! What was going on? My insides iced over.

"There's my bride-to-be."

My worst fears came true as Faraall rose from the water. I wanted to run, but my whole body felt frozen.

Fin yanked me to my feet, dragging me away from the edge of the lagoon, pushing me behind him.

My heart lurched into a more rapid beat.

Five more mermen, all of them soldiers in my father's army, slithered out of the darkened water. Traitors. Where was their loyalty? I was their princess.

Fear hooked its claws into me. "I'm not your bride." The words tumbled out of my mouth.

"Yes, you are," Faraall sneered.

I fired back with another question. "How'd you find me?"

Faraall gave his men a nod, and they fanned out around us. We were outnumbered.

"The sea witch has many talents," the commander bragged. "When word reached me that you'd escaped and had returned to the sea, well, I had to ensure your safety."

"The princess is safe," Fin declared, positioning himself between me and his commander.

Faraall sneered at Fin and motioned with a curt wave for me to join him. "Come, my princess. Don't make this hard. Remember what happened last time?"

How could I forget the bruise he'd given me? Or the pain and swelling in my cheek? Only lies spilled from that mouth. I'd rather die than go with him.

"Touch her, and we'll kill you," warned Nemo as he emerged from the shadows gripping his trident. His enormous size was even more hulking as he stood straighter, his muscles tensing. He tossed a second trident to Fin.

Faraall's gaze drifted to what I assumed was Nemo's tattoo. "I'll have your head for that threat, soldier."

A growl rumbled in Nemo's chest, making him seem more like a wolf than a merman.

Fin placed a firm hand on Nemo's shoulder and squeezed. "Fall back, soldier."

"There's a good fish," Faraall snarled. "Obey your superior."

"Listen, Commander." Fin adopted a reasoning tone. "We'll be happy to escort the princess back to Tritonia if that is the wish of our king."

"What?" My attention snapped to Fin.

I felt like a spear had penetrated my heart. How could he use me for his own pleasure them betray me like that?

A hollow, empty laugh burst from Faraall. "What a kind gesture. But I would prefer to escort my bride myself. I'm dying to make a woman of her before our big day."

His soldiers sniggered. One rubbed his crotch. All of their eyes blazed with the promise of my rape.

Vomit clogged my throat.

The slimy slug had said the right words to trigger Nemo. He aimed his trident at his commander.

My fingernails dug into my arms.

"Now, now, that's no way to speak to a merlady." Fin sauntered up to Faraall. "Especially not the daughter of your king."

Fin smashed a fist into Faraall's face. A loud crack rang out, most likely the sound of his nose breaking. He hunched over, whimpering.

I made a choked noise.

Faraall's slimy soldiers stepped back. I bet none of *them* had ever dared to defy the commander or attack him.

Blood stained Faraall's teeth. "Protecting her honor like

that, either you're both fools, or you fancy her. I'll find out which when I let my men mount her like the dog she is."

Fin kneed the creep in the head, and the commander collapsed to the ground, his trident ringing as it smashed the rock.

The soldiers readied their tridents.

My breath wedged somewhere between my throat and my lungs.

"Run," Nemo whispered to me.

My brain screamed at me to go. But my heart begged me to stay and fight with my mermen, to not leave them to face certain death. My heart won out, and I snatched Faraall's weapon, which had fallen from his grasp.

I'd had some basic training in defense. Only because I'd begged my father to let me have lessons, and he'd complied to end my nagging. But whenever I fought any of the practice instructors, they'd go easy on me because of who I was. This was eight moon cycles ago, though, and my mind scrambled, trying to remember everything my instructor had taught me.

"I'll take her first," said one of the soldiers, stepping forward, and grunting as if he prepared to rape me.

Palms sweating, heart fluttering, I stood my ground with the trident aimed at the traitor. Sorry. I wasn't that easy. Nor was I a dog. This guy was going to pay for assuming he'd rape me.

Fin defended my honor, batting at the mersoldier with his trident, thrusting him back. Another jumped into the fight, and Fin deflected their attacks. His motions reminded me of a sea horse doing a mating dance—graceful, effortless, and mesmerizing.

A mersoldier to my left issued a vicious snarl and twirled his weapon. It was time for me to battle, too. Our tridents clashed. The creep hammered me like a cruel storm battering the waves. My breaths burst in and out of my lungs. Heart jolting, I swung left, and he blocked me. Like the cocky brute he was, he swung at me over and over, pushing me back. In the end, his sheer strength won out, and he shoved me to the ground. My trident clanged beside me.

An ache claimed my spine. My heart tripped madly with mindless panic, but I wasn't giving up. As he loomed over me, I groped for my weapon, but it had fallen from my grasp. My stomach churned like a storm-tossed sea. By the grace of Poseidon, my fingertips encountered something warm and solid. One of the rocks we'd used to create the fire pit! I hefted it in my hand. With all my might, I hurled it at him. It caught him in the jaw, and he stumbled backward. I scrambled for my weapon as more soldiers closed in on me.

Nemo's roar deafened me as he lunged at the soldier, thrusting him backward and piercing him to the wall. Blood spurted everywhere.

My frantic gaze found Fin.

Menace flashed in Faraall's eyes. I knew that look. He was up to something.

For the briefest moment, a terrible fear rose in my heart. I thrust it into the very darkest corner of my mind. "Watch out!" I screamed, trying to warn Fin.

But it was too late. Faraall swept his leg in a wide arc parallel with the ground, catching Fin in the back of his knees. He crashed to the ground, and Faraall leaped on top of him, punching him in the face.

I let out a whimper.

Two more soldiers attacked Nemo. He beat them away with vicious swipes of his trident.

That left one soldier for me to deal with. Keeping one eye on Fin as he wrestled with Faraall, I faced my opponent. I swung the trident and struck his stomach. He bent over in pain but quickly recovered and slashed my arm with a prong.

I screamed and brought the shaft of my trident down on his back repeatedly until he sagged to the ground.

As I turned back to Fin, Faraall tugged a dagger from a sheath on his leather sash.

My fingers tightened around the trident.

"Fin," I cried.

Faraall and Fin wrestled for control of the blade. Fin strained from being underneath the commander. Blood poured down Fin's upper arm from a gash he received when slamming Faraall in beneath the armpit. Fin grunted and punched the commander in the jaw, knocking the weapon aside.

Dark thoughts crashed in my brain. My breaths came in fits and starts. Faster than a lightning bolt, I raced over to them. With all my strength, I jammed the triton into Faraall's chest.

Someone grabbed me by the arm and yanked me around.

I spun around and faced the soldier. In a panic, I kicked him in his privates. He moaned and hunched over. His grip on his trident grew slack, and I snatched it away, quickly flipped the weapon, and used the shaft to deliver a sharp blow to the soldier's thigh. According to my instructor, the move deadened the muscle. Down the soldier went as his leg buckled. Holding the trident at my chest level, I prepared to finish him off. But Fin pushed me out of the way and snatched the weapon from my grasp. He drove the trident into the man's back and twisted.

I closed my eyes at the sight all the blood.

Fin's big, warm hand landed on my back, and he rubbed my tightened muscles. "Where'd you learn how to fight?"

"Lessons." I offered him a smile, even though I felt sick inside.

"Explains everything," he muttered as he spun around, hurtling his trident through the air

The weapon's blades pierced one of the soldiers in the back. The man wheezed and sank to his knees. Fin moved up behind him and kicked him to the ground.

My eyes snapped shut, my mind blocking out the sight of all the blood and gore.

Nemo screamed. My heart seized, and my eyes flew open. I spun around to find him on his knees with a trident wedged in his thigh.

Above him, another soldier drew back his trident, preparing to pierce Nemo through the chest.

Fin snuck up behind an approaching soldier, put his trident over the man's throat, and choked him.

While the mersoldier was subdued, I called upon my aqua, and the power of the sea rose in me. The magic poured out in the form of a spear, which I directed at the traitor, piercing him between his chest and shoulder. His weapon fell from his grasp. He dropped his head to his chest.

This provided Nemo the distraction he needed, and despite being stabbed, he drove his weapon through the soldier's heart.

Flipping hell. They were all dead but the one I'd knocked out.

"Shit, Princess." Nemo collapsed to the ground. "That was awesome."

The praise washed off me. I was more concerned with his wellbeing than fanning my ego, and I rushed to my merman's aid.

Movement caught my eye, and I looked over my shoulder in time to watch the merman I'd battled drag Faraall into the lagoon. The two men disappeared below the water.

"Shit." Fin glanced between the escaping mersoldiers and Nemo. In the end, Fin's concern for his friend must have won out. He came to us, grabbed Nemo by the back of his collar, and dragged him into the water.

Nemo groaned.

"Sorry about this, my friend." Fin wrapped both hands around the trident's shaft and yanked the weapon from Nemo's leg.

Nemo's pain-filled bellow echoed off the cavern walls. Water splashed up in our faces as Fin dropped the bloody trident into the water.

I stuffed a fist into my mouth to keep from crying out as Nemo writhed in agony, his hands covering his wound.

"Hurry—get into the water, Princess," Fin ordered. He grabbed Nemo, wrapped an arm around his chest, and dragged him in deeper until they were both floating.

I stumbled into the lagoon to join them. My shaking hands reached for Nemo's face. I held it tight, forcing him to focus on me and not his pain.

"Leave me, Captain," Nemo mumbled. "Check the princess's wound."

Fin grabbed my arm and inspected the slash one of the soldiers had given me.

I pushed him away. "It's not that bad. Nemo needs our attention."

Blood darkened the crystal water. Sea god. My knees weakened at the sight. The liquid glimmered as Nemo's transformation took hold of him.

"Fuck," he said, scrunching up his face and groaning. A few moments later, his eyes widened. "Poseidon. I just swore in front of the princess."

Fin chuckled. I glanced in his direction and frowned. Sometimes, he scolded others for their language or vulgarity; other times, he laughed at it. His inconsistence drove me crazy, but in this case, he'd probably decided to give his wounded friend a break.

Nemo floated over to me and grabbed my hand. "Shit, I'm sorry, Princess."

I brushed the sweaty hair from his eyes. "Shh. I don't care. Just heal."

"Oh, mighty sea god," I started, pulling Nemo close. "Please do not take this merman from the sea so young. Fill him with your merciful healing power."

Nemo's arm found my back. "Don't talk like that. Everything's fine."

I wasn't sure I subscribed to his sunny outlook. He might bleed to death with a wound this serious. But I prayed that wouldn't be the case.

Fear burrowed under my skin like a thousand sea parasites. Would the water make him well again? Or would he die from such a wound?

"Stay with him," Fin told me as he climbed out of the water to grab a trident. "I'm going to hunt down the two that got away."

My stomach turned to stone. What if Faraall was still alive? Surely, that was why the mersoldier had taken him—to get him into the water, as we'd done with Nemo, so Faraall would have an opportunity to recover. But a wound like the one Faraall had sustained would take days, maybe longer, to heal. Dread built in my chest. The longer he was alive, the worse off my father and kingdom were.

"Back soon," Fin shouted, then he dove into the water, leaving the surface shimmering from his transformation.

Stomach churning, I dove under the water and retrieved the trident Fin had removed from Nemo's leg. Just in case any of the other slime bags were still alive. I'd finish them off if I had to. On my way back to the surface, I took a quick glance at Nemo's thigh. The wound no longer bled, and the water was working its magic, slowly healing him.

Thank the sea god!

I broke the water's surface and floated beside him.

Each moment Fin was gone, my blood pressure spiked. A

burning sensation, like molten lava, churned in my gut. I clung to my merman's arm and waited for Fin's return.

"It's okay, Princess," Nemo assured me. "They're dead."

I wasn't too sure. My gaze darted between each of the motionless soldiers littering the once beautiful, lagoon cave floor. Pain stretched through my hand from gripping the trident too tight.

"Talk to me," Nemo said. "Distract me."

"Err," I said, scrambling to think of something to say. "I like red sea blooms. I sneak out of the palace to go exploring. Dolphins are my favorite animal. I have a pet flounder."

Sea god, I was blubbering.

"Keep going," Nemo said through gritted teeth.

"My favorite food is lobster," I continued. "I love wearing silks made from the sea spider."

"Fancy taste," he said.

"My favorite color is orange," I said.

"Orange?" he scoffed. "Only weirdoes like that color."

I chuckled and rested my chin on his shoulder. "Well, what color do you like?"

He squeezed my arm. "Every hue of blue in the ocean."

I'll admit, those colors were hard not to love.

"Had any boyfriends?" There was a distinct note of inquisitiveness in his voice. The same tone the nosey noble mermaids used when fishing for information.

"No," I said. "Never had one stick around long enough. I tend to scare them off with the stupid things I do."

Nemo slipped from my grasp and spun to face me. The intensity in his eyes had me under his spell. I wasn't sure if he was mad or pleased.

Oh, well. I'd started now, so I might as well finish what I wanted to say while I had the chance.

"I still have feelings for you," I said, glancing over my shoulder, checking on the soldiers. They hadn't moved.

Surely, they must be dead. "I'm sorry I hurt you. Please, forgive me."

He slid his hands behind my back, pulling me into his embrace and holding me close in a way that told me I was his. The thought filled me with joy; I would be his if he'd have me. But there was the awkward whale in the room. My feelings for Fin. I couldn't deny I cared for both men. I didn't want to pretend or hide my true emotions.

"I don't like this situation between you, Fin, and me." Nemo raised a finger to my lips before I could say anything. "But I'll try to accept it if it gets me closer to you."

I laughed and wove one arm around his neck. "Good. I want that, too."

Our lips met, softly and sweetly, in the kind of kiss I never wanted to end. But I had to make sure none of the other soldiers crawled back into the water and escaped. Reluctantly, I pulled away to keep guard. Nemo released a frustrated groan. I patted his arm.

"We'll pick this up again when we're safe somewhere," I told him.

***

Fin returned a short while later.

"Did you find them?" I asked, the moment his head breached the surface.

"No." His eyes were dark and troubled. "Wait here while I tie these traitors to a tree and leave their corpses to rot in the sun."

Soldiers scraped along the rocky cavern floor as he dragged them outside.

When he was finished, he collected his and Nemo's tridents, entered the water, and floated beside Nemo and me.

"We mustn't linger. We must leave," Fin said.

I didn't exactly want to stick around a gravesite. But Nemo was still wounded and needed to heal.

"Why the rush?" I said. "The soldiers are dead, aren't they? They're not going anywhere."

"Military protocol," Fin explained, handing me the tridents and wrapping Nemo's arm over his shoulder. "When a squadron does not return, more soldiers are dispatched to find them." Fin hauled Nemo out of the lagoon.

But one had survived and had taken his commander's possibly dead body back with him. Would my father send more soldiers to find us?

I hurried out after Fin and Nemo. "If the merarmy knew of Faraall's plans to claim Tritonia, he'd have a rebellion on his hands."

"We can't be too careful, Princess," Fin replied. "I won't take any risks with either of you."

Perhaps Fin was right. I did not pretend to know military affairs better than he did. But I still doubted that anyone besides the corrupt traitors who'd accompanying Faraall knew of his plans.

Sweat still covered Fin's skin. He ran one broad forearm across his face and sighed. "Nemes, are you well enough to depart and help us find the dark pearl?"

"Yes," Nemo growled.

Fine. I didn't fully support this plan—not when Nemo remained unhealed—but still, now was our chance to save my father and be rid of that slimy slug for good.

CHAPTER 15

The horses' pace slowed as we emerged from the forest on the outskirts of the next town. After we'd left the cave, we'd ridden bareback for countless leagues—Nemo on one horse, and Fin and me on the other. Fin had ordered us to stay off the road to the Darkwoods to avoid being seen and to avoid leaving a trail in case more soldiers pursued us. If it weren't for the tired horses in desperate need of a rest, or Nemo, looking pale and sweaty, we could have slipped right past this town. But Fin felt it best to stop, seek water, and find some medicine to help Nemo's wound heal faster.

Rays of golden sunlight pierced the horizon. A sweet chorus of birds danced in the branches above. They probably responded to the song Nemo sung, trying to distract himself from the pain. The delicious smell of baked goods—a scent I recognized from previous trips to other realms in Haven—greeted us as we reached the edge of town.

Fin kicked the horse, and it clomped forward slowly. I clutched him tightly, my arms secure around his rock-hard stomach. Throughout the whole journey he'd kept one hand linked with mine. It was perfect. Being so close to him sent a tingle up my thighs.

Mud and brick thatched houses lined the road. A three-story tavern rose up among them, in addition to a bakery, butcher, and a tailor shop. The murmur of voices called us deeper into the town square, where a crowd was amassed around a cobblestone well. What were they doing there at the crack of dawn?

"What's going on?" I whispered.

"Let's take a closer look." Fin nudged his horse to carry him closer.

A stick of a man with a face as red as magenta coral climbed onto the well. He wore a long overcoat, pants that reached just beyond the knees, boots, and a vest. His hands clutched a long piece of leather attached to a handle.

"Bring da' prisoner forth." His voice boomed through the cobbled square.

Chains rattled behind us. Someone's boots scraped along the ground. The man groaned as if in pain. I prayed to the sea god that he hadn't been mistreated.

When I turned to look upon the poor soul, my heart pounded so hard, it threatened to burst through my ribcage. "Gill!"

Two officers dragged him along. But why? Couldn't he walk? His boots and shirt were missing. Pants covered his bottom half. A gray hue had captured his skin. His scales had all but vanished. Merscales were akin to flower petals curling during intense summer heat, and they vanished during severe dehydration.

A drowning sensation captured my gut. Where were they taking him? Why was he a prisoner? What were they going to do to him?

Gill's eyes flashed with a combination of regret and shame, and he hung his head.

Fin descended from the horse and hurried to his friend. "What in the name of Tritonia is going on here? What are this man's charges?"

"Who the 'ell are you?" the slim man asked.

"Get out of our way." The other shoved past Fin and continued to the well.

"Stop. Release this man," I shouted, gaining the attention of everyone assembled in the square, including the red-faced drunkard bellowing Gill's charges. "As a Princess of Tritonia, I order you to obey my command."

The lawmaker laughed at me, exposing a mouth full of stained, yellow teeth and several dark gaps were some were missing. "You ain't no princess. You're noth'n' but a trollop in a filthy dress."

Well, I'd give him that. I was a trollop in a dirty dress.

Fin stepped forward, squeezing his trident. "You will apologize to the princess for your disrespect."

If my heart weren't going mad, it would have done a little leap in response to Fin standing up for me. A man who would defend my honor—and look gorgeous doing it—was appealing as hell.

The man tapped his leather handle in his palm. I recognized the item now. A whip. Used for punishing those who disobeyed. "Who's gonna make me? You, and what army?"

Smartass. I'd love to punch him in the mouth and knock out a few more of his teeth. Fin would probably consider that kind of behavior beneath a princess, but I didn't.

Well, if this clown didn't believe I was royalty, then only one thing would convince him. Despite the dry conditions, I let my transformation overcome me, and the townsfolk shrieked at my glimmering skin. Without my legs, I collapsed to the ground, muddying my skirt even further.

A few gasps rang out. Everyone stared at me.

"Mermaid," someone whispered.

"She's a royal," another said.

Many in the crowd fell down on one knee to bow to me.

I waved them away. There was no need for formal etiquette.

Still, the man refused to submit to my demand. "Princess, huh?" He eyed me up and down, hitched up his pants, and licked his cracked lips. "Mistook you for a moment there. What can I do for you, Your Highness?"

"Let my merman go," I said as Fin and Nemo stood by my side.

"Can't do that, I'm afraid," he said, gesturing to Gill. "Caught 'im stealing from the bakery. On Haven, we have rules, and those rules must be upheld." His bloodshot eyes darkened, carrying a threat.

He jerked the handle of his whip as if to say, "Clear out."

What a fool to think I'd be dismissed so easily. I wasn't going anywhere. A man like him could be bribed. I took one of the pearl clips out of my hair. "How much is the bread worth?"

The man's eyes bugged out as they panned over to Nemo. "Your gold ain't worth nothing here, Princess."

Shellfish. I was running out of options. If I couldn't come up with another solution, I'd have to order Fin and Nemo to fight the man and his officers, grab Gill myself, and run.

The man smirked at me and lifted the whip above his head. He flicked his wrist, sending the whip flying at Gill's naked torso. The rope carved marks into his flesh, and he screamed.

My heart tore in two.

"Stop that," I shouted, forcing my transformation back into a human.

But the man only laughed and whipped Gill again.

An invisible force struck me, as if the whip had hit me.

Fin lunged at two of the officers, striking at them. Metal clashed as the soldiers defended themselves.

I scrambled to my feet and dove at the red-faced man, grabbing his whip and yanking hard. He shoved me in the chest, pushing me to the ground. His whip rose above his shoulder as if he meant to strike me. Fire whisked through my blood. The ocean would freeze over before I let him have the honor.

Magic welled in my palms. I unleashed it into the soil, calling to the water to rise, and it obeyed my command, causing the ground to rock.

The man tumbled head-first onto the cobblestones. People screamed and lost their balance, falling on top of each other. Splinters formed in the cement binding the stones together. Liquid dribbled from the fractures into the square. The shaking continued, and logs on a nearby pile tumbled everywhere. Tiles on the roofs smashed onto the ground. The bricks in the well crumbled. All the townsfolk scattered except for a few stragglers.

Weakened from my effort, I stumbled forward, falling to my knees and cradling Gill's head. To release him from the iron shackles on his wrists and ankles I'd need a key.

The man collected himself from the ground. His face turned purple, and the vein in his forehead throbbed. "You will pay for that."

Spit flying from his mouth hit me in the forehead, and I wiped it off.

He sprang at me, but Nemo swung his trident, hitting the man low on his legs and tripping him.

"I don't think so," Fin said, seizing the officer's upper arm and yanking him to his feet. "Threatening a princess is treason."

"That's enough, Pascoe," said a tall man with an authoritative voice. He was dressed like his associate, but this man had kinder eyes and cleaner teeth. "Only a fool would invite trouble from the sea king."

"But, Verita," the fat man argued.

Verita held out a palm. "Release the merman." He turned to me. "Take your men, and be off with you."

The man pulled out an iron key from a side pocket. I sprung to my feet and snatched it from his hand.

"This merman disobeyed an order. Let me deal with him." My glare sent him and his officers scampering away faster than sea rats.

Unsteady and woozy, I wobbled on my legs.

"I'm Verita, mayor of this town," said the taller man, offering me a hand and to help steady me. "I apologize for harming your kin. We did not recognize he belonged to the merfolk." Verita's voice was wary and probably aimed to soothe the wild beast inside me and prevent me from destroying the whole town.

"Thank you," I replied. I just wanted away from there and to hold Gill in my arms until he was well again.

Gill groaned as Fin lifted and supported him. Nemo ignored his own pain to help his comrades.

"I'm sorry, Captain," Gill whispered, his voice burning with lament.

And so, he should be, the fool. He could have died there.

"We've never been blessed with the presence of a royal before," said Verita, examining the scales blazing on my arm from the magic I'd called upon. "We would be honored if you would stay and rest for the day."

Gill was in no state to travel. He needed to rest in a bath. Nemo needed some herbs for his wound. And I needed to lie down for a few moments.

"Verita," I said, using my sweetest voice. "Would you be so kind as to show us to accommodations for the four of us, and I'll need access to a bath for my soldier?"

"Certainly. You can use my cabin. I often rent it out to travelers."

Verita bowed and traipsed out of the town square with Fin, Nemo, Gill, and me at his heels.

"Mira," the mayor called out to a young woman with a funny hat on her head. "Bring water to the princess's lodge next to the bank."

"Yes, Mayor." The woman bowed and scurried away to lower a bucket hanging from the well.

"Princess, is this wise?" Fin asked from behind me.

I held up a hand to silence him. This time, I would deal with Gill. It was time to settle a few things first. Such as the importance of obeying an order.

A few moments later, Verita showed us around a modest, little cabin consisting of a kitchen, two bedrooms, and a bathroom.

"I will call the maids to pour your man a bath," Verita advised, his eyes careful and alert.

"Very much appreciated." I flashed my friendliest smile to assure him my rage had passed. "Could I also trouble you for a healer?"

"There's a doctor next door." Verita bowed and exited.

Great news.

"Princess," Fin said when the front door closed. "We should leave. They could mount an attack on us."

"And go where?" I snapped. "Look at Gill."

My gaze fell to him. He was deathly pale, his skin cracked and blistered. Precious moisture bled from him in the form of sweat.

Fin and Nemo carried Gill toward the bathroom.

"Wait," I said. "As your princess, I order you to leave him in that chair."

Three pairs of eyes drilled into me.

"Princess, he needs the water." Fin's voice burned with agony for his friend.

I stared at Fin until he and Nemo set Gill down as requested.

Gill stared at the floor, refusing to look at me.

"You disobeyed your captain's order." My voice shook with rage. "My order."

"I had to save my sister," he growled.

Anger surged through me like a powerful swell. I paced the floor, clawing my fingers into my palms. "How could you be so reckless? You could have killed yourself."

Fin grabbed my arm as if trying to calm me down.

Gill's head hung low. "Just get me out of these shackles. My legs are cramping."

Why, the little sea weasel. He wasn't even remorseful. Well, he was not getting in that bath until he apologized. I'd just flooded the town square and destroyed public property to save him. Where was my thanks? We were lucky to receive the mayor's hospitality after what I'd done. He was probably only being kind out of fear I'd do something even worse.

"I'm sorry," he said with no hint of sincerity whatsoever.

My anger built like an underwater volcano about to explode, and it came pouring out. "Sorry? For what? For leaving your men? For disobeying an order? For stealing? For putting me in danger by forcing me to rescue you? Or for being downright rude to me ever since we met?"

I was about to spew fierier words when a knock sounded at the door, interrupting us.

"Come in," I said, restraining the anger in my voice.

Mira and six other girls entered with pitchers of water. Once they'd emptied the water into the tub, Mira returned to stand before me.

"Will there be anything else, Your Highness?" she asked.

"No, thank you." I nodded my thanks as they left.

I turned to Gill. "I should have left you at the well to rot."

It felt like rocks pounded my brain. My body trembled from expending my energy earlier. I needed a drink and to lie down.

"If you ever do that again," I said, "sea god, help me, Gill, I will leave you behind." Without looking at any of them, I grasped the door handle for the room closest to me. "I'm taking this room. You can have the other one." I entered my room and closed the door behind me.

Through the thin walls, I heard the shuffled movement of my men as they transported Gill into the bath.

I lay down on the bed and closed my eyes.

Water splashed in the room next door. Gill groaned with the delight of a merman reunited with water. Any noise he made stirred something in me and made my skin tingle. But I pushed those feelings away, intent on ignoring my building attraction to him and my yearning to go and bathe with him. Guys like him were too much trouble and not worth my time or effort.

"I'm sorry, Captain," I heard Gill mumble.

"You already said that," Fin replied.

"Tell her I'm sorry."

"Tell her yourself." Judging by his tone, Fin was just as pissed as I was.

A few moments later, there was a knock at my door, and Fin entered.

"May we talk?" Fin asked, standing still like a soldier by the door.

I didn't care to hear any excuses Fin might have come up with to explaion away Gill's reckless behavior. That merman had deserved every word I'd said. But I wanted Fin near and patted the bed. He sat beside me, caressing my hair, and I rested my head on his legs.

"Princess." His voice stroked my insides. "Can you watch Gill while I take Nemes next door to visit the healer?"

I rolled off him. "Shellfish, no. I don't want to be anywhere near him. That merman infuriates me."

Fin wasn't letting me go and crawled over to me, running his fingers through my hair. "Deep down, he means well."

Sea god. If Fin kept up with that hair stroking, I'd do anything for him.

"Upon my return, I shall bring breakfast back for all of us." He kissed the top my head.

For several moments, I lay there contemplating Fin's request. Why should I be kind to someone who showed me absolute contempt? Someone who'd defied an order from his superior officer? Someone who'd refused the sage advice of a friend. On one hand, Gill putting his life in danger to save his sister was admirable, but on the other, it was incredibly stupid.

I rolled over again. Maybe those things weren't really stopping me from going to my merman's side. Perhaps I sought an excuse not to go in there. Because as much as I hated to admit it, a deep, dark part of me wanted him, and with every fiber of my being I fought and denied these feelings. He both infuriated and appealed to me, and I couldn't walk away and close my heart to him completely.

Against my better judgment, I allowed my feet to carry me into the bathroom. I told myself I'd swallowed my pride and wanted to be the bigger merperson, but my heart knew that was a lie.

Gill stared at me as if he hadn't expected to ever see me again.

I picked up a sponge from the windowsill, kneeled by the side of the brass bathtub, and dipped it in the water. It dribbled as I brushed his arms and chest. Bathing him gave me the perfect excuse to stare at the magnificence of his chiseled chest. The blisters on his skin had already started to heal.

"I apologize, Your Highness." Regret stained his voice. "For being a right royal ass."

For the briefest moment, he had me fooled and thinking he was being genuine.

When I didn't say anything, he said, "Of course, not as good as *your* royal ass."

He gave me a nervous smile that was slightly crooked on one side but perfect, nonetheless. Sea god, it was beautiful. He needed to smile more often. It transformed his dark, broody face into that of a god.

But I was having none of it. Tritonia would have to freeze over before I let him worm his way back into my heart so easily. "Do you always joke to deflect?"

A wounded expression flashed across his face. "I joke when I'm nervous or flirting."

I pushed him forward to dab at the wounds on his back. Raw red flesh greeted me, and I swallowed back bile that rose in my throat. "Which one is it right now?"

"Both." He hissed as water trickled onto the wounds left behind by the lash of the whip.

Sea god. He was flirting with me. My heart took off like a bird. There was no chance of stopping it now. The tide that I'd held back flowed free.

He leaned back and grabbed my hand to stop me. "You don't have to do this. I don't deserve your kindness." His honey-brown eyes radiated sincerity. "I shouldn't have spoken to you like that. I regret not listening to Fin. He's always my voice of reason."

"Believe me, there's plenty of other places I'd rather be." I cleaned the dirt from his arms.

"Ouch." He touched his chest. "You're really cute when you're cross."

174

Cute? He'd better stop throwing around terms like that, or I might jump in the bath with him. "Stop toying with me, or I'll leave."

Gill sat up a little straighter, giving me more of a better view of his chest. I had to use all my restraint to keep my gaze fixed on his eyes and on the flashing reawakening of the scales across his temples.

"I'm not very good with authority, Princess. Never have been."

His admission caught me off guard. I didn't know why he'd felt the need to tell me that, but his admission explained a lot. I supposed I couldn't begrudge him his point of view when we had a lot in common on the rebelling and disobeying orders front. Maybe I shouldn't have been so hard on him and should hear him out.

"Then why don't you leave the merarmy?"

"Because I can't," he replied. "Not until I've finished my probation. But even then, I wouldn't quit—I love it. I love my team. Fin's turned me around. Nemes helps me remain positive."

I'd love to see this positive side he referred to because all I'd been privy to was the guy grumpier than a walrus.

"Why did my father force you into the army?" I continued to dribble water across his chest to give me the opportunity to admire him. Shadows in the water concealed the rest of him. Pity. I was quite enjoying the view.

"I was a pretty messed-up kid," he said, rubbing the shadow of growth on his chin. "Despite my adopted parents' love and support, I held this deep-rooted anger at my birth mother for abandoning me."

My heart sank a little for him. I couldn't imagine not knowing my parents or having them in my life. My father had always been there for me when I needed him—until Faraall and his spell came along.

"I acted out," he continued. "You know, breaking things, graffiti, getting into fights. My parents called me a disappointment and sent me to a boarding school to straighten me out."

I'd heard rumors about those. Kids didn't get to see their parents often. I was lucky I had tutors in the palace. But most of the nobles' children were sent off to boarding schools.

"At school, the kids teased me because I didn't read and learn as well as they did. I got into a lot of fights." His finger traced the top of the brass bath. "I was expelled from every school. Took up stealing. That got me in and out of court. Finally, the magistrate took my case before your father."

My insides were raw with emotion. His upbringing had been a stark contrast to mine. I'd rebelled to escape the constraints of my duties and the nobles who'd surrounded me.

"Did you find your birth mother?"

A fierceness sparked in Gill's eyes. His heavy brows drew together. His lips turned into a snarl. "With her new family."

I didn't begin to understand his mother's reasons, nor did I want to. That was her business. But I wanted to take him in my arms and strip away his pain.

Despite his hard façade, his rough demeanor, and all the multiple jagged edges, he was one of the most beautiful mermen I'd ever encountered. He was like a raw, uncultured pearl before it was polished into a shiny, smooth jewel. To me, that was one of the rarest and most precious finds.

I didn't get to delve deeper into Gill's psyche, as Fin and Nemo lumbered back into the cabin.

"Over there is fine, Mira," Fin said, and something—possibly a chair—scraped the floor.

"Anything else, sir?" Mira asked in her childlike voice.

"No, that's all. Thank you, Mira."

"Good day to you, sir."

The cabin door closed as I finished cleaning the rest of Gill's face and shoulders.

"Sit, my friend," Fin said. "Eat until your heart is content."

"Thanks, Captain," mumbled Nemo.

"Princess," Fin called out. "I bring news."

"What news?" I asked, standing, eager to hear it.

Fin burst into the room with eyes dazzling like the sparkle of morning water. "The doctor who treated Nemes told us that the collector has a storage trove of magical items somewhere nearby in the Darkwoods."

My heart had lifted from my talk with Gill. "Where is this trove? Does the collector have it guarded or protected with magical spells?"

"Maybe," Gill said, rubbing his forehead. "Blade and the resistance might know where it is and how to get inside."

The assassin? Sea god, no. After landing in his crotch, I never wanted to see that man again and be reminded of my shame. The event still haunted me, contributing to my nerves when I was around each of my mermen. But if that was our only hope of finding the dark pearl, then it was an avenue worth chasing.

"Go and speak with Verita," I told Fin on my way to get Gill a plate of food. "Have him prepare four horses for us. We leave at first light."

CHAPTER 16

Something thumped in my darkened room, and I startled awake, sitting up in my bed.

Moonlight streamed through the window, allowing me a little light for guidance. I groped for the dagger beside me on my bed table.

Shellfish. Damn, Fin. I should have listened to his warning. The townsfolk had probably come to harm us in revenge for my little display of power yesterday. But we were not meeting our end in this cabin.

I scanned the room. Coals in the fireplace glowed a deep red. An armchair sat by the fireplace. Everything seemed in its place except for the candle that had fallen from its holder. Somehow, it had knocked over. I leaned out of bed and picked it up, replacing it in its stand on the carved wooden bedside table.

"Sorry to wake you, Princess," a rough, dry voice said.

Startled, I leaped out of my bed with the candle in my grip.

Someone was seated on the floor, his back leaning against the wall.

"Nemo?" I said, rubbing the sleep from my eyes. "What the hell are you doing in here? Where are the others?"

"Sleeping," he replied, gesturing over his shoulder toward the snoring coming through the walls. "Gill's making a racket. I came in here to escape it, but you're just as bad."

What? He lied. None of my servants had ever mentioned I snored. Nor had any of my friends when I'd had sleepovers as a teen. "I don't snore."

When he laughed at me, as if to say, *oh, yes, you do*, I threw a pillow at him, hitting him in the head.

My reaction only made him chuckle more. Oh, how he enjoyed teasing me. This was like another of his *royal ass* jokes.

"Yes, you do." His smile was cheeky, sinful as hell, promising me an ocean of heartache if I didn't stop falling for him. "Like a whale. Lots of grunts and snorts. If we were in water, I'd add bubbles, too."

Why, that guppy! I picked up another pillow, ready to assault him for the unjust accusation.

But he was already armed with the first one I'd tossed at him. "Two can play at that game," he told me.

I quirked an eyebrow. "Is that a challenge?"

"You know I love one," he replied, his eyes radiating his playful nature and scrolling down my chest and stomach. "Get ready to be beaten—*again*, Princess."

Sea god. He hadn't let me live down my defeat at clam, seaweed, and rock. This time, I was going to win either way.

I liked a good game of poker with my friends down at Shark Bait bar. Putting a little wager on a hand added another layer of fun. One time, a Sharkrider had dared us to a stripping version of the game. Luckily, I'd worn several layers of undergarments that particular day. For my effort, I only got down to my bra. But Gellian had lost on purpose. Any chance to get her breasts out. Mad mermaid.

"What are the terms?" I asked Nemo.

"You like to gamble?" Nemo asked, playing up the mock surprise in his voice. "My, my… You're not such an innocent princess."

"What ever made you think I was one?"

He shrugged. "Just imagined you as one."

"Well." I traced a finger along the woolen throw rug. "You're wrong."

Nemo smiled, as if he liked the idea I might not be such an innocent. His terms came out in a rush.

"If I win, you have to bathe with me, and I get to wash you."

Flipping hell. The thought of that had me steaming up down below. Would we both fit in the bath? Who cared! How was I going to say no to something as sensual as that? I contemplated losing on purpose so I could be closer to him. Sea god. Was I turning into my horny best friend Gellian?

Then that nasty reminder in the back of my mind hit. The one that told me I couldn't be with him. That my father would never approve of our relationship, despite what I desired, no matter how much I begged him to change his mind. No matter how badly I wanted to, I couldn't forget that Nemo and I could never be a couple. I couldn't take a bath with him. That would undo me. I'd be lost to him forever. But I'd try one night of fun with him. A wonderful reminder of my adventure to save my father.

Damn me and my weakness for Nemo.

"I accept your terms," I said. "But if I win, you have to sleep outside on the porch."

"Even more reason for me to win." His lips pressed together in amusement. "Challenge accepted."

I didn't wait for him to tell me when the game had started and thumped him in the shoulder, earning me with a blast to the stomach. My sisters always said I was the child who cheated in games. No sense in changing my ways now. Especially when such big stakes were at hand.

"Low blow," he said, a smile sounding in his voice.

"There's more where that came from," I promised, and a thrill skated along my back.

I slammed him in the leg. Reciprocating, he whacked me in the butt.

"Dirty tactics," he said.

I was loving the flirting firing between us as I hit him in the side. All-out war broke out. Our pillows clashed. Another sweep got him in the chest. He got me back with a strike to the arm. We pummeled each other frantically, pillows whipping through the air, and I couldn't stop laughing. We were making so much noise, I was surprised Gill and Fin hadn't bust in to see what was going on.

For my final assault, I pounded his head. He got me in the back, and I fell face-first onto the bed. When I rolled over, he climbed over top of me, clutching both the pillows.

"It seems I won." Damn him and his eyes, which were smoldering with desire.

His gaze stirred something inside me. A longing to have him near, to wrestle with him, and for our actions to turn from fun to foreplay and fornication.

"No, you haven't," I said.

I tried to snatch back my pillow, but he held both of them over his head and away from my grasp. Now, he played dirty. I leaped up, trying again to secure my pillow, accidentally scratching him in the face.

Sea god not again.

"Im sorry..." But he didn't care for my apology.

He tossed the pillows aside. A warm arm hooked around my back. His lips found my neck and gently caressed it. I leaned my head back, letting him dust my throat in his love.

"I believe you owe me a bath." His words fanned my skin, bringing out the goose bumps.

By now, an underwater volcano raged below. I was willing to do anything for him as long as he didn't leave. "Very well. Come collect your prize."

He scooped me into his arms and carried me to the bathroom. My arms found his neck and stroked it. Soon, he set me back down on the cold stone floor. His shirt and pants came off in a hurry, and he stepped into the bath, his legs stretching the entire length of it.

Mira and the maids had replaced the water after Gill's bath, so it was cold but fresh. The temperature didn't bother merfolk because of our thick and insulated skin.

"Your turn," he said, motioning for me to get undressed.

He didn't take his eyes off me as I removed my skirt. His gaze lingered on the curls between my legs.

"The corset, too," he told me.

Really? Things were sliding more out of control by the moment. But I dived in with total surrender. To hell with my earlier concerns. I was going to remember this night for the rest of my life. Might as well enjoy it.

Slowly, I untied the laces of my garment, and I smiled, enjoying building the anticipation. He seemed to like it too, leaning back, rubbing his jaw. I pried the corset free from my body and let it fall behind me. Nemo took all of me in as I grabbed the sponge from the nearby sink. He held me steady as I sank into the water in front of him, squishing between his legs. I leaned back into his chest, savoring the sensation of being cradled there.

After a few moments, he pushed aside my hair and swept the sponge across my neck. I delighted in each stroke trickling water down my back. Poseidon, I loved being treated like a princess by him and him alone. If I weren't careful, I could really get used to this. His sweet and considerate nature kept drawing me in further. Sea god, he made it hard for me not to fall deeper for him.

"I have to ask you this," he said, "because it's driving me crazy."

"Aha," I said, enjoying what he was doing to me.

"You like Gill too?" he growled, making me stiffen. "I see the way you look at him."

Flipping hell. Talk about ruining the moment.

I shifted to face Nemo.

"I can't help it." I ran my hands across his giant chest, doing my best, and my worst to comfort him. "He calls to me. A darkness inside me. I can't explain it. Besides that I'm attracted to him. To all of you. This is a crazy situation for me, as much as it is for you, and I don't expect you to understand. But I don't want you to go."

"I don't like it," he said, twirling my wet hair around his finger. "But I'm not leaving. You're mine."

I loved the way he claimed me as his. He wasn't about to hear any complaints from me. But I wasn't denying I wanted to be all of theirs. I didn't like hiding anything from Nemo. If he wanted me to be his, then he would have to accept it.

I moaned and leaned my neck to the side, and his warm lips danced across my flesh, leaving it blazing in his wake. Nemo was almost undoing me with his tender kisses. As he traced circles on my back, the crest between my legs burned with desperation. I dug my fingers into his thighs as he nibbled on my shoulder.

"Enjoying your bath?" His seductive whisper in my ear left the rest of me scorching.

"Yes," I croaked, barely able to get a word out over my arousal.

The sponge floated in the water in front of me.

Nemo's keen hand surfed along the curves of my stomach. His hardness pressed into the crevice between my buttocks. I yearned for him to take my breast in his mouth and suck it. At last, his hands found my chest and fondled my nipples. I kneeled and turned to face him, allowing him better access.

"More than a handful." He squeezed my breasts together in both hands, twirling his tongue around the tips of my nipples.

My head rolled backward. He ran his palm over my breasts and up my neck. Gently, he lifted my head and crushed his mouth on mine. His urgent tongue parted my lips and found mine. We swirled together in a sea of ecstasy. I never wanted it to end but was just as satisfied when he took my left breast and sucked it so hard, all the while cupping my right.

"I don't think we're going to finish this bath," I said, my voice tight, my body thirsty for him.

"Oh, yes we are," he told me in a voice that made it clear he was in charge.

Flipping hell. He enjoyed teasing me, making me wait for it. That would teach me for letting him win the challenge and capitulating to his demands. Next time, we'd do it my way.

He smiled and slid an arm beneath mine, grasping the sponge, which had disappeared behind me, grazing my hip as he drew it slowly back.

Shellfish. This was turning me on like crazy. The space between my legs and my belly were tingling with desire. I wanted to make him mine right there and then. But at the same time, I didn't want this bath to ever—*ever*—end. All of me also ached to wash him down, trace every muscle, all his skin, lapping up the droplets left over after I rinsed away the soap.

Soft strokes skimmed across my chest. With each caress Nemo's smile grew. His eyes feasted on me. I couldn't look away, and I drank him all in. The beautiful, upside-down,

CLAIMED

half-moon shape of his eyes. The darkened pigment of his
skin. The lips that tightened as if they yearned to kiss me.
The power in his jaw and body, as if crafted by the sea god
himself.

The sponge wandered across my stomach and up and
down my arms. Nemo abandoned it to cleanse my fingers,
instead linking his with mine and sliding them together. The
friction drove me wild. Being washed made me feel amazing...wanted and adored. Shellfish, I almost came at the
thought.

Desperate for him, I leaned forward, sliding my arms over
his broad shoulders, and kissed him. After a brief moment,
he pushed me away, leaving me craving more. So
much more.

"Not yet," he whispered.

Flipping hell. I was going crazy here. My body raged out
of control. If I didn't have another piece of him soon, I'd
explode. How was he able to control himself when I knew he
coveted me, too?

"Stand up," he ordered.

I was practically melting from his scorching caress. Using
his shoulders for balance, I climbed to my feet. The sponge
danced along the lines of my legs. All the while, he kissed me
between them. My fingers curled through his hair. Sea god.
I'd never felt pleasure like this before. If I had known how
perfect it was, I'd have lain with a merman much earlier.

"Show me your delicious sea pearl," Nemo said, spreading
my legs.

I trembled at his touch and at the thought of him gazing
on me there.

"Let me taste it. Suck it. Fuck you until you scream
my name."

The vulgar words spilling from his wide lips charged my
arousal, owning me, overpowering my body. Without hesita-

185

tion, I welcomed his tongue, and it lapped at the entrance of my sea pearl. I pressed him harder to me, and he gripped my ass, burying deeper into my moist folds. My knees weakened from the pleasure, and I clung to him with all my strength. I was so aroused that I didn't last long, coasting over in a matter of moments, him leaving me breathless and unsteady on my feet.

Soft kisses trailed along my body as Nemo rose to meet me. His hardness was on full display. One touch was enough to tempt him. His hands clamped on my behind, and he lifted me to meet his swell. My legs enfolded his waist, and I relished the feel of him between my thighs, of being entangled with him. Carrying me, he took me from the bath to the wall, where he slammed me against it, his kisses just as hard to match.

"Now," I begged him, panting from the arousal possessing me.

Flashing me a sexy smile, Nemo sank into me deeply, bringing out a long groan. As he drove deeper, I cried out, loving every perfect moment. Crushed beneath him, I tangled my tongue with his, our kiss in perfect rhythm with our bodies. He yanked my hair, stretching my head backward, exposing my neck. His lips feathered me in kisses, and I moaned at each caress.

My heart thrummed from each pump he drove in and out. I rocked to his steady beat. Not too slow. Not too fast. Just perfect. He liked to take things slowly, like he had in the bath, and I wanted my orgasm to last the whole night.

Pleasure surged and spread across my body. I met each thrust, needing him deeper, losing my breath as he filled me completely. All of me drifted on an intense wave, and I drowned beneath his passion.

"Come for me, Princess."

His whisper nearly sent me over the edge.

Squeezing my hips, he drove deeper into me, stretching me to my limits. Fire consumed every inch of me. I raised my pelvis, meeting his quickening thrusts, demanding more.

"Nemo. Yes!"

My head rolled backward as he tipped me over.

At that exact moment, his body tightened against me, and he howled as he exploded inside me.

We remained like that, entwined, panting, our heartbeats erratic. I could never have imagined a more perfect moment than that one. A single thought filled my mind: when could we do it again? I rested my head on his shoulders, inhaling his scent. A layer of sweat glistened on his back and coated my chest.

"My turn to be scrubbed," he said, carrying me back to the bath.

I tingled all over, hoping to repeat the same exercise.

CHAPTER 17

The gentle rocking of the horse I rode shook me awake. I brushed hair from my face and sat up straighter. Our trip through the Darkwoods forest had been uneventful, and throughout the afternoon, I kept drifting off. The previous night, Nemo and I had made love all night long and had barely gotten any sleep.

Gill and Fin kept glancing at us, smirking, seeming to understand what had happened but saying nothing. Nemo was in an extra good mood, singing practically the whole ride through the Darkwoods until his voice turned hoarse.

By the time we arrived at our destination, night had descended, and everything was still and silent. Moonlight crept through the blanket of trees. Dried leaves crunched under the horses' hooves. Mist crawled along the ground. A little critter scrambled along a log in hunt of its meal. Trees began to thin out along the edges of a clearing.

Fin's horse led the way, followed by Gill, and they left Nemo and me to trail alongside each other.

Laughter and shouts floated on the still night air.

"We're nearly there," Fin announced.

Several hundred feet farther into the forest, the glow of firelight stretched through the trees. In a few moments, we reached a well-trod path leading to a town. Instantly, I knew which building housed the tavern—a two-story building in the center of the town, from which came the sounds of raucous voices and clinking glasses. Smoke curled out of its chimney. Even from half a league away, the smell of beer, wine, and horse urine tainted my nostrils.

"If I know Blade," said Gill, "then thieves, mercenaries, thugs, and murderers will frequent this establishment. Just looking a patron in the eye might get you stabbed."

A cold chill slinked down my spine. At Shark Bait bar, the customers were rough and often got into tussles. But no one ever got murdered. A thick glue plugged my throat, making it hard to swallow. What kind of scoundrels frequented this Haven tavern?

"Stay close, Princess." Fin claimed my hand with his and squeezed tight.

I stumbled backward, seizing Nemo's arm, my stomach exploding with nerves that seared me. "Perhaps it might be best if we stayed outside." Out of all of them, Nemo made me feel the safest and most protected.

"Don't back down now, Princess." Gill's deep voice descended into a lower octave. "We've come all this way."

Thanks a million for throwing me in the shark pit.

The glue in my throat expanded, and I struggled to breathe. *Poseidon, give me strength. Let me and my mermen leave this place alive and unharmed.*

"No one will touch you when you're with us." Gill wrapped an arm around my waist and pressed me close to his side.

Something had changed between us during our conversation the day before. He now regarded me with respect. This morning, he had lifted me onto my horse and given me a faltering smile.

But even with his confident assurances, I wasn't wholly convinced. Should anyone recognize my silver scales, we might be in deep trouble. A sea princess and four fit mersoldiers would fetch a fair price from the collector.

"This'll be fun," Nemo said, cracking his knuckles, flaring the dread scratching beneath my breastbone.

Fun? Was he mad with seasickness? There was nothing fun about the prospect of entering this venue when one wrong move could cause us to be killed or recaptured and sold into slavery.

A woman screamed inside, and something smashed.

I flinched and jumped backward. Trembles took hold of me. My knees buckled, and I almost lost my balance. *Shellfish. Hold it together, Nyssa. Otherwise, you'll never leave this place.*

Gill ran the backs of his fingers along my arm. "Showing weakness in this place is like leading a moth to a flame. Pretend you're my whore." He grabbed my breast and ass and squeezed, making me swoon for a split moment. "If anyone asks, you suck my cock all night long and fuck me until I'm spent."

Part of me was disgusted by his filthy words. Only Faraall had ever spoken to me in such a manner. The words were degrading and below me. Yet that deep, dark part of me ached for Gill to speak to me that way again. She wanted to scream his name as he claimed me. Whisper dirty words into his ear. My mind fogged over with filthy sexual thoughts. All of it had me burning below. *Sea god.* What was Gill doing to me?

What were they *all* doing to me? My world felt as if it was spinning, and I couldn't control it. Having sex with two mersoldiers in a matter of days wasn't like me at all. We'd just ridden through the Darkwoods as if my relationship with them was natural. Sure, Fin seemed fine with the way things were between us, and Nemo had jealousy issues to deal with but had agreed to go along with the status quo, but what would they think if I threw Gill into the mix, too? Only one thing seemed certain: my attraction toward them was as unstoppable as the tide.

My thoughts flew back to Gill's suggestion. "I'm not acting like some cheap floozy!" I told him.

"No one will dare try anything with you with a vicious face like that." He gave me that crooked, gorgeous smile that instantly convinced me to follow him anywhere.

Fin snickered behind us.

I flushed with heat. Gill was worldly and street-wise compared to me and my somewhat sheltered and naïve palace life. If anyone was the merman to help me understand the ways of Haven, to not fall victim to it, it was him. And if a little roleplay saved my skin—and those of my companions—I was totally up for it.

"No, you don't," said Nemo, trying to snatch me from Gill's grasp. "I'm with the princess."

Gill whisked me in the opposite direction and thumped Nemo on the chest. "My turn now, big boy."

I can't deny that something about Gill claiming me did something to me. Turned me upside down and spun me 'round and 'round like a forceful beach wave. A part of me still longed to be in Nemo's arms after everything we'd shared last night. But that was at odds with the dark Nyssa who wanted only Gill by her side tonight.

Gill pressed me protectively to him, dragging me into the tavern first.

Fin followed, his steps light compared with Nemo's stomping; the big merman was making his annoyance clear.

Having the three of them with me did little to comfort my fraying nerves. I was well out of my depth in a place like this, and I wasn't afraid to admit it. My mermen wouldn't be able to fight our way out if the whole place turned on us.

Smoke from cigarettes and cigars filled the room with a thick haze. Fire lamps coated everything in a reddish glow. Broken glass littered the rotting wooden floor. I could hardly breathe from the hazy smoke, body odor, bad breath, and the aroma of alcohol filling the air. All eyes inside the tavern landed on us. Half the patrons stopped talking and laughing. Lecherous gazes panned across my body. Every cell in me screamed at me to get out of there.

Gill leaned into me and whispered, "They can smell innocence like yours a mile away. Hang off me like you want to fuck me."

Despite my terror, his dirty words lit a fire in my panties and set my juices flowing. His hand found my ass and squeezed.

A whore to our left slid her hand down her man's body, and he leaned back and sighed.

Copying her, I draped myself over Gill like seaweed curtains, pretending he was my lover. I ran my hand along his rock-hard chest, circling his nipples, turning them hard beneath his white shirt and vest.

"Keep doing that, Princess," Gill growled in my ear, "and I might have to take you on one of these tables."

That idea did two things to me—one, it filled me with disgust and shyness, and two, it turned me. The thought of all these people watching us made my knees weak. I smiled a wicked, sexy smile and ran my fingers through his hair.

"You're good at this," he said.

His tone of voice coaxed a darkness out of me, one that wanted to play, get dirty, talk filthy, and I wanted to dive into it and explore.

This experience was both terrifying and exhilarating at the same time.

Some asshole blew his cigar smoke all over me. The urge to cough and sputter pounded at me. But I held it in, causing my lungs to burn. A whore should be used to that foul stench.

Nemo leaned in and said to Gill, "You know I'm going to kill you for this, right?"

"Oh, yeah." Gill thumped him on the chest again.

Previously, I'd found Nemo's jealousy over Fin kind of cute. But having both Nemo and Gill fighting for my affections was really turning me on in a twisted way. Sea god. I was turning into a hussy.

A waitress served drinks to the table behind us. The customers tossed back their shots three in a row, obviously seasoned drinkers.

"I'd love a piece of that ass," one man snarled as we went past.

Gill took out his knife, backtracked with me in his arms, and jammed it in the wooden table. "Over my dead body."

My heart pounded so hard, I feared my chest cavity might explode. What was he doing? Was he asking for a fight?

The man stood and kicked his chair aside. "Want to start trouble, friend?"

"I ain't no friend of yours," snarled Gill. "Don't go looking at my whore like that, or I'll peel the skin off your face and eat it."

Gill's violent threat startled me. Would he really do such a thing if the situation called for it? Or was that part of his act?

The bartender kept on pouring drinks as if these kinds of conflicts were regular occurrences. I imagined his job wasn't easy, witnessing people being beaten and killed daily, leaving him with the responsibility of cleaning up the mess. Was the wage really worth it? I guessed I'd never know.

Keeping in character, I wove an arm under Gill's and over his chest. "Come, my love. Don't waste your time. He couldn't afford me. He'd taste like cheap wine. I bet his cock is covered with scabies."

In the back of my mind, the good little Nyssa gasped, shocked to her core. But the adventurous side of me sailed on the thrill of it all.

The man's hand balled into a fist, as if he were considering punching me in the mouth for my comments.

Fin and Nemo stomped over to stand beside us.

The man ran his gaze across Nemo, and the sight of my huge merman was enough to prompt the man to take his seat again.

The breath I held rushed out.

A gentle tug from me got Gill walking again.

"Don't do that again," I whispered, blowing a kiss at some feral fool staring at me.

"That's the way, sexy," Gill said, licking my lips, making a show of our writhing tongues and the fact that I was all his.

His hands found my butt again, and the folds between my legs glossed with excitement. I rested a hand on his shoulder, enjoying playing my part as I stroked his face.

This time, Fin took the rear the way the palace guards did at functions.

Nemo, on the other hand, was apparently very bothered by what Gill was doing to me and had decided not to cooperate.

I wriggled free of Gill and threw myself at Nemo.

"I don't like this," he growled, squeezing me tight to show I was his.

"I'm playing my part in our effort to find the pearl; that's all." I ran my hands across his giant chest, but it did little to soothe the jealous beast inside him.

"It's more than that." He refused to look at me.

The sadness in his eyes had me choking up, but I had to hold it together. For our mission. To find the pearl and save my father. All I could do was pull his head down to mine and kiss him, hard, quick, like I meant it, showing him I was his, as well. When I pulled away, his expression had lightened a little.

"I'd like it if you did that again." A hint of a smile tugged at the corner of his lips. "And if you stayed with me."

Gill swept me back into his arms, taking away my choice in the matter.

"Enough of that, Sugarfins," he said.

My heart almost snapped in two at the look Nemo gave me as Gill pulled me along.

"Blade's at the farthest table in the corner," Gill said.

I shoved aside the haunting image of Nemo's face, trying to concentrate on my role.

The gloom in the tavern cast harsh shadows along the scar on Blade's face. *Poseidon*. Trust him to be at the table farthest from the door...from escape if things turned deadly.

Upon our arrival at his table, he didn't even glance up from the hand of cards he played. He tossed in some round pieces of wood with numbers on them.

"I raise you fifty," he said.

"You really want this boat, don't you?" chuckled the man opposite him, revealing gold fillings on several of his front teeth. He was a fat, leathery, old fellow dressed in long, cotton sleeves—typical pirate's regalia. He tossed in the same quantity of wooden chips.

"Give me a moment, friend," the assassin said to Gill, not looking up from his hands. "I'm about to win myself a new ride."

Gill nodded.

I glanced at Fin. He gave me a wink and returned to scanning the tavern like the pretend thug he was.

Nemo swallowed hard and rubbed a fist in his palm.

The assassin laid down his fan of cards on the stained table.

"Fucking asshole." The other man slammed his palm on the table then yanked at his necklace, tearing it off and smashing it on the table beside his cards. His chair scraped along the wooden floor as he stood. Angry stomps accompanied his retreat from the premises.

Blade scooped up his prize and tucked it inside his shirt. "Sit down." He held out a hand of welcome to Gill.

We all took a seat at the booth. Unfortunately, I was the lucky one to land on the chair the fat pirate had vacated, and his sweat soaked into my skin. Every instinct in me wanted to brush it away with a napkin, but that wasn't what my whore character would do. Cringing inside, I suffered in silence, smiling, nibbling at Gill's ripped shoulder.

"You've changed, Princess," said the assassin.

"The name's *wench*." I took one of his shot glasses and tossed back the alcohol. The burning liquid warmed my throat.

Everyone stared at me in surprise.

Good. If my act was shocking them, then it must be convincing everyone else, too.

"What can I do for you, *wench*?" Blade gulped down the contents of his last glass.

Fin answered for me. "We're looking for the collector's trove."

Blade leaned back in his seat and grabbed a handful of nuts from a woven basket. "Do you want to go back to the trade market?"

The assassin's words cut deep. My imagination ran riot at the thought of being caught again. I had to use all my concentration just to focus on Gill. For him to hold me in the moment. I squeezed his thigh, and he returned the pressure on my hand.

Fin remained level-headed as always, never showing his fear. "We believe the collector might possess an item we wish to acquire."

"The collector owns all manner of magical items," Blade said, plucking a dagger from beneath the table and shoving it inside his boot. "Or she could find it for you. That's her specialty."

That was good news. But would she be willing to bargain with four merfolk who'd escaped her? That was money out of her pocket. I'd bet she'd sooner apprehend us again and have us back on the market.

The assassin took a swill of his beer. "But do you trust her?"

I certainly didn't.

Fin leaned in and said in a low voice, "We're not below stealing."

"Maybe we can bargain for my sister," Gill chimed in, "and the rest of the merfolk."

A few people at the tables surrounding us stared as if their suspicions were aroused. I'd let down my guard and abandoned my act. To redeem myself, I licked Gill's ear, liking the salty taste of his lobe. My hand glided over his chest and down into his lap, squeezing his leg and then his groin, the way I'd seen many a whore do in the past. His privates twitched, encouraging me to rub it further, but this was neither the time nor the place...despite the fact that the idea of doing it in front of all these people turned me on. Such was the effect he had on me.

"Do you know where it is?" The apple of Gill's throat bobbed, as if he was having a hard time concentrating.

The deep, dark part of me expanded with disappointment as he pushed my hand away. She really wanted the excitement of getting him off in the bar.

Gill pulled me into his body so I leaned against his chest, enjoying the way his rocking breaths comforted me.

Nemo glared at me from across the table. I blew him a playful kiss and winked at him. This time, my efforts failed miserably, and he turned away, refusing to look at me again. We were really going to have a talk about this. Jealousy was not becoming. Not on a man as sweet as Nemo. Sea god. Nemo was making the guilt eat me up inside right when I was starting to enjoy myself.

"No one has ever gotten into the collector's trove," said the assassin. "And don't think I haven't tried."

I slumped against Gill. Now, how were we supposed to get the pearl and save my father and Gill's sister?

"Well, I'll die trying," growled Gill.

I was willing to do the same for my family if it came to it.

Blade scooped all the round wooden chips into his palm as if he prepared to leave. "Tomorrow is Sunday. The day she visits her mother's grave. The trove will be empty for a few hours."

My mood brightened, and I sat up straighter.

"Go to the old ruins in the Darkwoods," Blade said. "Head east for two leagues. Look for the twisted trees. There, you will find the entrance. Good luck, my friend."

He stood up, approached my side of the table, and gave me a kiss on the cheek. "If you ever want to spend a night with a *real* man..." He tossed a chip on the table in front of me.

Nemo stood up and blocked his path.

Blade huffed and squeezed past the hulking merman.

"Asshole," mumbled Gill.

My sentiments, exactly. Thank you, but no, thank you, Blade. I was quite content with my two mermen...maybe three if Gill allowed it. A man who wasted his money on whores was not exactly the kind of man I'd take to my bed or consider for my lover.

The assassin dumped his winnings on the bar, where the barman exchanged them for gold coins and a beer bottle. Blade stuffed his prize in a velvet pouch dangling from a leather tie around his neck. Then he took a slug of the beer on his way out.

Gill nudged me in the arm. "Time to leave."

I scooted along the chair and got out of the booth. All my fear outside the tavern returned in a giant wave that crashed down on me. The prospect of breaking into the collector's facility—and potentially not even finding what I needed— terrified me even more than entering this tavern had.

Gill lifted me over his shoulder, gave me a hard slap on the ass, and carried me out of the tavern. Poseidon, he was really not helping the situation with Nemo.

The swinging doors on the tavern creaked as they closed behind us. Outside in the cool night air, he set me back on my feet and smacked me on the ass again.

"You did well, wench."

Thank Poseidon. We'd made it out alive. While I'd played my part, I'd lost all my inhibition and anxiety about what could go wrong. Now, being back outside, I kept glancing over my shoulder, expecting to see some murderer stalking us in the dark.

"Hurry," said Fin. "This is not a place where we want to linger."

I concurred wholeheartedly. He helped me onto my mare. Verita had kindly given us four horses in exchange for one of my gold hair clips with the pearls.

When my companions were on their steeds, we raced off into the night, headed for the old ruins in the Darkwoods. With each strike of the horses' hooves, my terror grew. Had we just left one deadly place for another?

Back home, the worst threat a mermaid faced was a shark. They were too dumb and bloodthirsty to get smart and not attack merfolk. Whales, dolphins, and seals were among the smartest sea creatures. Sharks, we could deal with, using our sonic vibration powers.

But what dwelled in this forest, ready to attack us? This thought did not sit well with me. When I was young, my tutors had told me stories of all the lands of Haven. Fae dwelled in the southern part of the Darkwoods. The witch queen had taken control of the White's kingdom in the northeast. Voodoo witches and pirates settled in the south near The Cove. On the borders dwelled the panther shifters. To the east, dragons lived in the Wildfire mountains. Any one of those creatures could wander into the Darkwoods and claim us as their next meal.

Haven was positively brimming with humans, witches, and magical species, and not long ago, war had waged between them all. The witch queen could consider our presence in the Darkwoods an invasion. Poseidon only knew what she'd do with us. Rumor spoke of her bathing in the blood of virgins to preserve her lifespan well beyond her human years. If they were to be believed, legend also spoke of her possessing a magic mirror that revealed to her the future and the intent within anyone's heart. My mermen and I were dealing with forces beyond our experience and power to control. That terrified me beyond belief, and I sat my horse stiffly, my legs cramping from squeezing the saddle too tightly.

"Princess, your royal ass sure is tight from this angle." Gill said from beside me, giving me a confident wink. "Don't tell me you're a little worried?"

Yes, I was, actually. But I wasn't about to admit it. My aunt always told me to never admit my fears or concerns, especially to the people in court. They'd twist it to their advantage. Not that I considered these mermen the same kind of people, but I still didn't want them to see my fear.

Fin chuckled. "Hurry up, and tell her you're fond of her."

Gill plucked an apple from a tree in the orchard we strolled through, took a bite, and then tossed the rest at Fin.

Fin slowed his horse to keep pace with Gill's and gave his friend a good whack on the thigh.

Nemo cracked his knuckles as he had with Blade. I could see Nemo swinging at Gill for his behavior back at the tavern.

Guilt nipped at my heart like a hungry salmon. Poor Nemo. He really didn't want to share me. A relationship with Fin had stretched the limits of Nemo's tolerance. Flirting will Gil was testing him even further. Controlling my feelings for all three was impossible; I could just as easily stop breathing air.

There was something about Gill that was a refreshing change from the crowds I'd been surrounded by at court. The simplicity of him was incredibly appealing to me. No matter how I tried to deny my attraction to him, a deep, dark part of me was excited to explore our feelings. I wondered what kind of lover he might be compared to Nemo and Fin. Judging by his reckless ways so far, he'd be quite the kinky partner, probably into the rough stuff, wrecking my body with pleasurable pain. I hated to admit it, but the idea had my privates steaming up.

"You'll have to try much harder to impress me," I said, returning his flirtation.

"Ouch." He pressed a hand to his chest.

The humor didn't distract me for long. Quickly, my heart turned dark again with worry about what lay ahead of us. The cramps in my legs returned. I squeezed the horse's reins so tight, I lost feeling in my hands.

"Nyssa," said Fin, his horse trotting beside mine. "You need not worry when you're with us."

Nothing frightened that merman. I wished I possessed but a fraction of his courage. Then I might not have been such a quivering mess all tangled in a tight ball.

Even with his reassurances, I wasn't so confident. My mind kept wandering back to the assassin's words. No one had ever broken into the collector's trove. I had to consider the possibility that this was a suicide mission. That my mermen and I might end up where we'd left—apprehended again, and this time, sold to the highest bidder. A fate my stomach could not digest.

CHAPTER 18

An early morning mist clung to the circle of trees surrounding the twisted tree Blade had mentioned.

"Wait here," Fin said, climbing down from his horse and taking the reins. "Let me investigate first."

I glanced at Gill and Nemo. Both of them nodded at their leader.

My stomach wrung as Fin secured his steed to a low-hanging branch and wandered to the edge of the circle, examining it.

"Be careful," I said. "What if the collector has set traps?"

Fin returned to me immediately. I was hypnotized by his tall, confident, strong stride and nearly fell off my horse. He clasped my hand, bringing me back to reality.

"I won't endanger you or my men by sending you all in there." He kissed my hand. Again, he left to stand by the edge of the trees.

Fin bent down and placed a hand on the ground. The sonic blast he sent out into the circle reverberated through me.

Our horses whinnied nervously and shifted backward.

"Steady," Gill said, trying to soothe his steed, but it still twitched with nerves.

The signal that returned, and which I'd picked up, was weak, and I didn't get a good picture of their exact locations because the sonic blast had not originated from me, but I received a vision of five objects buried inside the circle of trees. Probably traps set up to prevent anyone from entering.

Fin applied more pressure to the ground, and it vibrated more fiercely.

This time, the horses were well and truly spooked. Gill's stead trotted a few steps and shook its head. Nemo's took off, and nothing he did—yelling, yanking at its reins—made it stop. Fin's horse tossed its head and yanked at the reins holding it to the tree.

Mine rose onto its hind legs and tossed me backward. The layers of leaves softened my fall, but I still received several bruises, my ribs aching with every breath. Thanks to our shifter ability, merfolk were a little more resilient than humans were. I wondered how much worse this would feel for a human.

Gill was by my side, running his hands through my hair and rubbing my chest. Gill. His beautiful brown eyes were stained with panic. He squeezed my hand so tight, his grip cut off the circulation to my fingers.

Fin was at my side, carrying a leather flask full of water. "Roll her over and calm the horses."

"Yes, Captain." Ever so gently, Gill turned me onto my stomach.

Water trickled down my spine. My skin responded to the liquid, absorbing it, harnessing its healing power.

"More," I said, the words costing me pain.

Fin dribbled more onto my skin.

My fins and scales demanded to be released. No. Not now. I forced the energy of the water into the bruised parts of me—into my muscles and deeper into my spine. My body buzzed from the healing power of the water.

"All of it," I panted, desperate for it.

Fin squeezed my hand tightly and let the rest flow.

My body responded like a greedy shark, gulping it all up. Within moments, the pain in my chest had dulled, and I was grateful for the relief.

"Can she move?" Gill asked.

"Don't be silly." My voice came out hoarse. I demonstrated for him, moving my legs and arms, testing them. "See?"

"My apologies, Princess." The strain in Fin's voice told me of his regret. He clasped my hand and pressed it to his cheek.

Gill grabbed Fin's shirt and gave him a good yank. "Don't do that again, Captain. She could have broken her neck."

I needed to stop this before it elevated into an argument. "I'm fine, Gill." I sat up and put a hand to his chest.

His nostrils flared as he let go of his leader.

"Where's Nemo?" I glanced around the clearing. His horse and mine had taken off. Flighty creatures.

"He'll be back," Gill said, lifting me to my feet. "Can you walk?"

Each step I took hurt a little, but nowhere near the kind of pain I'd experienced earlier.

The accident had shaken Fin a little. I could tell by how quiet he'd become. He needed to snap out of it. We were so close to the pearl. A little mishap was not going to deter us.

"How do we get around the traps?" I asked him.

"Er," he said as if his mind was somewhere else.

"Set a few off, wait until the dust settles, and sneak in," Gill suggested.

Brilliant idea. I left the mermen behind and grabbed a few fallen branches. From several feet away, I tossed them through the circle of trees. Nothing happened on the first two. But the last set off a trap. Chains rattled, then a panel in one of the trees opened, and arrows fired from it. They flicked my hair as they whizzed past me and struck the ground behind me.

My heart sank into my boots. Sea god, that was close. I rubbed my arms, lucky to still be alive.

The horses whinnied again. Gill's mount retreated a few paces until he managed to get it to stay.

"Princess?" Fin was at my side, checking for any wounds.

"I'm fine," I reassured him.

His concern was touching, but I didn't want him to feel bad about what had happened before. He needed to focus on the mission.

"We need to get the horses out of here," I said.

Fin nodded. "You take them. I don't want you near this when more traps go off."

That didn't sit well with me. What if my mermen got hurt? We only had one pouch of water left, and if one of us was injured... I had better preserve it.

Fin kissed me long and soft, like it might be our last kiss before we perished. I held on to that moment, reliving it as I drew the horses away, looking back over my shoulder several times as I left the area.

Behind me, my mermen collected rocks, logs, and more branches.

I waved from a safe distance away, my stomach rock hard with dread.

Where the hell was Nemo? He shouldn't have been gone this long. Was he okay? I scanned the forest but found no sign of him.

Fin and Gill took turns throwing their objects into the circle. Three spears exploded at Fin's shot, one of which barely missed him, the other two striking the ground at the edge of the tree line. The arrows buried themselves several inches into the earth, their shafts wobbling madly from the impact.

For a moment, a terrible fear rose in my heart. Quickly, I thrust it into the very farthest corner of my mind. My mermen were not going to perish here.

The sound of gears and chains upset the poor horses, and one whinnied, the other yanking at the reins.

"Shhh," I said, stroking its long face, telling it telepathically that it would be fine, and this all would be over soon.

"Woooo!" Gill screamed, as if all the traps going off excited him. Crazy merman.

They moved to different positions around the ring of trees and threw more rocks. Spiky rows rose out of the ground when Gill took his turn. Daggers ejected and struck the ground at Fin's feet. Had he been inside the circle, they would have stabbed him in the guts.

My insides rolled over with fear each time they activated a trap. I wanted to close my eyes and pray for it to end as fast as possible, but my mind froze with terror.

Gill's horse chewed at the reins, as if trying to get free.

"Stop that," I told the frightened animal, patting its neck.

"One more to go," Fin yelled as he advanced to another position and heaved another rock.

Something snapped and then groaned.

"What was that?" I shouted.

Whatever it was, it whooshed through the air.

"Fuck." Gill grabbed Fin and threw him to the ground an instant before a giant log would have hit them. Ropes suspending it from the trees creaked as the wood swung back the other way. Three more logs oscillated in the same fashion at different positions.

My fingers curled into claws. The collector was very clever at protecting her property. What else did she have in store inside her trove? My chest seized at the idea.

"Is that the last trap?" I called out to my mermen.

"I believe so," Fin replied, watching the logs overhead. "But we should test it one more time to be safe."

Once the logs had ceased swaying, he sent out another sonic blast. I didn't detect any more traps when the waves hit me. But we couldn't be too sure. Maybe the collector had some magical traps set up, too.

Gill bombarded the clearing with a few more pieces of debris. No more traps activated, to my great relief.

Fin snuck in to double-check, stomping the ground, scanning the clearing.

My whole body tensed, ready to run to him if necessary.

"All clear," he said.

Thank Poseidon.

I led the horses back to the ring of trees and secured them.

There, Fin took my hand, leading me through the tree line as fast as our feet would carry us.

Even with Gill walking backward, scanning for any danger coming in the opposite direction, I kept glancing over my shoulder.

We reached the twisted tree, finding a door carved in its trunk. Gill stood guard, while Fin tried the handle, but it didn't give.

"There's no lock on it," he said.

"How are we going to get inside?" I asked.

"Step back." He motioned for me to move out of the way. Shoulder braced, he slammed into the door. The door rattled but wasn't budging.

Shellfish.

The horses whinnied and stomped from where they were tethered across the clearing. They were still rattled, and rightly so. I was, too, and I didn't know how else to calm them. But then when I heard a few birds screech and take flight from the trees, I knew something was wrong.

Then I heard it. The distant pound of horse hooves.

"Nemo!" I cried, spinning around, waiting for him to appear.

"Shh," said Gill, cocking his head. "There are several horses."

I listened; he was right. Had Nemo brought company?

A squadron of mersoldiers emerged from the forest ahead, led by Faraall.

The warmth of my blood was stolen away. How the hell had he survived? Better yet, how had he found me? Did the sea god hate me so much that he had led the commander right back to me?

The wound on Faraall's chest glimmered green. Magic. Now more than ever, I was convinced he and the sea witch were working together to rid the merrealm of my father. How sad that Faraall was probably just a useless pawn in her game. Once my father was dead, the witch was not going to let Faraall live; I had no doubt she wanted the kingdom for herself.

My blood iced over as I realized why Nemo had not returned to me. Faraall had probably killed him. Pain like I'd never felt stabbed at my heart, and I burst into tears. I was going to destroy that asshole. One way or another, I would have my vengeance.

"What the fuck is he doing here?" Gill growled. "Didn't you kill that prick?"

"Get us inside," I screamed, my pulse cranking up a notch.

"What if we get trapped?" Gill asked. "We should run."

"Where?" I cried. "We won't reach the horses in time."

"But we'll be trapped," Fin said.

The galloping pounded in my brain as the commander's team approached. There was no way he was getting his hands on me again. I'd rather starve and perish from dehydration inside the collector's trove than go back to Tritonia with him or be sold to the pirates a second time.

"With a fuck-load of magical items," Gill added.

Exactly. The only downside was that we had no idea how to use them. Would they even work for us if we weren't witches? What if the magic hurt one of my mermen or me? I supposed I'd rather die from magic than rape and murder.

Fin pressed his hands to the trove's door. It rattled as his vibrations shook it. Blazing red symbols of a strange language burned into the wood. Little embers flew off them. He hissed as one seared his skin but didn't let up on his attempt to break in.

I spoke four different languages, and I didn't recognize a single letter of this one.

Prickles crawled down my neck like an army of sea mites on the march.

I jammed my hands against the wood and shook with all my might.

More markings spread across the door.

Fin shoved the door and it began to give. "It's working. Keep going, Princess."

I put all I had into my sonic blasts. The door shook so hard, I was terrified it was going to shatter into a thousand pieces. Somehow, it didn't, which was a miracle. Because my powers were known to smash small shells to bits.

By the time Faraall and his men hit the tree line, the door finally gave. Fin shoved me inside and hurried in after me, followed by Gill. My mermen tried to barricade the door with their bodies, but the whole door glowed red hot, burning them, and they pulled away.

Shellfish. Now we were well and truly trapped, whether we liked it or not.

I heard the horses slow their pace.

"Get my beloved bride," Faraall ordered. "Kill the other two."

"Quick," Fin said, dragging me down a short flight of stairs into darkness.

Strange markings glowed on the tree's wood, allowing us to see a little. At the end of the stairs we emerged into a darkened room. My mervision kicked in, allowing me to see a desk by the wall, cabinets, and even nooks carved into the wall, storing all sorts of weird and wonderful-looking objects.

Someone screamed outside the tree. One of the mersoldiers must have touched the fiery door.

My heart wrenched even though the traitor of a merman hunted us.

"Get a ram to break the door down," Faraall barked. "She's not getting away this time."

Dark thoughts crashed inside my mind. They could use one of the swinging trees. What if they managed to get in? We'd be trapped. My mermen slain and me taken hostage again. A fate worse than death.

Gill wrapped an arm around my shoulder. "I won't let him touch you."

Despite his promise, I wasn't so sure. We were outnumbered and confined to a small space. The horrific reality of the situation deadened my insides.

"Find the pearl and anything that we can use against the commander," Fin ordered, and he and Gill got to work, searching among all the items.

I tried to distract myself by examining all the jewelry, weapons, headpieces, masks, spears, chalices, small statues carved from stone, what looked like various kinds of animals' teeth and skulls, and even a gnarled branch.

The headpiece made me think of my own, and I touched

the last remaining hairclip with the purple pearl. Sparks flashed upon my touch.

"What the hell?" I jumped backward.

Fin pulled it from my hair, and it glowed green. "Magic," he whispered.

That same word rested on my tongue, but I couldn't spit it out. Faraall's shell, the one that held my father's mind captive, glowed the same color. Was he using more magic on me? Had the bastard cast a spell on my hair piece? I was willing to bet my crown that this was how he'd tracked me down. There was no other way to explain how he'd found me.

Thumps sounded from above. The mersoldiers were trying to break down the door. At each strike, I jerked. I gripped one of the cabinets hard and didn't let go.

"Think I've found it," Gill announced.

Fin and I rushed over to the cabinet where Gill stood. Atop it sat a bowl carved from marble and filled with water. A golden pearl was immersed inside, giving off a glow. A dark power radiated from the pearl, a force that made me sick to the stomach and lightheaded.

"Do you feel that?" I asked my mermen.

Fin shook his head as if he'd been punched. "Can't think straight," he said, rubbing his forehead.

"It makes me feel like my skin's peeling off," Gill said, twitching as if sea slugs crawled on his back.

Shellfish. If this thing affected us like this, then how were we going to carry it back to the sea?

Fin left me for a moment to rummage around on a few of the shelves, returning with a square piece of silk large enough to wrap up the pearl and stuff it inside his pocket. He grimaced as he removed the magical totem. The instant he stuffed it inside the silk, his face relaxed, and the horrible sensation I'd felt lessened.

"I'll carry it," he told us.

Selfless and always protecting his men. I stretched up on my tiptoes to kiss him.

"Grab as much as you can carry," Fin ordered. "We might need to sell some of these things on our way back."

Good idea.

My mermen grabbed a couple more handfuls of items and stuffed them down their boots and inside the pockets of their vests.

But the more I thought about the pearl, the more I convinced myself this was a bad idea. With all that power, the sea witch could bring the merrealm to its knees.

The sound of muffled voice penetrating from above added to my worries. "It's not working, Commander."

"Set fire to the tree," Faraall ordered. "Four of you stay in case the rats manage to escape."

My blood congealed to ice.

CHAPTER 19

*G*reen flames circled the exit, blackening the wood, shrouding it in fire. The blaze quickly spread along the door, consuming it.

Shellfish. Faraall, that pig! We weren't going to get through the door without burning ourselves.

"How are we going to get out of here?" I asked.

Fear and hope chased across Fin's face. "Everybody hunt around for another way out."

Clutching their tridents, the guys started examining the room. I could barely hear my own thoughts above my pulse pounding in my ears. *Think, Nyssa, think!*

Back at home, the architects who had built my father's kingdom had constructed secret tunnel exits in the event of an emergency. This way, the royal family could escape the palace. Secret corridors were hidden in every royal family member's bedroom, the library, the banquet hall, the throne room, and my father's hall, where he met with dignitaries, and in the gardens. The tunnels led to three escape routes. One led to the southern lands of Tritonia. A second to Wildfire and a third to The Cove. I prayed to the sea god

214

that the collector was clever enough to have done something similar.

"There might be a secret panel or door somewhere," I said, running my fingers across the walls, looking for indents or hollow spaces. Nothing.

The air was thickening with smoke, and I coughed.

"Hurry," said Fin, adding to the darkening in my gut.

We had to get out of there. Too much depended on us. The merfolk kingdom would descend into chaos if Faraall claimed the throne.

Something scraped behind me, and I turned to find Gill shifting a shelf full of magical items.

"Found something," he said.

I rushed over to see.

A door. Locked by a great, big padlock and bolt across the center.

"Let's see if I can bust it down," said Gill, slamming it a few times with his weapon. The lock rattled, and the door thumped. It sounded like something heavy was resting against it on the other side. He pushed me out of the way and rested his trident against the wall. Then he backed up and rushed at the door, thumping against it with his shoulder.

Poseidon, please, get us out of here.

Something crackled behind us, and I spun around. Fire the color of the sea witch's magic licked at the ceiling, consuming the wood with incredible speed. My stomach sank as I shielded my eyes from the roaring heat. We didn't have too much longer before it reached us.

One of the wooden beams in the ceiling tore from its joist and came crashing down. I flinched and shrank away. The heat was drying out my skin, turning it taut, and every movement was painful. I needed water to soften and moisturize it.

"Shit," puffed Gill after another pound against the door failed to open it. He wiped sweaty hair from his face and pressed his palms flat against the door. It shook from the vibrations Gill pounded it with.

Fin held me, protected my head from the fire's intensity.

The black smoke created a haze in the small space, and I lost sight of Gill.

Ice spread across my whole body. I couldn't shake the feeling that we might meet our end in this trove. Oh, the irony. Dying whilst trying to save my father and our people. None of the merfolk would ever know. Faraall would claim another of my sisters and marry her, kill my father, and seize the throne. Dread locked my stomach tight at the thought of being so helpless.

The fire crawled along toward us, and Fin squeezed me to him.

"I've got it," Gill shouted.

Sweet Poseidon! Please let it lead out of the trove.

Gill's next words ate a hole in my stomach. "But we're not getting out of here easily. The fire's starting to eat at the door."

"What about using a water shield to go through the fire?" Fin suggested.

A water shield was something we merfolk used to protect us from heat and desiccation. It might prolong us on land for a few extra days, but it cost us great energy to maintain it.

"It's too hot," I protested, coughing back the smoke choking my lungs. "The water will turn to steam. We won't make it."

"Never say never, your royal ass." Fin gave my cheek a quick kiss. "Hold my hand. Pool our power together."

His optimism reminded me of Nemo, and my heart stung. If he'd taught me one thing, it was to remain hopeful. I had to hold on to that with every part of my being.

Fin dragged me over to the hole in the wall. We found

Gill waiting with both mermen's tridents. Gill handed one to Fin and grabbed my hand.

"Ready?" Fin asked, squeezing my other hand.

"Yes," Gill and I both replied.

My skin tingled as I called upon the water within to shield me. A thin, watery film washed over me. I forced it across my mermen to cover and protect them, too. Their rippling liquid flushed across me like a current bringing fresh water.

Fin sent us all a message. "Time to go."

My heart pounded against my sternum so hard it hurt.

Gill jerked me forward. Flames curled at him, hissing, spitting embers at him as if the trove didn't want him to escape its grasp. He pulled me into the tunnel.

A beam crashed down behind me, and I jumped, breaking my bond with Fin. Shellfish. What had I done?

"Fin?" I screamed in my mind. "Fin?"

He didn't answer.

Gill's calls to his comrade echoed in my head.

I continued to cry out for Fin. Where was he? Had the wood fallen on him? Sea god, no! I groped for him, but the heat penetrated my shell, drying my skin further.

Gill yanked me forward, and I fought him, not wanting to leave Fin behind.

"Princess, we have to go," he insisted in my head.

"Not without Fin." My efforts to draw Gill backward were useless.

I had two options. Let go of Gill, and try to find Fin—and possibly lose them all—or keep going with Gill but be left devastated, my heart sliced in two. That choice wasn't afforded me when suddenly I was lifted off my feet and carried away. I wailed for Fin, scratching at Gill to put me down, but he refused to respond to my cries. I'd likely already lost Nemo. I couldn't lose Fin, as well.

Another slab of wood slammed onto the ground, sealing off the tunnel behind us. The impact rocketed through my bones.

"No." I kicked at Gill, wanting to go back and check.

His hold was so strong. He carried me all the way out of the tunnel and into the forest, at least three hundred feet from the trove's entrance. Under his arm, he squeezed his trident.

Green flames had burned half of the tree. Soon, it would fall, too, leaving my beloved burning inside it. The knife in my chest threatened to cut the rest of my insides.

Gill released his liquid shield, and I felt his magic drain from me. I did the same. My skin was so sore and dry. Every muscle in my body ached. I could barely move, I was so tired. We needed water desperately.

When he set me on the ground, I collapsed, my heart heavy with grief. So heavy I could hardly breathe. I'd failed Fin. Failed my father. Failed my people. Warm tears trickled down my face. I couldn't afford to lose the moisture, but I didn't care. My chest shook with my sobs, and I cried against Gill's powerful shoulder.

"Fin. Nemo." I buried my head in my hands.

Gill cradled me and whispered, "Fin's coming. I know it."

Fin's death was all my fault. I should have gone back to search for him. If he'd perished in the trove, I'd never forgive myself.

Gill kept repeating, "They're coming."

But with each passing moment, my hope diluted.

Even Gill stopped repeating his positive mantra's when a big boom exploded. Fire hissed and spat out of the secret entrance. Smoke poured off the tree.

Hot, bitter tears poured down my cheeks.

Then I heard something else—sounds like a cough and a grunt.

I snapped to attention and swiveled away from Gill.

Someone emerged from the mass of smoke and fire and fell to the ground.

Before I could think clearly, my feet were carrying me forward. Something deep inside the pit of my stomach told me it might be my merman.

"Nyssa." Gill's footsteps thumped after me.

"Fin? Nemo?" I shouted.

Another grunt sounded.

A breeze swept through the clearing, fanning away some of the smoke.

And there he was, lying on the ground, breathing hard. Soot-smeared skin. Pink skin, inflamed and blistered from the heat that had scorched his shell. Two tridents rested beside him on the ground.

"Captain," said Gill.

He dragged Fin some hundred feet farther away from the blaze and rested him against a tree.

I grabbed the two weapons and hurried after them.

Wheezed breaths pushed in and out of Fin's lungs. "Water," he moaned.

I kneeled in front of him and ran my hands along his grimy face. "I'm so sorry I let you go. I can't believe you're alive." I pressed my lips to his forehead. My heart was bouncing with joy.

Fin's shaky hands reached out for me and pressed me to his firm torso. "Don't be." Our chests melted together as he kissed me like it was our last moment on Haven together... and it almost had been.

"That's enough of that," growled Gill, pulling me onto his lap, supporting my back with his arm. "My turn."

His kiss was demanding and rough, taking all of me, and I let him. I felt like jumping over the moon, knowing he had feelings for me, too.

But my delight was short-lived, sliced in two by someone shouting, "There they are. Kill them!"

I glanced up to find four mersoldiers racing for us. With all that had happened, I'd forgotten the commander had left a few mermen behind to finish us off if we escaped.

Gill picked up his trident but rocked on his feet, unsteady from using his energy for the shield.

I clutched Fin, who hadn't moved and now shivered in my grasp.

Shellfish. We were sitting sardines, waiting to be eaten by a much bigger predatory fish.

Gill's trident defended a stabbing blow directed at him. He swung, blocking another blow. One soldier's next attack struck him with such force, it sent him reeling back. But he didn't give up and jabbed at them. They laughed, taunting him.

"Give us the princess, and let us fuck her," one snarled, earning a whack to the wrist.

I winced as I heard the bones in his hand smash.

"You'll pay for that, soldier," one of the others growled.

All three of them lunged at Gill. He wobbled as he attempted to block their strikes, but he wasn't fast enough. With a sweep of their weapons to the back of his legs, they took him to the ground. Three tridents aimed at his throat.

"No," I shouted, standing up. "Leave them. Take me."

One of the mersoldiers glared at me. "That wasn't our order. We don't take orders from you. The commander is our new king."

Shock sucked the air from my lungs. King? Had he killed my father and family already? Invisible tridents pierced my stomach and twisted.

Two of the soldiers dragged Fin and dumped him beside Gill.

"Say *goodbye* to your friends," one said, pulling out a dagger.

Fear jacked up my heart rate. Breathing was close to impossible. I was about to say goodbye to two of the mermen I'd come to deeply admire and love. Yes, loved. Their deaths were going to split what was left of my heart after Nemo's likely death into two. I couldn't bear the thought.

Something thumped in the distance, catching my attention. I could barely see a thing through the smoky haze surrounding us.

"What's that?" I asked, trying to distract the mermen. "I think your master has returned."

"Don't try to delay the inevitable, Princess." A sinister gleam captured the soldier's eyes.

"Which one shall we kill first?" one of them asked.

He grabbed Fin, and I whimpered, moving forward, but another soldier jabbed my stomach.

"Stay back, bitch," he warned me.

But I no longer cared about death. If I couldn't have my mermen, then my life wasn't worth living.

The approach of horses' hooves grew louder. One horse, this time. A lone soldier, perhaps, come to collect the commander's prize.

My stomach twisted.

Fin jerked as the soldiers nicked his face with the sharp edge of a trident.

"Get it over with," he demanded, his breathing slow, his skin very pale.

"Oh, no," replied the soldier. "We're going to make this nice and slow."

Sadistic bastard. I lunged at him, scratching his face, tearing at his flesh. He pushed me to the ground.

Gill grabbed one of the soldier's legs and tripped him up.

A trident flew out of the dark, striking the last soldier in the chest.

The rider was upon us, bursting through the smoky haze, and my breath hitched upon recognizing him.

"Nemo," I whispered.

My great, big, lug of a merman was alive, albeit covered in blood and sweat. He leaped off his horse, onto one of the soldiers, and they crashed to the ground. Nemo sank his teeth into the soldier's neck and drew blood. Large fists pummeled the soldier with such ferocity, I had to look away.

Gill was atop another soldier, strangling him with his bare hands.

I hurried to the horse and collected Nemo's pouch of water. Out of all my mermen, Fin was in the most desperate need. Back by his side, I lifted the pouch and poured the liquid into his waiting mouth.

"Save some for Gill and Nemes," he said, pushing the rest away.

"No," I said, forcing him to drink it. "We passed a stream about half a league before the collector's trove. They can drink there."

Fin refused. Stubborn merman. Always more concerned with the health and safety of his men than himself.

When I turned around, all the mersoldiers were dead.

"How? Where? What?" I couldn't get a proper sentence out.

Nemo laughed as he rushed over to pull me against his chest.

I buried myself in his arms. "I thought I'd lost you." The blood all over him was of no consequence to me. Him returning alive meant more to me. "I can't lose you."

"You'll never lose me."

Nemo lifted me up and wrapped my legs around his waist. The passionate kiss he gave me had my head spinning.

"I'm going to marry you," he added.

This time, I didn't laugh at his statement. I wanted some sort of future with him. With all of them. Even if I had to give up my title and all that came with it.

"My turn now," Gill said.

His statement earned him a challenging glare from Nemo.

Reluctantly, the hulking merman set me down, allowing Gill to sweep me up and lay a gruff kiss on me. I wasn't going to say no. Something about him screamed power, and the deep, dark part of me wanted him to command me. Turn my already-weak legs to jelly.

"Come on, Captain," said Nemo, lifting Fin to his feet. "Let's get you to the stream."

Nemo lifted his leader onto the horse. Fin sucked in a breath, possibly from the agony of his burns.

I was a little disappointed that I hadn't won a kiss from Fin, too. But there would be time for that. I'd rather him save his energy and put it into healing himself. And I didn't want to hurt him if he was burned.

Nemo disappeared into the smoke, returning with the two horses.

I blinked, astonished that Faraall hadn't cut them loose and chased them into the forest.

"Thank Poseidon," I said to myself.

Gill carried me to the second horse and lifted me onto it. Then he jumped up behind me, holding me tight with one arm as we crossed through the veil of smoke into the forest.

Nemo took the remaining horse, and he and Fin trotted beside us.

I hoped like hell we didn't encounter Faraall and his men again. We were in no state to be fending them off. If there was another battle anytime soon, I didn't think we'd be victorious.

CHAPTER 20

*G*ill kneeled at the bank, scooping a handful of water and drinking it. The stream wasn't very deep—perhaps halfway up my calves. Rocks decorated sections of the banks and even the stream itself.

Nemo carried Fin into the water.

"Sea god," Fin exclaimed as he lay back in the stream, the water bubbling over his head and shoulders. He pulled the cloth containing the dark pearl from his pocket and placed it on the bank.

His blue eyes had paled, along with the rest of him.

I smiled, glad we'd made it to the water so he could heal. Each time he'd grimaced along the way, I'd felt pain, too.

"I'll get us some food," Nemo said, squeezing my shoulder, leaving a sweet kiss upon the crown of my head.

For a while, I sat with Fin, not caring if my dress or boots got wet. I held his hand, and we sat in silence until the skin of his blisters began to peel. Fresh skin reformed in their place, creating pink spots.

I glanced at Gill, who had stripped off his shirt to rinse it in the water. His muscles glistened with the water he tossed over his chest.

"Checking out this god of a merman?" Gill's waggling eyebrows implied all the wrong intentions.

Suddenly, a crippling shyness overcame me, and I ducked my head, watching him from beneath my hair. He made me feel like a teenager with a crush on a handsome merman way out of my league. Where was that deep, darker part of me when I needed her?

"Don't be shy, Princess," Gill said as he scrubbed his shirt and skin. "We've already seen each other's asses naked."

"I don't want to see your ass again," Fin said.

He laughed, and Gill tossed a bit of mud at him, and they did it back and forth until they tired of their little game.

I burned up when Gill took off his pants and flashed me a wicked smile before resting them on the banks. Sea god, he was bold. But that was what I admired about him. Plus, he was sexy as hell. Probably just as sinful.

"Bring your sexy, royal ass over here, and scrub with me." He tapped the rock beside him. "Your dress is stained and highly inappropriate attire for a princess."

He was right. Parts of my dress were smeared with charcoal, and sections of it had burned away. It reeked of smoke, too. Damn the fire. I'd need to take it off and wash it. That meant getting naked. Fin and Nemo too had seen me nude. But something about Gill made me nervous as hell all of a sudden.

Regardless of my nerves, every instinct inside me demanded I go to him. But my head said otherwise. I glanced at Fin, not wanting to leave his side.

"Go on," Fin said, patting my leg. "Check out his fine ass."

I laughed, smoothed hair from his eyes, and kissed his forehead.

My feet carried me over to Gill, and I kneeled beside him.

Together, we washed our clothes, me still dressed and him naked. Some of the soot came out, but I suspected the fabric had burned and was left with a permanent stain.

I had to use every ounce of restraint I had not to keep looking at him, admiring every inch of him—the angle of his jaw, the lines of his stomach muscles, his flexing arms...even the package between his legs. Sea god. He was perfect.

"Like what you see?" he asked.

My insides lit awake from the sound of his voice.

When he looked my way, he did more than simply undress me with his eyes. His gaze said he was imagining ripping off the rest of my clothes and positioning me on all fours as he claimed me. Just as I had presumed, he reached out and tugged on the string of my corset. My breath caught in my throat. He tore it off in moments, leaving me bare and vulnerable. The back of his knuckles brushed along the skin of my arms. A spark ignited in my chest and then heat exploded across my whole body.

"This is hot," Fin said.

Fire tore through my body. Was something going to happen between Gill and me while Fin watched? Something about that idea had my libido tingling. I'd wanted an audience ever since we visited the tavern to find Blade. The thought turned me on more than anything.

Gill leaned in to kiss me, and I reached for him. Our heads smacked together, and we pulled away. Pain cracked down my forehead, and I massaged it.

Shellfish. Why did this always happen? Right at the intimate moments.

The impact didn't seem to bother Gill, and he smiled, returning for another smooch. My anxiety got the better of me, and I retreated.

Gill stroked my arm. "Don't be nervous."

I wanted to explain, but my mouth seemed fused shut. If I

was to get past my nerves and progress to the next level with Gill, I had to do something drastic before I did something humiliating again. Doing the first thing that came to mind, I clenched my fist, said, "I'm sorry," and punched Gill in the jaw.

"What'd you do that for?" he said, rubbing his chin.

Fin chuckled. "It's better than being kicked in the balls."

"What?" Gill's brows knitted together.

"Trust me," I said. "It was bound to happen in some form."

"What are you talking—?"

I ended his sentence with a long kiss, parting his lips with my tongue and swirling it with his. When I pulled back, Gill smiled like a dolphin that had caught a wave.

"For that, it was definitely worth it." His brown eyes blazed with passion, as if he'd forgotten all about Fin, or possibly he just didn't care.

I left a trail of kisses along the spot where I'd punched him.

"You awoke something in me," Gill whispered. "The moment those pirates threw you in the wagon, I wanted to claim you. Protect you. Never let another man put his hands on you. I'm drawn to you in a way I've never been drawn to another woman."

His admission was at odds with the way he'd treated me. "Then why were you such an asshole?"

He ran a finger along the lines of my collarbone. "You're way out of my league."

I felt a stirring in my chest and a warmth in my core. Part of me couldn't believe he was confessing this in front of Fin. But then, I didn't think Gill cared what anyone thought of him. That was one of the many things that attracted me to him.

"I've tried to fight it." Those delicious, roaming hands of

his clasped my behind and squeezed. "Tried to push you away."

A little mewl escaped my mouth. A raging fire ignited down below. It stormed through my body, setting me alight.

Fin was resting his chin in his hands, delighting in being a spectator, and I loved every second of him watching us.

Gill's hand slid between my breasts all the way down to my belly. "It just makes me want your juicy, royal ass even more." He cupped my generous bust in his hands.

I moaned as his fingers tweaked my erect nipple.

His eyes glimmered with longing as he stripped off my skirt.

I shivered at his touch, unable to get a word out. My voice had disappeared into a chasm beneath the ocean.

His lips were inches from my neck, making my need for him intensify.

"Like a perfect little flower, opening up to the sunlight." He kissed my neck, rough and hard, matching his demeanor.

I tilted my head back and moaned. "More, more, more."

"Fuck yes, little princess," he purred in my ear.

I bit my lip and closed my eyes.

"I want to summon that sexy, royal ass from the tavern and make her scream my name."

Flames licked at my neck and face. How had he known about that? Could he see into my soul? *Poseidon*. I felt so exposed in front of him, and I curled away. But he wasn't letting me go. His grip was commanding and holding me captive.

"I want to watch you touch your tender pearl for me," he commanded. "Stroke it back and forth. Real dirty for me."

A laugh rumbled in his throat at my gasp. I'd never touched myself there. Didn't know how to do it. What if I did something wrong, and he laughed at me? The thought had me tensing.

Gill's smile softened his features. "Like this."

He extended my forefinger, guided it down to my wetness, and pushed my wrist back and forth. The friction made me gasp. It wasn't as good as when Fin or Nemo had touched me there, but having Gill guide me had my arousal spiking.

"Yeah, like that, beautiful," he said, eyes glued to the motion of my hand.

The roughness in his voice and the firm way his hand touched mine had me craving more of him. Right now, I was willing to do whatever he asked of me. Fingers thrumming along my folds, I groaned, and he smiled as if he liked what he saw.

I glanced over at Fin. He'd reclined back in the water. His dick was hard, and he stroked it. Sea god, that was hot.

I bit my lip as my pleasure rose. The stimulation of them both watching me intensified my pulsing pearl. My whole body belonged to them both. This was primal, animalistic, raw, and all consuming. It hit a deep urge inside me. One that had wanted to burst free a long time ago.

Gill pressed his mouth to mine. Hot, hard, and demanding, rendering me powerless in his hold. He tasted sweet and sour, like underwater berries and seagrass. His hands explored my curves. Mine kept going, delicately stroking my wetness, brushing his privates, and pretty soon, his excitement dug into my thigh. I gripped him, and he grunted as if he enjoyed me touching him that way.

"You before me, beautiful," he whispered, winding the curls between my legs in his finger.

Sea god. He nearly undid me from that small motion.

"I'm a gentleman," he added with a wink.

Hardly. Did a gentleman make his partner fuck herself? No, only a dirty scoundrel would.

"You, a gentleman?" I panted, twitching as I milked the pleasure from my body.

"A gentleman only in the bed."

His deep, husky growl teased my body and coaxed sensations I'd never felt before. The instant his hand returned to my wrist, I exploded. Wave after delicious wave.

"Gill," I screamed as my body shook from the pleasure he'd extracted from me. Unable to breathe, I slumped into his arms and leaned into him.

"I'm going to make you scream again," he said, kneeling then splaying my legs over him.

Every inch of me smoldered, and the blazing inferno between my thighs submitted to his control. Having someone so strong-willed, so wild, so demanding, unraveled me.

My gaze fell on Fin. He was sitting up now. His hardness glided between his hand. Flipping hell, that was sexy. Was it wrong of me, dirty even, to enjoy having him watch?

Gripping my hips, Gill entered me, his hardness striking me fast and forceful, making me gasp. There was nothing tender about him. Only his heart. This was a pure merman. Hard and unyielding. Each strike brought me closer to my peak. I curled my legs around his hips, rocking to his furious beat like a drummer. My nails raked down his back, and he groaned.

"Fuck, do that again," he said.

His dirty words had my mind swimming. I obeyed, completely sinking into him. Neither Fin nor Nemo had been this rough. What Gill asked of me frightened me a little. I didn't want to hurt him. But I did as he asked, for him, much harder, and he grunted.

Every one of his plunges into me pushed me farther over the edge into his oblivion. Into his darkness. His rawness. I didn't want it to end. Each hard and demanding kiss had me melting farther against him, barely able to breathe and keep up with his pace. This animalistic coupling both thrilled and alarmed me.

"Gill," I screamed in his ear, my fingers yanking at his hair.

I was completely lost in him. Under his bedazzling spell.

"Like that," Gill grunted, pounding into me with ferocity that would leave me hurting in the best way tomorrow.

Over his shoulder, I saw Fin, his gaze locked on mine, rubbing his pulsing cock. He groaned, speeding up his beat, and I rocked, pretending I rode him, too.

I dragged my nails so deep into Gill's flesh I swore I drew blood.

"Fuck, that's amazing," he cried, hurtling me closer to the brink. "Don't stop."

His dirty words ricocheted me over the edge, and I shrieked as my body trembled from the pleasure he buried in me. Soon, his body tensed as he followed me over the edge. He lifted me off him, pulling out before he came and then ejaculating on my stomach. His strong arms called me back onto him. For a few moments, we lay tangled together, our chests pumping hard, catching our breaths. His heartbeat thrummed against my skin.

Soon, Nemo would return, so I curled into Gill's hold, loving every second of being his, even if it was just for a moment.

Fin's stomach locked tight, his muscles bulging as he, too, spilled over into oblivion.

"Sea god, that was hot," he said as he cleaned the mess from his leg.

Hell, yes! I wanted to do that again. With all three of them.

"Let's clean that dirty, royal ass of yours," Gill said.

I climbed off him and moved to kneel in the water.

Fin came over and nuzzled my neck. "Do that for me again sometime."

"Anytime," I said, smiling, still trying to come to terms with what I'd just done and with the fact that both of them had enjoyed sharing me in that way.

Fin rested his back against the bank of the stream, observing me as Gill scooped water into his palms and washed the mess off me. His gentleness shocked me. I'd never expected such a light touch from someone like him. But I guessed even the hardest of soldiers had a soft spot. I floated on a cloud of contentment as his hands glided across every inch of me. I giggled as they touched my sensitive parts below, sore from what he'd done, still throbbing and filled with blood.

He kissed my neck, and that, along with Fin's intense gaze, nearly undid me again. I ran a wet hand along the scars on Gill's arms and chest. He smiled, his gaze trailing my fingers, as if he enjoyed me exploring every muscle, every curve, and even the fresh bulge waiting for me below.

Together, we cleaned each other, washed away our pasts. Bathed in our mutual darkness, no longer afraid to set it free.

"You didn't take me up my royal ass like you promised," I said, shocked by the words that spilled from my mouth.

"Not on our first time, beautiful," he said, slapping me on the ass. "There's plenty of time for that."

Plenty of time? So...he wanted to do this again and again? I hadn't taken Gill for a "relationship" kind of guy—not the kind of merman who'd escort me to royal balls. He was more the secret-lover type who usually only stuck around for a few months then broke a girl's heart when he left. But a part of me didn't want to hide him away. I wanted to show him off to the world. That part of me didn't want him to leave, either. Something had bonded me to all three of the mermen.

Something strange and unfamiliar, exciting and terrifying, all wrapped up in one.

"Maybe Fin and I can have a three-way with you," Gill suggested, slapping my ass hard. "I'll take you up that royal ass of yours."

My friend Gellian loved two partners at once. She always told me to try it if I could, that I wouldn't regret it. The way Gill said it sounded so dirty, but I was willing to try it once for him.

"On a more important note." Gill grabbed my hips. "Where'd this dirty mouth of yours come from? I'm gonna have to spank you for that."

He whacked my ass hard with his hand, and I gasped.

"Be a dirty girl again for me."

"Only if you fuck me now," I teased.

"Oh, I'll fuck you and make those perfect titties shake."

"Wait a moment," Fin interrupted. "Doesn't the commanding officer get the first honors?"

Gill bent over with an arm outstretched. "Of course."

I kneeled in front of Fin to give him a long and luscious kiss. When I glanced over my shoulder at Gill, he grabbed my corset from where I'd left it beside the stream and dunked it in the stream.

"Oh, look, gorgeous," he said, "your clothes are wet. Looks like you'll have to stay naked a little longer. Let the captain and I admire that gorgeous ass and those curvy hips of yours."

Wearing the sexiest of grins, he tossed aside my corset, scrambled over, and then bit my bottom. He followed up by licking the same spot and then smacking me again.

I shoved him in the shoulder with my hip.

He flashed that grin of his again, almost knocking me over.

Leaves crunched and bushes rustled behind us, signaling

Nemo's return. He approached the stream, the bottom of his shirt folded up to carry a load of berries.

"All clean?" he asked with a smile as bright as a neon starfish.

"She's all dirty now." Gill slapped me on the ass, hard, and I yelped.

"You slept with him, too?" Nemo groaned, collapsing beside me and stuffing his face with so many berries, his cheeks puffed out.

I slumped to the ground next to him, and he slipped his arm around my waist, resting his hand on my stomach.

Once we returned to Tritonia and saved my father, I'd no longer see any of my mermen. A princess with three suitors was unheard of. We could meet in secret, but someone was bound to find out. Then what? Would my father lock up my mermen for daring to lie with a princess of the realm? Take Fin's hands for claiming my virginity? Exile all of us? While I often harbored the notion of running away from everything, it was unfair to steal my mermen from their loved ones. Either way, I doubted Gill's willingness to stay with me long-term, regardless. A wildness resided in his blood, like it did in mine, and I knew it couldn't be tamed. Yet, I wanted more, so much more from all of them than just an adventurous tryst. For the foreseeable future, I wanted to be afforded the chance to explore my relationship further with all of them.

Sea god, why did I have to fall for all three of them at once? If it was just one of them, Fin, perhaps, we might have stood a chance with my father.

A heaviness settled under my ribcage. With Nemo's firm cuddle and soft kisses on the side of my head, the thickness turned into a dull ache, leaving me wanting to crumble into a thousand pieces of sand. Every part of me wished I could stay forever in his arms, finding comfort, love, and honor.

"What are you thinking about, Princess?" Nemo pressed a berry to my lips.

I accepted it, savoring the sweet taste, avoiding telling him my thoughts. He didn't like it when I dwelled on the bad. Nemo's head was up in the clouds, and I hated dragging him down with my troubles.

"Nothing." I brushed the back of my hand along his bulging upper arm.

He forced my chin up so our gazes met. "Don't lie to me."

One question in particular burned a hole in my tongue, and I just had to ask. "What will happen when we get back to the palace? My father won't allow this. The three of us." I shook my head, fighting the blockage in my throat. "I can't lose you."

Nemo kissed me on each eyelid. "Don't think like that."

I loved how he remained positive even in the darkest of times.

"The king isn't keeping Nemes apart from his future wife," Fin joked, running his hand up and down my back.

"Damn straight." Nemo's chest muscles twitched, as if he was ready to fight every soldier in the kingdom for me. "I'll kidnap my future wife if I have to."

His positivity gave me a shred of comfort. A hiccupped laugh burst forth, and my men joined in, too.

Gill surprised me by kneeling in front of me. "I'd kill anyone who tried to stop us from being with you."

Sea god. He stole the breath right from my lips. I remembered every single word he'd said earlier. Words any woman desired to hear from her mate. For so long, he'd fought everyone and everything: his parents, teachers, the merkids at school, anyone in authority, including Fin. Had he now found direction and something to fight for in me? I hoped to the sea god he had, and I nestled into the tender hold of his hand on my face.

"She's mine, too," Nemo said.

The way he elbowed Gill and they mucked around, nudging each other back and forth, told me Nemo was finally coming around to the idea of sharing me.

"Children." Fin nuzzled my neck.

I shivered with delight in his embrace.

When Nemo and Gill finished, they threw their arms over each other, hugging and laughing. Brotherhood. Camaraderie. Respect. Values I admired and honored in my mermen. *Shellfish.* I still couldn't believe I had three of them. Talk about the luckiest girl in the world.

For too long I'd been told what to do. Obey court protocol. Attend meetings regarding the realm. Comply with my father's wishes and the expectations placed upon me as a princess. Now, it was time for me to do something just for me. My happiness was all that mattered. From that point on, I was determined to keep my mermen. Losing one was like losing my scales...my fins...I couldn't survive without them. I'd do anything to stay with them, and I prayed to the sea god they felt the same way.

Somehow, I had to convince my father the mersoldiers were worthy of my love.

More than anything, I just wanted to get back to the sea. My skin craved the salty water to soothe and moisturize it. My fin and scales begged for release. My heart wanted to exchange the pearl for my father's freedom. The longer we lingered in the Darkwoods, the more an icy tentacle of dread took residence in my chest, strangling my sternum.

CHAPTER 21

Fin cocked his head as if he'd heard a noise. "Halt," he ordered, pulling his stallion to a stop.

My stomach contracted. Who was out there? Wolves? Bears? Hunters? I knew we shouldn't have gone searching for Gill's sister based on a tip from Blade. We should have saved my father first, then returned to the tea plantations in Wildfire armed with more men.

Gill's horse sidled up beside Fin's. I hugged Gill tighter from my position behind him, inhaling his stormy ocean scent.

"Do you hear that?" Fin asked us all.

Mermaids didn't exactly have the best hearing. We didn't really need it underwater because we used different senses. But I caught the mumble of words.

"It's coming from over there." I pointed east.

"Stay here with the others," Fin instructed, reaching over to take my hand and leave a kiss on my palm. "I'll scout it out."

With a longing glance, he reluctantly nudged his horse into action and they took off at a trot, disappearing into the foliage in the distance. Normally, my eyes would be glued to his bouncing ass, but my gut sank like wet sand, and I wished I'd done something to convince him to stay.

My belly was on fire with nerves as we waited. Was Fin in danger? Was he hurt? I wanted to go with him, but I wasn't in control of the horse. I hated us being this vulnerable, out in the open no less. Back in the sea my instincts served me well. But they didn't work the same way on land. The Darkwoods were foreign. Beautiful and breathtaking. Yet frightening as well. They left me feeling terribly out of my comfort zone and yearning to return to the sea.

Clouds passed overhead, shrouding the forest in a blanket of gray gloom. A vicious wind whipped my hair and skirt. A storm was coming. An electrical charge tickled my skin—a warning sign all merfolk possessed to warn them to dive deep and not return until the coast was clear.

The horses whinnied as something made them nervous, and they shifted uncomfortably. A thickness enveloped the air, and I felt like I was being strangled by jellyfish tentacles.

"Anyone else sense that?" Gill's words sent shivers trailing down my spine.

"This place makes me nervous," I answered.

"What the hell is that?" Nemo pointed to a tree thirty feet away.

A bubbling, black ooze crawled all over it, turning the bark black and the leaves gray. It had spread along the ground, consuming the moss and undergrowth. All the area around it on the ground was gray, as if it had been frozen.

"It's killing the trees," I said, hugging Gill tighter.

"I don't like this," Gill said, moving our horse away from the strange black mass. Nemo followed suit.

The wind picked up, scattering leaves and thrashing branches. All of a sudden it felt like all the air had been stripped from our very spot. It reminded me of being at the sea witch's cave. I glanced around, expecting her to enter the clearing, but she didn't.

"Where is he?" I said, every muscle in my body tense with anxiety.

"Relax," Nero reminded me. "He'll be back soon."

Always calm. Always positive. My beautiful Nemo. We fastened gazes, and I held onto that, trying to remain steady like him.

At last Fin returned, and my locked stomach released.

"There's a camp of creatures not too far from here," said Fin, brushing his golden air from his eyes. "Bloody and bruised. Escaped prisoners perhaps. There're a few merfolk there."

"What?" said Gill.

Before any of us could find out any more information from Fin, Gill prod his horse into action, and it raced down the track. I clung to Gill so I wouldn't fall off. We hadn't rode this fast two abreast, and I wasn't used to it.

"Gill, wait!" shouted Fin.

I heard the other horses chasing ours.

Gill was wild, reckless, and headstrong. Not good qualities when it came to preparing an attack.

We both ducked under a low-hanging branch as our horse galloped. Wind blasted my eyes and flung my hair over my shoulders. Our horse burst into a clearing where a bunch of creatures rested against trees, logs, or on the forest floor. A lady and seven small men fed them food and water from three wagons parked on the edge of the glade. The seven little men were all wearing tights, vests, and hats, and were armed with small blades. The woman's clothes resembled mine; a long skirt like mine and a corset. She too carried a sword in a scabbard around her waist.

At the accouchement of our horses, the humans spun

around. The woman and dwarves pulled their swords, and surrounded my men and I.

For a moment I almost didn't recognize the beautiful woman. Skin as pale as snow. Hair as dark as the night. Lips as rich and red as the coral beneath the sea. But she was different. Dark circles hung beneath her eyes. Bruises and lacerations laced her arms and neck. This was Snow, the daughter of my father's ward, and every time my father visited land, we would stay at her manor. What was she doing in Wildfire? So far from her apple orchards and manor in Tritonia.

After the ancient wars, the sea king was appointed ruler of Tritonia, a land that included the merrealm. A millennia ago, my ancestor appointed a ward to rule the land region of Tritonia in his stead, and to this day that arrangement remained. Snow's father was Triton's current ward. But where was her? Last I had heard he was ill. Over the last few moon cycles, Snow had met with my father to discuss the governing of Tritonia on her own papa's behalf. Snow was like a second sister to me. When we were young we played together and even slept in the same bed on visits. My father had to drag me away crying each time we departed for home.

"Kaya," said Gill, trying to rush our horse forward. "Kaya!"

"Stay where you are, pirate," shouted the woman.

"Pirate?" said Gill, turning around to smirk at me.

"Snow?" I said, descending Gill's horse.

"Nyssa." Shock clouded Snow's voice. Her eyes were bloodshot as if she hadn't slept. "Thank the sea god. You got my message?"

"What message?" I reached out to embrace her, but she gasped and took a few steps backward.

What was wrong with her? This wasn't the girl I knew. She was meek, startled easily, and her eyes burned with suspicion. A far cry from my bold, brave and sassy friend. Why hadn't she recognized my men as merfolk? She'd grown up around them.

"Papa is dead," she said, her blue eyes welling with tears.

My heart felt heavy. I'd known Snow's father since I was little. He was always very kind to me. Gave me baked treats and sweets from his kitchen. Cuddled me, kissed me, treated me like his daughter. Now he was just a fond memory. Tears welled in my eyes. Now I understood why Snow's father had not met with mine in many moon cycles. Triton had even ventured to the ward's manor, seeking answers, but both Snow, and her stepmother had refused to see him.

"I'm so sorry, Snow." Again I tried taking her hand, but yanked them away as if she were frightened by my touch. "What's wrong?"

Her gaze fell to the ground.

I didn't get my answer because Gill slid off the horse, and a dwarf accosted him with his blade.

"Whoa," said Gill, raising two palms in the air, smiling as if he found this amusing. "Take it easy there, little man."

One of the dwarves poked Gill's stomach with his sword. "Who you calling little?"

Gill snatched the weapon from the dwarf and threw it at the soil, making the handle of the sword wobble.

The motion startled Snow, and she flicked her sword to Gill, making a gash in his shirt. "Don't touch them."

"Snow," I said. "This isn't like you."

My friend was very warm and loving. Not withdrawn and jumpy. What had happened to Snow to make her this way? Worry ate away at me and I could barely think past it.

Gill's gaze panned Snow up and down and his eyes narrowed. "Trying to get me naked, sweetheart?"

She treated him to another jab in the guts, warning him to back off. "You're not my type."

"I'm taken anyway." He swung his trident at her.

Poseidon. Stupid merman! What was he doing escalating the situation?

But then I couldn't stop thinking about him saying he was taken. By whom? Me? He'd never indicated we were a couple. And he didn't seem like the settling type. Adding more fuel to my already spinning head, he left me a kiss on my cheek, and departed to search the merfolk crowd to our right.

"Where's Kaya?" he called out. "My sister. Has anyone seen her?"

Two of the little men hobbled after him.

Fin disembarked from his horse, but the four remaining little men swung their blades at him too. "I mean you no harm," he told them, and they swarmed protectively around Snow. "We're just here to retrieve our own kidnapped by the collector."

Nemo smiled as if amused by the thought of dwarves attacking him. It wasn't a fair fight by any stretch.

"Lower your weapons," Snow told the dwarves, replacing her sword in her scabbard. "They're merfolk, they won't harm you. Nyssa is princess of Tritonia, and my friend."

Slowly and reluctantly the dwarves lowered their blades.

"I've never met a princess," the one with the orange vest said, stepping forward, staring at what I assumed was the scales on my temples.

Humoring him, I thought of Faraall, feeling the anger pulse through my scales. The dwarf gasped and stepped backward, probably as my scales changed color, bumping into one of his friends.

"Did you see that?" he said, nudging his friend again.

Fin, Nemo and I exchanged a smile.

"Quit it." His friend in the red vest jabbed him back.

Orange vest rubbed his stomach. "No need to poke me so hard."

"You hit me!" red vest cried.

"Guys," said Snow, dragging them apart. "How about you help the rescued?"

The dwarves mumbled as they dawdled into the crowd.

Over to my right, Gill bent down beside a brunette mermaid and lifted her chin. The mermaid shook her head. I couldn't hear what they said to each other. But she pointed to another mermaid seated at the end of the group.

"Kaya," Gill cried, embracing a brunette mermaid at the end of the group.

My heart swelled. He'd found his sister! I couldn't wait to meet her. Would she be like him? But first I had to help my people and the other shifters.

"How can my mersoldiers and I help?" I asked Snow.

"Distribute the water, food and blankets," she replied, pointing to a wagon full of barrels.

I jerked my head, signaling for my men to aid the rescued shifters.

"What's happened here?" I asked, tailing Snow to grab some clay goblets from a sack on the back of a cart.

Snow moved to the barrels on the back of the wagon, and filled her goblets with water.

"My stepmother has taken control of the manor and of Tritonia," she snarled, handing out two goblets to shifters. They nodded and gulped down the water. "The resistance tells me she's amassing an army of shifters. Probably to take over the rest of Haven."

My body numbed over with shock. Stories Snow told me about her stepmother bombarded my mind. The time the wicked bitch slapped Snow's face. Or the time she had Snow thumped by one of the guards, for taking a sweet pastry from her own bakery, which was intended for visitors. All of it she had done out of sight of Snow's father and the servants. So when Snow confessed to her father she wasn't believed.

"Nyssa." Snow's eyes welled with tears. "That witch murdered my father. Imprisoned me and tried to have me executed before the resistance saved me."

Snow's explanation sure clarified why she had turned suspicious and untrusting if those closest to her betrayed her. Had her stepmother been cruel to Snow, causing the bruises and cuts on her face?

The crushing news scratched inside my head like the witch's claws. I'd fallen in a crevice between words. Nothing I could say would make up for what had happened to Snow. To bring her father back. Destroy the source of my friend's devastation and pain.

"I promise I will help you get your home back," I pledged.

Despite her earlier unease, and resistance to my affections, I held out my arms, signaling my intentions. Her body stiffened as I embraced her, but she did not move away, nor return the hug like she used to. Warm tears spilled onto my neck. Sobs shook her body.

My mind spun with everything she had told me. An army? What was wrong with Haven? First Farrall tried to seize control of the merrealm. Then the sea witch wanted the dark pearl to wreck sea god knew what havoc. Now Snow's evil stepmother had claimed Tritonia, and prepared for some sort of war.

Urgency pumped through me to save my father. He had to know what was going on. A revolt was coming, and he had to stop it.

Snow pulled away suddenly, wiped her face, and stalked away into the woods.

I wanted to go to her, to hold her, tell her I would fight for her. But Gill stood before me, his arm curled around his sister's back, holding her steady.

Sea god. An introduction was the last thing I needed right now. I was still reeling from everything Snow had said. But I had to hold it in. It was unfair of me to disregard the ordeal Gill's sister had also experience. To my people, I represented, unification, stability, and a beacon of light. Today she, and the rest of the merfolk needed me, and I couldn't let her down.

"Nyssa," said Gill. "I'd like you to meet my sister, Kaya."

Kaya looked a lot like Gill. Dark features and hair. Her golden brown eyes flickered to me, then the ground. But because she'd been in a wagon for several days or two, she could barely stand, her skin was awfully pale, her skin blistering as if she had sunburn.

"Your highness," she squeaked.

"Call me, Nyssa," I said, taking her hand between both of mine.

"Yes, your..." said Kaya, giving me a nervous smile. "I mean Nyssa."

"Come," I said, linking arms with her, slowly escorting her to the wagon to get her a drink. "Have some water."

Kaya nodded, her innocent eyes swinging between the cart and me.

While I poured Kaya some liquid, I spotted Snow to my right, tending to one of the shifters, draping them in blankets.

A newfound sense of duty swelled in me. Before I'd run from my responsibilities, scared of the weight of them, and of the judgment that accompanied them. But something had changed in me over the course of my land adventures. Call it a change in perspective. Bigger things were at play than my ego and reluctance to embrace them. Now I had to protect my people. Get them back to the sea safely. Ensure they were never harmed again. To figure out who was behind the kidnapping of shifters, including my merfolk, and put a stop to them forever. I also had to help my childhood friend from whatever trouble she was in.

I returned Kaya to Gill, and crossed to Fin, who was crouched nearby, offering the merfolk portions of cheese and bread.

"Could you please get me the treasure from the trove?" I said, running my fingers through his hair.

With a nod, he stood and returned to the horse, removing the items he'd taken from the trove, and bringing them to me.

"Thank you," I said, stretching up to brush his lips with mind, before taking the items, and crossing to where Snow was by one of the wagons.

At my arrival, she shuffled sideways, holding her chest.

"Take these," I said, pretending not to notice her jitters. "Sell them. Buy what you can to feed these people."

Snow stared at the gifts I offered her. She refused to take them, so I rested them on the side of the wagon. Slowly, she selected a hand held mirror from the small pile of magical items, and looked into it for a few seconds. It glimmered gold at her. She gasped and dropped it. Amazingly it didn't break.

I picked it up, and replaced it in her hands, making her tense, and breath hard. "Take it."

It glowed again at her touch, but this time she didn't make a sound nor move. She seemed transfixed by the mirror as if it called to her in a strange way. The dark pearl had done the same to me.

"I can't stay," said Snow, not looking at me. "I've got to get all these shifters to a safe place."

My gut sank with disappointment. After so long of not seeing my friend I wanted to spend more time with her. But I understood her reasons. I too had to take my people and return them safely to the ocean.

"I can spare you four horses to carry your merfolk," offered Snow.

It wasn't going to be enough. But it would carry half of them.

"Thank you. That would be wonderful." I watched as my friend disappeared into the woods, carrying the mirror, glancing at it occasionally.

Snow returned some moments later with the steeds she'd promised.

"Thank you, my friend," I said, taking the reigns of one horse.

Snow nodded and left, scooping up the rest of the treasure I'd given her.

"Gill," I called to him, and he came over to me. "Get my people on the horses. We're walking back to the sea."

CHAPTER 22

*I*t took my merman and the rescued camp of merfolk two days to reach the ocean. Half of the group, including my men and I, traveled on foot, while the others who were exhausted and could not walk rode the horses. On our journey, we had stopped at a river for a few hours to rehydrate, but we didn't dwell long because they longed for home and their families.

The salty wind flicked my hair into my eyes from my position on the dunes. Waves crashed onshore, calling for me to join them. Headlands rose up around the small inlet we'd found. Birds squawked over by the rocky pools to my right. Palm tree leaves rustled behind us.

The group of merfolk crowded around me as if they wondered why I had not entered the water. My mermen stood off to the side. Gill rested his arm on his trident. Nemo and Fin held theirs to their sides.

Now that we were back at the sea, it was time for my mersoldiers and I to depart. But before we did, I had to seek the safety and silence of this group.

"Shortly, we must go our separate ways," I said to them. "I

wish I could return with you to the kingdom, but I have pressing business to attend to."

I hadn't wanted to frighten them further with the horror of what Faraall had done to their king. Not after everything they'd been through. But I couldn't risk word getting back to my father of my return to the sea. If he knew, he might dispatch soldiers to retrieve me. I could not let that happen before I removed the spell Faraall had placed on the king.

"Stay in your homes," I said, looking each one in the eye. "You will be safe there. Promise me you will not go to the king before the sea horn tolls."

The horn was the palace's way of calling all it's people to the square for announcements and celebrations.

They bombarded me with questions and statements.

"Why aren't you coming with us, Princess?" one young woman asked.

"Where are you going?"

"Why can't we tell the king that his people are being kidnapped?"

"How will we save the rest of the merfolk?"

I silenced any further words by holding my palms in the air. "All I can tell you is that the king is in danger. These mersoldiers and I must eliminate that threat first. Only when the sea horn sounds, may you go to the king."

All eyes flew to my mermen standing behind me.

Only one young man, who reminded me of Gill but who was a few years younger, said, "Yes, Princess."

The rest of the crowd stared at me with pensive brows, confused eyes, and tight mouths.

I didn't like what I was about to do, but it was the only way to get their cooperation. "That is an order, you understand?"

The rest of the group nodded.

"Come," said Gill's sister, placing her arms around the

backs of two of the merfolk and leading them down the beach. When she glanced over her shoulder, I waved at her.

Gill rushed down the beach to see her off. She stayed until last, ensuring the rest of the group departed, then she and Gill hugged for a few moments before she, too, vanished into the ocean.

My stomach sunk for them all.

"Sea god," I said to the wind and waves. "Grant my people safe passage home. Protect them all from harm. Give me and my mermen the strength to rescue my father and defeat the evil that has infiltrated the merrealm."

Fin picked up his trident as if preparing to leave. It was time. He removed the cloth holding the sea pearl and handed it to me. I unwrapped it, checking it was still there, and then shoved it down inside my corset.

"That's my sexy girl," Gill said, giving me a slap on the butt and then stripping off his clothes.

Poseidon, I hoped to be able to enjoy that gorgeous body again before I died.

***

THIS WAS THE DEFINING MOMENT. We'd been through hell and back, had traveled all this way to save my father, but I couldn't move. My mind was a blur of fear. The sulfur, thick in the water surrounding the sea witch's lair, choked and burned me, and I couldn't think straight.

Now, the time had come to cut a horrible deal with her to free my father. But in doing so, I'd be giving her the one item she needed to overthrow my father's rule and take the sea kingdom for herself. Who was the lesser of two evils? Faraall or the witch? I made certain the peal was tucked between my breasts. There it would be safe until I needed it.

The murky water of the witch's cave surrounded us like the claws of a terrifying beast. Gas bubbles poured out of the rocks forming her lair. Hundreds of red eyes watched our every move from their hiding places in the rocky wall. I wondered if they warned the sea witch of our presence. Nothing else but these strange monsters survived for long in this land. The sulfur was poisonous and the sand infertile.

"This place is the definition of creepy," said Gill.

He jabbed at a hole, and one of the red-eyed creatures snapped at him.

Yes, definitely creepy. As soon as we were done, we were out of there.

"Formation, soldiers," Fin ordered.

Nemo and Gill readied their tridents.

I came armed with only the pearl, so I wasn't going to be much use in a fight. Unless I was able to harness the power of the pearl. But I'd already tried a hundred times on the way back from the Darkwoods, and nothing happened.

"Princess." Fin's voice sounded in my mind. "You stay at the rear."

I took two deep breaths, building the courage to move forward. This was for my father. For the realm. And to destroy Faraall.

"Very well." I squeezed the pearl so tight, I was surprised I didn't crush it.

"Forward, soldiers," Fin ordered.

My mermen and I propelled into the sea witch's lair. Sulfur tainted the water, replacing the oxygen. My lungs and scales clouded, and I gulped for air. Darkness descended upon us as we pushed deeper into her filthy grotto. Eyes in the walls of her cave blinked at us. Despite the screams in my head telling me to turn back, I couldn't.

Inside the grotto, we found the sea witch lounging in her chair, with Faraall and his men by her side.

The berries I'd eaten at lunch scratched in my stomach. Shellfish. They were working together.

"Welcome, Princess. I assume you brought me the pearl."

The sea witch's voice rang in my ears like nails scraping down rock, and I shuddered.

Now, I definitely did not want to give her the pearl. With it, she and Faraall would possess immense power. My mind ran riot, imagining what they'd do with it. Instead of removing the cloth from between my breasts, I turned to leave. Something sharp jabbed me in the side, and I froze and looked down at the cold, hard metal prongs of a trident.

Shellfish.

Twelve mersoldiers. We were vastly outnumbered. A hammer blow forced the air out of my lungs. Fin and Nemo had beaten back six men, including the slimy general, at the cave. But how would they fair against an even bigger battalion? My merman spun around, ready to fight back.

"Bring the traitors to me," Faraall's voice growled in my mind. "I'll kill them all in front of the princess. Especially the two who want what's mine."

My insides iced over, colder than the mountains of Whitepeak.

A rough hand squeezed my shoulder so hard it would leave a bruise.

Gill ripped the soldier off me and threw him against the wall, slamming a fist into his jaw. Three mersoldiers sprang at him. One stabbed him in the fin. The other two seized his arms and pressed him to the rock.

Nemo's hands clenched into fists. I could tell by the look on his face he was ready to pound the mersoldiers' faces to pulp if the chance arose. But he was smarter and more calculated than my reckless Gill. Some plan was probably forming inside that beautiful, optimistic head of his. One ending with much happier odds than I was imagining, I was certain.

All sorts of hideous creatures emerged from out of the gloom, things with spiked protrusions on their bodies, jagged fins, sharp teeth, and slimy eyeballs. They swarmed around me, showing teeth, nipping the water between us, and one even sank its fangs into my wrist, drawing blood.

I gasped, yanked my arm away, and bumped into the guard behind me. He grabbed me and held me on the spot.

The sea witch sauntered over, her overpowering, sulfurous stench stinging my nostrils, throat, and scales.

Her long, gray tongue stretched out to sample my blood. "Delicious," she said, showing very sharp and stained teeth.

My stomach turned.

The witch floated back to a shelf behind her whalebone throne. One of her tentacles snapped out to seize a jar. At once, she was back at my side, collecting a sample of my blood into the canister and then jamming it closed with a lid.

"For use later in a spell, sweet princess," she hissed.

Her clawed finger traced my cheek, and I batted her away.

She cackled. "Royal blood is most powerful."

"Don't touch her," barked Gill, lunging forward, but two of the mersoldiers blocked him with their tridents.

Poseidon. I wanted to yell at him. *Just stay still and stay alive, you stupid merman!*

"Where's my father?" I demanded. "I brought you the pearl. Now bring him to me at once."

Faraall's nasty fingers grabbed my jaw and squeezed so hard, I cried out.

"You no longer give the orders around here," he said.

He painted his disgusting tongue along my lips. I struggled against him, but his grip was so strong. Unable to break his grip, I whacked him in the pouch below his privates. He hunched over and wheezed. That'd teach him to touch me.

One of his guards pushed me so hard I thumped into the wall behind me.

This set Nemo off, and his elbow cracked into the side of one mersoldier's head. Fin joined the fight, yanking the trident from the guard to his right. He cracked the butt of it on the back of soldier's neck. The soldier slumped to the ground. On the other side, Gill wrestled the two mersoldiers restraining him.

Time for me to join the fray. I snatched Faraall's weapon and stabbed the mersoldier who had hit me right in the guts. He swatted me away with a punch to my waist. Pain sliced down my side. I thought he'd broken a rib. But I couldn't give up now. My father's life and my kingdom were at stake.

Someone snared me by my hair and yanked my head backward.

Faraall. His eyes blazed with hatred and a promise of death. Like the nasty slime he was, he bit into my neck and drew more blood.

I screamed and punched him between the eyes with the end of his dagger. He stumbled backward, clutching his forehead. A pink lump had sprouted on his forehead, making his left eye swell. That didn't stop the look of utter contempt and malice aimed at me. He sprang at me with full force, pounding me against the wall. He twisted and dug his forearm into my throat, crushing my windpipe. I gasped for air and slashed at him, creating two deep cuts in his arm and torso, making a mess of the water between us. One good kick got him off me.

But another mersoldier awaited. He grabbed me and twisted my wrist backward. Splinters of pain shot down my arm, and I dropped the dagger.

Before the soldier could do more, Nemo moved in and stabbed him in the back.

Faraall and I lunged for the dagger at the same time. He punched me in the cheek. Blinded by pain searing my face, I staggered sideways.

For that, Nemo smashed Faraall over and over in the face, spilling more blood.

"I'll kill you for that, soldier." Faraall's horrid threat rattled in my mind as they thrashed it out, throwing punches, and whacking each other with their tails.

Two mersoldiers rounded on Nemo. Faraall smirked, no doubt thinking he'd won this battle. But when the soldiers thrust their tridents at Nemo, he swung Faraall at them, and they stabbed the commander in the side and tail.

The sea witch's laughter echoed in my mind. This was all a game to her. Faraall was just a pawn to aid her in claiming the sea realm.

The mersoldiers' expressions froze somewhere between shock and confusion.

The witch rubbed her hands together, still laughing.

The soldiers straightened again and tightened their grips on their weapons.

I left it to Nemo to take care of them. Ignoring the pain swelling in me, I growled. I'd never wanted to destroy something more than I wanted to ruin the witch and Faraall.

By the wall, the commander clutched at his weeping wounds.

In an instant, I snatched up his dagger and flew at him, weapon raised. He wrestled me for control, and I bit his hand. A firm grip squeezed my throat, strangling me. Now or never, I thought. I raised my arm then brought it down hard, jamming the dagger into his heart. Green flared in his wide eyes, and then the light fluttered and died.

The evidence of the witch's magic confirmed my earlier

suspicions; the sea witch had healed him with her power. That was how Faraall had survived the attack at the lagoon cave. But would she save him again? That was not going to happen if I had a say in it.

Leaving that creep behind, I lunged at her, scratching at her face like a ferocious lion. *Poseidon.* I didn't know where the rage in me sprang from. Perhaps from being kidnapped and traded to pirates, being attacked in the lagoon cave, and almost burned to death. But I unleashed my anger with a torrent of fury like a vicious storm sent by the sea god himself.

Green blood spurted from several scratches I'd made upon the witch's face. Her mouth twisted into a snarl. She hadn't expected that of me, I'd bet. I could tell she was normally the one in control. Green magic shimmered on her fingertips. Her rage steamed the water around me, scalding me. Any moment now, she was going to turn me into dust to powder her filthy cavern floor.

I refused to go out so easily. I called upon my merpowers and whirled up a wind that tossed her away. She struck the wall and slid down it. The violence within me terrified me. Where had I kept this inner demon buried before all this?

I glanced at my mermen.

Two mersoldiers wrestled to control Gill. His muscles trembled as he struggled to get free of their grasp.

Nemo grabbed a soldier in a headlock and slammed his skull into the nearby wall. The mersoldier slumped to the sandy seafloor.

Fin was fighting attacks from two soldiers. He took a blow to the gut from the butt of a trident, but it didn't slow him down. He wrenched the weapon free and drove it into the soldier's stomach.

My chest ignited with the hope that maybe, just maybe, we might be able to win this battle.

Movement flashed in the corner of my eye. I swirled around to find the sea witch missing.

Damn it!

I scanned the murky waters, looking for her. Eyes blinked in the depths of her caverns. A shadow passed above me, and my head snapped upward.

The sea witch's tentacle slid around my throat and squeezed.

I clawed at her limb.

"No," Nemo screamed. He ran toward us, his dagger raised. A moment later, he slammed into her, burying his knife in her back.

The witch lifted her face toward the water's surface and howled, the sickening noise scraping down my every nerve. The grip on my throat released, freeing me. Eyes narrowed, she twirled to face Nemo and aimed her finger at him. She threw out a bomb of magic that slammed him against the wall and held him there.

My evil, inner mermaid took control, and I raced to his defense. I yanked her hair back. My other hand found the wound in her back, and I jammed a finger in it. She screamed and spun to face me. One of her tentacles seized my neck and squeezed. Desperate for breath, I slashed her with my nails.

From behind her, Fin punched the witch in the back of the head, but her tentacles smashed him against the wall beside Nemo.

"No!" I shrieked, hating seeing my mermen injured.

Fire whisked through my blood like a tornado. I summoned my merpowers and unleashed another current that flung her across the cavern.

This time, she clapped to taunt me. Her eyes flashed green as she stalked toward me.

We couldn't keep playing this game. I had to destroy her

once and for all. Palm pressed against the seafloor, I poured out my sonic vibration, willing it deep into the bedrock. Soon, the cavern was shaking. Items tipped off the sea witch's shelves. Her throne toppled over. Encouraged, I put even more power into it, my whole body shaking from the force I exerted. All this required too much energy, and fatigue clawed at me. I wasn't sure how much longer I could keep it up. Releasing my last blast, I loosened a torrent of rocks that cascaded upon the sea witch's head. One large one crushed her tentacles, pinning her to the spot. Her scream boomed in my mind. More stones struck her and piled around her. She shielded her face an instant before one smashed her head. The wails in my mind fell silent.

Was she dead? I hoped so. For too many years, she had haunted my people. Luring them into deals and then stealing their souls to fuel her own dark powers.

I shuddered at my violent but necessary actions. Gill's ruthless influence had rubbed off on me. But I'd done what I'd needed to do to save my father and my kingdom.

Now that the witch was taken care of, I had to redirect my efforts to my mermen. I powered forward into the fray. Someone's trident lay on the sandy floor. I snatched it up and charged at a mersoldier. Using all my strength, I drove the weapon at him, piercing his tail to the floor. His shriek clattered in my head.

I snatched his weapon and threatened him with it. "Yield," I roared.

His brow pressed down in a hard line. Surrendering was not in a soldier's nature. To them, giving up was a fate worse than death. But I was handing him the choice—life or death.

"Yield or die," I screamed, the rage in my voice startling me.

Fear flickered behind his gaze. He raised his palms in capitulation.

I gave him a nod and moved on to the soldier fighting Nemo. As I raised the end of the trident to hit the mersoldier in the shoulder blade, something wrapped around my neck and tightened. Pain radiated down my throat as I was crushed.

The sea witch's laugh thundered down my spine.

Blood froze in my veins.

Tentacles ripped the trident from my grasp, grabbing both my arms and holding them out wide.

"Now you die, sweet princess." The slippery voice crawled along me like sea snails.

Without my hands free, my powers were useless. The way she compressed my neck, I didn't have long before she crushed my throat and my life along with it.

"Nemo," I called to him since he was closest to me.

He responded to my desperation, harpooning the sea witch, and she retaliated by flicking him away with her magic.

My gaze flew to Fin, desperate for him to save me. His eyes burned with pain that said he couldn't help...not with three mersoldiers holding him to the ground.

To Fin's left, a soldier stabbed Gill in the back of his tail. Blood poured from the wound, and he curled over.

I cried out in pain inside my mind. My men were going to die if I didn't do something and fast.

The witch's tentacle tightened, and I bucked, unable to breathe.

Everything flashed before my eyes. My fake engagement. The spell on my father's mind. My kidnapping. Meeting my mermen. Losing my virginity to Fin. Finding three mermen I loved.

The sea witch was not going to take them from me!

An explosion went off inside me. My power came out in a deluge that swept the witch across the cavern and whisked the mersoldiers off my men and tossed them into the wall. The witch's landed on the throne, where a prong pierced her chest. The witch's mouth flew open, and her eyes grew wide. After a few moments, her eyes closed as her body went limp.

Magic drained from her body and fizzled, going out forever. Dark swirls of octopus ink leeched from her, staining the water. Her flesh disappeared as if made from the very dye itself. In a few short seconds, she was no more than a blob of ink floating in the water.

CHAPTER 23

*G*reen fireworks popped throughout the cavern as merfolk she'd turned into creepy monsters returned to their original form. They cried out in joy that they'd finally been released.

I clutched my throat and gasped for air. Water cooled the bruises she'd left on me. But it wouldn't erase the pain or the memories she had left me with.

The shell necklace around Faraall's neck—the one that contained the witch's spell that had held my father hostage—crumbled into dust and drifted away.

Poseidon! I'd saved my father and my kingdom. Immense relief charged through me. Thank the sea god for his mercy and for hearing my prayers.

Gill cried out as he tried to float but couldn't get off the sea floor.

Fin and Nemo had rounded up the weapons of the other mersoldiers and cornered them. They held their hands up, signaling they yielded.

My throat ached from being choked three times. It hurt

just to breathe. But I managed to get a few husky words out. "Get my father," I told several of the merfolk I'd freed from her magical prison. "Tell him to bring the healers."

"Yes, Princess." They bowed and left with haste.

"Hold on there, my friend," Fin said, clutching Gill to his chest as if he was a dying brother. "I've got you."

Gill gave a pained laugh. "I'm not going anywhere."

In an instant, I was by their sides. My hands trembled at the sight of Gill's wound. I touched the back of my wrist to his forehead. His skin was so cold. He'd lost a lot of blood. This kind of injury would heal in time, but a brew of herbs would prevent infection and speed up the process.

"Let me find something to help you," I said.

But before I could leave him, he clasped the back of my neck, pulling me to him gently. The kiss he laid on my lips was soft and grateful. The kind you gave when you'd survived death. I surrendered to it, returning it with all the force I could muster, spent from using my sea gifts.

"Fuck," he said. "I've never seen a merlady fight like that."

I gave him a cheeky smile. "I'm not a merlady."

"No, you aren't." The grin claiming his face made me soar.

I ran my hand along Fin and Gill's lightly stubbled cheeks.

Nemo snuck up behind me and clasped me against the front of his body. His warmth soaked into me, calming and invigorating me. I reached up and stroked the back of his neck.

Thank Poseidon for saving my mermen.

I wriggled free of Nemo and hunted around the witch's cavern, digging through her shelves and tools for anything I could use to bandage Gill's wound. Next to a preparation table, I found a few potted plants of seaweed and snatched one. With frantic motions, I tied several strands together and wrapped them around Gill's tail.

Gill took my hand and gave me a weak squeeze.

Unfortunately, I didn't have time to sit with him. There were other wounded soldiers needing attention. Yes, they'd committed treason, but until such time as they were judged and sentenced for their crimes, they were a part of my kingdom's merarmy. By the time I finished bandaging the last one, my father and the healers arrived.

"Nyssa," my father said, his gaze scanning the mess and wounded mersoldiers. "What happened here?"

I'd never been so glad to see him. I jumped into his strong arms. In a way, his build reminded me of Nemo. His arms were huge, powerful, and comforting.

Behind us, the medical team attended to the wounded, disinfecting cuts and dispatching doses of herbs.

I began explaining everything, but my father pushed aside the hair floating around me.

"You're bruised and bleeding. Who did this to you?" he asked.

"Faraall." I pressed my palm to my father's hand. Everything that had happened poured out of me in a rush.

Each word mounted Triton's anger at his most trusted ally's deceit and betrayal. The vein in his forehead pulsed. Skin on his face and neck flushed a deep pink.

"That would explain why I've not been feeling myself lately," he said.

As I came to the end of my tale, relaying the part about my kidnapping, threatened rape, and trading to the pirates, my father's face was twisted with horror and shock.

"How could he?" he roared, slamming his magical trident against the wall, smashing off a bit of rock. "After everything I did for him. That swine!"

I was used to his outbursts, but a few of the healers flinched, and Gill jerked as his healer stabbed him deeper with the suture hook.

Triton paced along the cavern. He always tended to stomp around—usually in the palace gardens—as doing so seemed to help calm his temper. The atmosphere thickened with tension. Nervous glances darted between everyone present. The poor healers jolted at each strike of my father's trident on the floor.

Nemo floated up behind me. He wrapped an arm around my waist and took hold of both my elbows.

Coming to a stop, my father cupped his chin between his thumb and forefinger. His expression softened as he crossed the cavern to me.

I pushed Nemo away. Now was not the time to reveal I'd taken not just one lover, but three. Perhaps later, when my father had sufficient time to process everything, we could discuss these things. But who knew how long that might be? Days. Weeks. Months. He'd devoted half his lifetime to nurturing Faraall, making certain he received an adequate education and training. My father had raised the slimy slug like his own son and afforded him one of the highest honors in the kingdom by making him commander of the merfolk army. Forgetting a betrayal like that wouldn't happen overnight. I knew I wouldn't lose those memories that quickly. Maybe not ever.

My father grasped my hands. "Oh, my precious daughter. Can you forgive me for not heeding your warnings?"

I sighed. None of this was his fault. He'd put too much trust in someone. I'd blame his desperate desire for a son.

"There is nothing to forgive," I replied, squeezing his hands in return.

"Nyssa." My father drew a long breath. "You know I would never force you to marry someone you didn't love."

Thank Poseidon! My heart twirled in my chest like sea flower seeds carried in the currents.

My father leaned in close and whispered. "Although, I have been waiting for you to find that special someone." His eyebrows waggled suggestively at me.

"Well…" I started, not sure how to answer.

Nemo embraced me again.

"This is your princess, son," my father said in a commanding tone. "You dare get familiar with her?"

I placed a hand on my father's chest.

"About that, Father." Words pressed to the back of my throat, demanding to be released. But I wasn't the best at being diplomatic and tactful. Speaking the truth often got me into trouble. This was potentially going to be one of those explosive moments. No better way to say it came to mind, so I just let my father have it. "There *is* a special merman. Three, actually."

My father reared back. "Sea god, help me. Three?" It was an unusual day when my father could barely speak.

"Yes, Father." I sailed over to Fin. "This is Fin, captain in your army." Next, I moved on to Nemo. "And Nemo, a mersoldier." Lastly, I was by Gill's side. "And Gill, also a soldier. All valiant warriors who were kidnapped by the pirates and helped me destroy Faraall and the sea witch."

"It's a pleasure to meet you, sire." Fin bowed, as was customary.

Nemo whacked Gill on the back, and he followed suit. I could tell Gill wasn't used to being in the presence of royalty and didn't understand the customs.

I held my breath, waiting for my father to give me his blessing, but it didn't come. The water between us stifled, and I stared at my father. He was not impressed. That much I could tell from his expression.

"You only met them not five moons ago," he roared.

"But, Father," I protested. "I've never felt like this about anyone. Imagine my surprise when I realized my heart beats wild for all of them."

I hadn't planned on finding myself in this crazy situation any more than I'd wanted to be kidnapped. My heart knew what it wanted and refused the advice of my mind. How was I to deny it?

My father's gaze panned over Nemo and Gill. "Every day you become more like my sister, Nyssa. A relationship with three mermen is unheard of. Over my dead body."

My temper flared. How dare he speak to my mermen that way? After everything we had done for him. Risked our lives for my father's and the kingdom's prosperity. This talk was not progressing how I'd imagined it would.

I raised my voice, refusing to bow down. "You owe them a great debt."

Red claimed my father's face and neck. "Get out of my sight. All of you."

The healers and mersoldiers scurried out.

My mermen stood by my side.

A splinter tore through the center of my chest. My father had just told me that I was free to choose, and when I did, he insulted my mermen. He might have been the King of Tritonia, but he was not the ruler of my heart.

"No," I told him. "They've claimed me as their mate, and I them. If you do not accept it, then I will leave the kingdom tonight and never return."

The stern gaze my father regarded me with cut me to pieces. That was my cue to leave. There would be no changing his mind.

"Goodbye, Father," I said, drifting out of the cave.

Fin met me at the entrance and swept me into his arms. "Princess, are you mad? You just defied the king."

Yes, I supposed I was going mad. Such was the effect these three had on me. They'd swept my heart into a tangled

266

mess and left me trapped in their love. I'd do anything to be with them, even if it meant leaving everything, my family included, behind.

I yanked free of Fin. "Let's leave before my father has us arrested."

Nemo blocked my way out. "Let your father cool down first."

"You heard what he said," I snapped, all caught up in the fury and sadness ruling my emotions. "He thinks you're not good enough for his daughter. There's no reasoning with a stubborn fool like him."

Fin took my hand and stroked it. "Don't speak ill of your father like that."

Poseidon. Where would I be without my beloved and practical Fin?

"He wants to tear us apart," I said, my voice wavering.

Emotions poked at my chest like a dam waiting to burst. A voice in my mind screamed at me to leave and never return. I couldn't bear the heartbreak of my father turning his back on me.

Gill held me tightly, and I buried my face in his chest. "Shhh," he whispered, brushing hair from my neck and laying light, feathery kisses there.

One of the other mermen took my hand. "Everything will be all right, your royal ass." Nemo. Always up for a joke. "You'll see."

For once, I hoped he was right. His optimism was a beacon in the darkness, and I clung to it for all hope.

Gill rested the top of his head on mine. His heart kept a soft, steady beat. I fell under its spell, listening to it, letting it fill me, calm me, give me strength. I clung to his strength, letting it wrap around me and give me courage to face my future with all my heart.

These three had changed me in profound ways. Fin had

shown me how to take charge of my own destiny and stand up for what I believed in. Nero's sunshine had filled me with cheer and joy. Gill's courage had shown me that taking chances paid off and that I should never apologize for being true to myself.

Someone cleared his throat behind us, and I jolted from Gill's arms to confront my father.

"Perhaps I was a little hasty," he said.

His admission had me rocking on the spot. It was a rare day for the king of Tritonia to admit he was wrong. "Maybe I ought to determine why my daughter is so fond of you all."

My jaw fell open. This I had not anticipated, as much as I'd wanted for him to give my mermen a chance.

"I remember you." My father pointed one huge finger at Nemo. "You were but a frightened little boy when my men presented your family at court."

No one could say my father didn't have a brilliant memory.

Nemo smiled and bowed his head. "That's right, my king."

My father laughed. "When my daughter entered, your eyes lit up and never left her. I recall you vowed to marry her."

Nemo stood tall and proud. "My intentions haven't changed."

His comment drew a smile from my father's stern countenance. I could tell he warmed to Nemo. "You saved my daughter?"

Nemo glanced at me, his eyes radiating that same love my father spoke of. "I'd die for her."

My father nodded and moved on to Gill. "A troubled boy with a dubious past." To this, Gill nodded. "Did the merarmy straighten you out?"

Shellfish. Gill was still just as headstrong, stubborn, and reckless as he'd always been. A lot like I was.

"No," Gill said. "She did."

His reply shocked me even more than my father's change of heart. I wasn't the only one staring at him. Nemo and Fin gazed at Gill, too, surprise written in their expressions.

"Mmm." This time, my father gave no indication of his feelings.

He was harder to read than a blowfish, and I wasn't confident he'd warmed to Gill as he had to Nemo.

Lastly, my father arrived in front of Fin.

My stomach cramped with nerves.

"I never heard the end of you disappointing your family by joining my army. To this day, I still get your father's sneers." He clapped a hand on Fin's shoulder and smiled like a dolphin cruising the waves on the bow of a ship. "Oh, you're as resolved, unwavering, and spirited as my daughter."

I held back a smile. A pat from my father was always a good sign.

"I can see why she adores you three." My father held his head high. He pointed to Nemo. "Your steadfast determination and hope." His gaze flew to Gill. "I've not seen your recklessness and stubbornness matched in anyone but my Nyssa."

"What?" I said, choking on the word.

My father didn't even look at me. "I know about your trips to the bars and the parties you've attended."

"Oh, Princess, you didn't," Nemo teased.

I nudged him with my hip, signaling for him to be quiet. Now was not the time to stir my father up when things looked somewhat positive.

My father smiled at Fin. "My daughter has always followed her heart."

Sea god. How had my father assessed so much from a short interaction with my mermen? When he couldn't read Faraall's wickedness right in front of his nose?

"That's why she'd make a terrible queen."

My father laughed at Fin's comment.

Good. I didn't want that responsibility. Ever.

My father's expression fell serious again. "Well, I know there's no hope of changing her mind. There's nothing for me to do but honor her wishes. But"—he held up a finger —"at this point, I'm not open to marriage between you all. Nor may I ever be."

Fin bowed. "We were not asking for your daughter's hand, my king. Just the chance to serve her, cherish her, honor her."

Nemo opened his mouth as if he were about to argue that point, but Gill slapped a hand over his lips.

They wanted to serve and cherish me? Poseidon, I truly was the luckiest mermaid. My heart blossomed like the coral blooms. I'd never wanted anyone to fuss over me. Call it my stubborn independence. But when the words were cast from Fin's mouth, I longed for my merman to do so. To treat me like a princess. Because now, I was ready for it with open arms and heart.

My father's expression softened as if he had not expected this news. He wrapped his arms over Fin's and Nemo's shoulders.

"Treat her well," he said. "Or I will have you executed." The last part he said while staring at Gill.

With that, he smiled and left.

We all laughed at my father's joke. Although, I had no doubt there was an element of truth in there.

Nemo smothered me kisses. I melted into him and wrapped my arms around his neck. I gave him a quick hug, then moved into Fin's embrace. He squeezed me tightly, and I clung to him, my body fitting perfectly against his. Gill was lucky last. Smiling like the cocky merman he was, he gave my behind a cheeky squeeze. I let him enfold me in his embrace, and I got lost in his hold.

For the moment, everything was perfect. My father was free, the merkingdom saved. I would have the chance to pursue my relationship with my three mermen. What more could I ask for?

EPILOGUE

$\mathcal{T}$he air was thick with anticipation. Everyone crowded in the throne room for a big announcement. Nemo squeezed my hand, and I smiled at him. Gill twitched beside me. He wasn't used to the pomp and ceremony of court. All eyes were on us as we stood atop the podium for my father's speech. Fin stood tall, proud, and incredibly handsome to Nemo's left. Fin gave me a wink, and I returned the action.

To my right, Nimian was fuming, her arms crossed, her lips and forehead tight. When Father had presented my mermen to her, she'd whined throughout the whole dinner about not being able to have her own harem.

"Hush, child. Go find your own mermen, then," our father had told her, and things had been tense ever since.

The rest of my family crowded beside her. Aquina with her snooty nose in the air. Lativa, my youngest sister, clung to her beau, the two of them hanging on each other like mating octopuses.

All eyes were on my family and my mermen. No doubt,

the assembled crowd wondered what the king prepared to unveil to his court. The noble mermaids were dressed in their finest silk corsets, their hair and makeup impeccable. Although many of them were the epitomes of beauty, my mermen didn't even notice them, their eyes belonging to me alone. Not that I would have minded them sneaking glances. They were mermen, after all. But knowing this made me that much more confident in their bonds with me.

To think I'd been here a few moon cycles earlier when my father had ordered me to marry Faraall. It seemed like a distant memory now. But the horror of it still haunted me. Every night, he came in my dreams to collect me. Nemo had insisted on staying by my side. My father had disapproved of the idea of a male staying in my quarters and feared any gossip escaping the palace, so he'd appointed my mermen as my personal guards. A very high honor in the kingdom. Each night, they would rotate, one remaining at my door, while the other two snuck in to stay with me. Whenever I awoke from my nightmares, they were always there to comfort me and stroke my hair until I fell back asleep. Having them there was the greatest comfort.

Music blared as the king sailed into the room. Everyone pressed a fist across their chests and bowed to him.

"Thank you all for coming on this momentous occasion." My father's voice boomed in my mind as he sat atop his throne. "Please, sit."

The nobles all took their places in the pews below the throne.

"I called you all here today," my father said, "to recognize the bravery and courage of four individuals in a matter concerning the safety and prosperity of the realm."

My stomach twirled with pride. Were my mermen to be rewarded for their valor in protecting me and saving their king? If so, my father had not said a word, the rascal! I hoped this was the case. They were Tritonian heroes and deserved recognition and thanks from the kingdom.

My father nodded at Fin. He'd really taken a liking to him. They talked for long periods of time in my father's library. Fin also attended council meetings concerning the safety of the realm.

In the corner of my eye, Fin bobbed in the water, and when I glanced at him, a grin illuminated his features. Did he know what was about to be declared?

Sea god, he was handsome. All shaved for once. Dressed in his finest sash. They'd all gone to extreme efforts for the ceremony...and to impress my father. Gill had put on this delicious aftershave that smelled like merspice, and Nemo had styled his hair with sea slug gel.

All three of my mermen attended dinners with us every week. My father adored Nemo's humor, and family gatherings were a lot livelier with him there.

As expected, my father took longer to warm to Gill, primarily because the stubborn merman didn't make an effort with the king. Their relationship would take time to grow, but already I'd seen huge improvements.

My father gestured with his hand, and one of the servants flittered forward carrying a plate with four medals.

Nemo squeezed my hand tighter. He'd always dreamed of receiving a medal from the king. I hoped for his sake that his dream was about to come true.

My father accepted the medal tray. "The kingdom was shocked to the core by the betrayal of the merarmy's commander."

Everybody in the crowd nodded their agreement.

"Despite these dark times, a light has emerged in the kingdom," my father said, his gaze flying to my mermen.

"Today, it is my intention to recognize the four heroes who saved the merkingdom from that darkness."

My stomach flipped again.

All eyes landed on my mermen and me. Many had heard the rumors of our fight with Faraall. To my surprise, many had reached out to me, sending me clam mail with their thanks for what we'd done or expressing their regret for my ordeal. I hadn't expected the outpour of affection.

My father descended from his throne and floated in front of Fin. "I present this medal in honor of your contribution to Tritonia. On behalf of the merfolk, I thank you, Fin."

The crowd erupted as my father secured the medal to Fin's sash.

My heart melted at Fin's proud smile.

"And," my father said, "it is also my great honor to appoint you the new defender of the realm. Everybody, please welcome the new merarmy commander."

Some of the mermaids held hands to their mouths and glanced at one another. Others smiled with raised eyebrows as if they'd set their sights on Fin. The only female in the room who wasn't excited was Nimian—she pouted and sneered.

The rest of the nobles applauded and nodded. Even Fin's father, who my father had forced to sit in the front row, begrudgingly clapped for his son.

Fin's proud smile rocketed me into the heavens. He was getting his wish; to prove his worth to his father and to show he'd made the right choice by breaking with tradition.

I wept tears of joy for my merman. What an honor to be appointed such a title. I only hoped it wouldn't mean I'd be seeing less of my love. Then again, the elevation in his status might mean he had a better chance of my father agreeing to a marriage between Fin and me. That thought made me ecstatic with anticipation.

Fin held a fist to his chest and kneeled at my father's feet. My father handed Fin a new trident, glittering with dazzling jewels.

"Congratulations, my son." He pressed his own fist to his chest, nodded, and then moved onto Nemo.

I swept to Fin's side and placed a kiss on his cheek, making sure all the mermaids knew he was mine.

By this point, Nemo jiggled with enthusiasm as his dream was about to be realized. As I swam back into line beside him, I wondered what my father had in store for him. *Poseidon, let it be a medal.*

"Dearest Nemo," my father said, his eyes gleaming with joy.

I'd never seen the king so pleased to be awarding a medal in one of these ceremonies. Typically, they were tedious, a duty he had to carry out, and he undertook them with all the seriousness of a king. But something was different this time. Perhaps he was just elated that he had been saved from the spell, but something told me there was more to his happiness. That my mermen spoke to a deeper part of him, too, like they did for me.

"I present you with this medal of honor for protecting my daughter and the realm." He pinned it to Nemo's sash.

Nemo was positively beaming, and he couldn't stop touching his medal.

"How could I ignore your contribution to Tritonia's safety?" my father added. "I'm appointing you Master of the Crops."

Master of the Crops was a role created after the devastating loss of crops back when the nutrients had failed to fertilize the plants one year. Recently, the former master had retired. It was the duty of the master to protect the realm from famine, to ensure the crops were not eaten by pest fish, and to make certain the plants were fertilized in times when the currents did not bring the nutrition.

Nemo accepted a staff made from molten sand encased with seaweed.

"This staff was freshly forged by a blacksmith on land," said my father. "Now, I entrust it to you."

Everyone, me included, went wild as Nemo thrust the staff in the air. Before I could move to congratulate him, he swept me into his arms, bent me over, and laid a long kiss on my lips.

A few shocked gasps carried through the crowd. From upside-down, I caught the mermaids leaning in to whisper to their friends. I smiled. Let them talk. I no longer cared for their opinions. They could gossip until they ran out of breath.

When Nemo set me upright, my father's eyebrows were drawn together.

"Yes, well." The king wasn't one for affection in public. He also appreciated the courtesy of respect, like a bow or some form of acknowledgement, and I nudged Nemo. Grinning from ear to ear, he fell to the ground in a bow.

Apparently satisfied, my father moved on to Gill.

Gill swallowed hard. I could tell all this made him uncomfortable. But if he wanted to be in my life, this was the sacrifice he had to make. Never a day went by without me thanking him for sticking by my side. Sea god, I was truly blessed. With all my heart, I hoped my father did not offend Gill and refuse him a title in front of the court. That would not help the circumstances between them. I wanted more than anything for them to find common ground and get along as well as Fin and Nemo did with my family.

"This one I am most proud to appoint," my father declared.

What? I'd never heard him speak so highly of Gill before. Was the king skipping Gill altogether and awarding something to me? I did not breathe again until my father lifted the second last medal and pinned it to Gill's sash. *Thank the sea god!*

Even Gill looked taken aback, and normally, nothing rattled him. "Thank you, great king." His lips trembled.

My father's fist found his chest. "For saving the merrealm, my daughter, and yourself."

The whole room exploded with applause.

I caught the eye of Gill's sister. She bounced as if she wanted to come up to the podium. I waved for her to join us. She was there in a flash and leaped into her brother's arms. Gill's adopted parents drifted up, too, embracing their son, crying with joy, no doubt happy about the way he'd turned around his life.

My heart was uplifted with joy for them all.

My father waited for the cheers to die down before he spoke again. "It is also my honor to declare you the Keeper of the Peace."

I'd never heard of this title before. It must have been created recently.

"It will be your duty," declared my father, "to bring harmony between the two merkingdoms. Be the voice of reason. Negotiate for prosperity."

I clasped my hands together. What a fabulous role and well-suited to Gill who, as a child, had struggled for his own inner peace.

Gill's jaw hung open. He hadn't expected the privilege.

I threw my arms around him and held him. This was the most wonderful news. Now, all three of my mermen had been elevated to important positions within the kingdom. Maybe, just maybe, there might be a chance for us to all stay together. Although I wasn't counting my fry before they hatched.

"And to my daughter," bellowed my father, claiming the last token, a trident pendant hanging from a gold chain. He did me the honor of lifting it over my neck and settling it at my clavicle. "Were it not for you bringing together this band of mermen, risking your own life, and battling evil most foul, I might not be standing here today."

I stroked the trident, the symbol of my father's merkingdom.

The whistles of my mermen topped the applause from the nobles. I glanced at my family. My mother clutched her hands to her chest. Aquina reluctantly clapped and rolled her eyes as if the ceremony were beneath her. Sea god, she was a bitch sometimes. Lativa and her beau were smiling and clapping. Even Nimian applauded, some of her ice having obviously melted.

"To my daughter," my father said. "I appoint you ambassador of Tritonia. You will deal with the ward on land and bring harmony to the two worlds of my kingdom; sea and land."

For once, I'd been awarded a burden I was happy to bear. To help Snow take back her home and appoint her as rightful ward of the Tritonian land would be an honor. The kingdom of Tritonia was no longer going to be victim to that evil witch wreaking havoc on my father's territory.

****

TODAY WAS THE BIG DAY. My stomach fluttered with excitement. I'd been counting down the hours, wishing for them to pass more quickly, and now the time had finally arrived! Crystal boxes, furniture, clothing, and various items were scattered across my quarters. Fin's arms were filled with two boxes of my belongings. On his way past me, I leaped up, grabbed the sides of his face, and laid a quick one on him. I didn't linger for long. Time was of the essence. We had a new life to commence.

After six moon cycles together, my mermen and I were moving into our new apartment. Thank the sea god! Ever since the king had assigned us our new appointments, we hadn't seen as much of each other. I had to be content to see my mermen at meals, after dinner, and when I snuck them into my quarters.

As an added precaution after the episode with Faraall, my father had posted an extra four guards at my door. After some negotiation, the new guards and I had come to an arrangement: they permitted my secret trysts with my mermen, as long as I awarded them extra paid days off. In return, I had their loyalty and silence. Should any of my family—or a person who might report the trysts to the king —approach, the guards sent out an aquablast. For their loyalty, I was incredibly grateful, as it had permitted me more time to spend with my loves.

My father had taken some time to convince when it came to me moving out. Each day, we'd built his trust, until finally, he'd given us his blessing to live together. His decision hadn't come a moment too soon either.

"Allow me." Nemo tried to snatch the corsets and pillows I carried.

"No, you don't." I playfully whacked him with a pillow. "I'm not a helpless princess."

"No. But you're a damn sexy one." He kissed me on the cheek and patted me on the behind.

I found his lips, and he licked mine.

"Captain Corny." Gill shook his head and exited with more of my things.

Nemo raised his hands in the air. "She loves it. Don't you, Princess?"

I rolled my eyes and left him behind.

"You love it in the bedroom," Nemo mumbled upon my exit.

"Aha," Gill said, hurrying to join me.

We both sailed together through the halls of the palace. I really appreciated their help in moving. The quicker we were out of my old quarters, the sooner we'd be together in our new apartment.

It was early morning, and the morning glow of the sun, reflected and enhanced by crystals, trickled through to the depths of the palace. The light caught on the tiled, mother-of-pearl mosaics along the wall. Sea plants swayed in the soft flow of water through the halls. Several servants carried platters of food to the dining hall.

I would miss this part of the palace. The whale song in the sea grass fields below waking me in the morning. The click of dolphins playing in the afternoon. Scents from the kitchen drifting in the water.

Gill and I arrived at the whale sleigh, where Fin was stacking boxes.

The whale hauling the chariot flicked its head in greeting. This was the king's personal escort for all official palace business. My father had loaned it to us to transport all our belongings to our new apartment on the other side of the palace. There, we had an even more spectacular view of the coral reefs, teeming with aquatic life, and our windows looked down on the palace gardens.

Once we were all packed, my mermen jumped into the sleigh.

I stroked the tail of the great beast and said, "To the palace gardens." I sat back into my seat.

The whale pumped its tail, hauling us through the water.

Fish scattered out of the way. Curious merfolk glanced at us as we sailed around the city to the opposite side of the palace. I gave them an excited wave. The children bounced up and down, waving back, until their mothers ushered them away.

Soon, we arrived at our new quarters, one of the guest-houses for visiting dignitaries from my uncle's merkingdom. The spacious, six-bedroom apartment provided us some privacy while being close enough should trouble break out. All of my mermen had a room of his own, with one spare room for a library and study, and the last room for visitors. We opted not to have live-in servants, preferring to limit their presence to delivering meals and cleaning. At my father's insistence—and this was non-negotiable—four guards always remained at every entrance.

My mermen and I carried some of the boxes inside and put them down in the living quarters.

"I can't believe this is really happening," I said, twirling with my arms outstretched.

With this new arrangement, I was getting my space and freedom from my family, the palace, and the nobles, while also inheriting a new role I'd grown to relish.

Fin found a platter of treats—a selection of fresh meat, fruit, vegetables, and even sea cake—awaiting us on the kitchen bench. He picked up a clam mail accompanying the gift.

"A welcome gift from your father," he said.

Four sea cucumber sacs rested beside the platter.

I sailed over to my merman to read the note.

A CONGRATULATORY SERVING of merchampagne to celebrate the occasion. My blessings and love to you all. Welcome to the family, my sons.

"Oh, how sweet of him," I said.

Every day, my father's affections for my mermen grew. He treated Fin like his own son, Nemo, like a fun, lively friend who entertained everyone at a party, and Gill with the admiration and respect for a man who improved every day. Everything was perfect. I'd never expected it to turn out so well or for my father to ever welcome my affections for more than one merman. And I had Faraall, the sea witch, and the pirates, of all people, to thank for it.

Fin handed us each a cucumber sac. "To us and new beginnings."

I connected my pouch to his. Gill and Nemo joined in.

"To new beginnings," we all said at the same time.

Together, we sipped at the contents of our pouch. What a commemoration. The best one so far.

"I'd like to toast my sexy, royal ass," Gill said, raising his drink.

"To *our* sexy royal ass," Nemo chimed in.

Fin to raise his pouch and nodded.

Sea god they made me laugh. My stomach hurt from it.

"Well, I'm going to be a gentleman," Fin said, sliding his arm around my waist and toasting me. "To our beloved, sweet, and stubborn merlady." He kissed the top of my head. "And her sexy, royal ass."

I nudged him for being cheeky and encouraging the other two...even though I loved every minute of their teasing me.

"Time for a song," Nemo announced. "A theme song for our new place."

He cleared his throat and put a hand to his chest.

"Every morning I will wake," he said. "Next to me, her ass will shake."

Gill and Fin repeated the lines.

I giggled. This was going to be a hard song to forget. The last one he'd made up about me had stuck in my head for at least three moon cycles. But I wouldn't have had it any other way.

Thanks for reading Claimed.

Reviews are super important to authors as it helps other reader make better decisions on books they will read. So if you have a moment, please do leave a review for Hunted, HERE.

Are you curious to read the next Haven Realm instalment? Discover more in **ENTANGLED**, a Rapunzel retelling.

Subscribe to Mila Young's Newsletter to receive exclusive content, latest updates, and giveaways. Join here.

HAVEN REALM SERIES
Hunted
Charmed
Cursed
Claimed
Entangled

Continue the Haven Realm series.
www.amazon.com/Mila-Young/e/B077QT5J5M

HUNTED

Little Red Riding Hood. Three Big Bad Wolves. A Poisonous Scheme.

Scarlet, a healer, lives nestled in the forest surrounded by humans on one side and wolves on the other. But when a rogue wolf attacks her, she's rescued by another pack and taken deep into their den to perform her healing magic on an injured Alpha.

The wolves in the forest are under threat from a mysterious affliction, and Scarlet is the only hope they have left. Faced with a mixed pack of threatened shifters, Scarlet must use her wits and magic to survive and unravel the strange affliction now affecting the wolves... All while trying to navigate an overpowering attraction to not just one, but three of the Alphas.

Witches, wolves, magic and love intertwine in an exciting mystery that finds its own, unique, 'Happily Ever After.'

Click To Read Hunted

CHARMED

Aladdin. Three Dangerously Sexy Genies. A Deadly Sorcerer.

In the depths of the Sultan's cave, tenacious street thief Azar steals a bunch of jewels and a brass lamp. Sure, stealing has no honor, but she'll do whatever it takes to feed her brother, buy the medicine he needs and get them out of the slums of Utaara.

When Azar releases three gorgeous genies from the lamp, her first wish is to save her brother. Except the genies magic is weakened from being trapped for hundreds of years, and they must wait for their power to recover. A growing darkness in the kingdom is hunting Azar's genies, desperate to claim their power for his own dark plans. Now Azar must fight to save her brother and the genies that have charmed their way into her heart.

Family, magic and love intertwine in an action packed romance with a 'Happily Ever After.'

Click To Read Charmed

CURSED

Beauty and the Four Beasts. A Deadly Curse. A Fallen Kingdom.

With magic banned in the human realm, Bee, a powerful witch, has had to offer her services in secret. When a request to break a curse comes from the dangerous mountains and royal bear shifters, Bee is hesitant, but winter is coming and funds are tight.

At the castle, Bee finds things are not quite what she was led to believe. The curse Bee is meant to break has reached its zenith, siphoning off the Prince's life while preventing him from controlling his shifting abilities. He is volatile, angry, and far stronger than she had imagined. His brothers, who commissioned her, present her with a challenge - fix it, or lose everything.

Soon the curse is spreading throughout the castle, taking brother alike. It's a race against the clock, buffeted by dark magic, intrigue, and a strange attraction that has her looking at the four brothers in a new light.

Click To Read Cursed

Continue the Haven Realm series.

www.amazon.com/Mila-Young/e/B077QT5J5M

HUNTED EXCERPT

Chapter 1

"SCARLET, GET A LOOK AT HIM." Bee nudged me in the ribs.

I gritted my teeth, my hands juggling the jar of chamomile I'd just pulled off the shelf. "For the love of wolfsbane."

Honestly, Bee had the boniest elbow in all the seven realms of Haven. No matter how often I protested, she insisted on jabbing me right in the side every time she had something to say. Her idea of grabbing my attention wasn't tapping my shoulder but inflicting pain. I twisted around and my gaze flew through the arched windows of my store, Get Your Herb On.

A huge guy marched out of the woods, arms swinging in an over-exaggerated motion. His chest stuck out, and with his chin high, I had him figured out in two seconds flat. I'd seen so many of his kind leaving the priestess's palace.

Guardians, full of cockiness and attitude, taking what they wanted without paying for goods.

Yet he wasn't wearing a uniform, but the strangest clothes. A gray tunic falling to mid-thigh; no pants or boots. Goddess, his legs were the size of tree trunks.

"Who wants to bet his muscles aren't real?" I said. I'd heard of people using magic to enhance their physique. It was the latest trend in other territories.

Bee glanced at me with disbelief pinching her expression. With her braided red hair and ivory skin, most called her beautiful and always referenced her green eyes. But the real Bee was also tough. I'd once seen her scare off a bear with a glare, and there was a reason most in town kept their distance from her. Sure, it might have a little something to do with Bee insisting most of the folk were uneducated swine breeders—her words, not mine—but hey, she was a best friend who often popped into my store, and I loved her company. Even if she didn't know when to keep her mouth shut.

"How can they not be real?" Her gaze turned from the man and back my way. "He's not wearing pants. What could he possibly be padding—" Then her eyes widened, and her lips curled upward into a wicked grin. "You filthy girl, Scarlet. Never knew you had it in you." She whacked me in the arm, her strength intimidating, considering she stood five-foot-two and reached my nose.

"What are you talking about?" I slouched, a hip pressed against the counter, and pushed several sample bowls of tea leaves up against the ceramic cups that I had painted with different stages of the moon cycle. I called them my night collection series and regular customers tended to buy a new one whenever they purchased their regular healing herbs. If I had more time, I'd paint all the time.

"You're referring to his junk, aren't you? And well…" Bee

glanced outside. "With the wind blowing against his clothes, there's definitely a healthy package in his arsenal." Bee wiggled her eyebrows and broke out laughing.

Fire scorched my cheeks. You'd think I'd be used to Bee's dirty mouth; after all, this was normal for her. "I wasn't talking about his... his privates."

Bee gripped her hips, cinching in the long, blue tunica dress she wore. The outfit had a V-neckline and tiny buttons ran down the front. I admired her flowing sleeves, and I needed to re-examine my wardrobe. My black pants and sea-green blouse beneath the leather vest with a belt made me look more like a thief. But when I chose my clothing, I prior-itized comfort. Most days, I lifted boxes at work and a skirt would get in the way.

"Just say it, Scarlet," Bee continued. "Dick. Cock."

I rolled my eyes. I had no issues with such words... As long as I didn't say them. I blamed my grandma, who'd brought me up strict, no cursing or vulgarities. Heavens bless her soul.

"Penis." Bee licked her lips. "Blowjob."

A squeaky male's voice came from behind Bee. "Eww." Santos walked out of the storage room carrying several boxes. "I can hear you out the back. That's called sexual harassment of men."

I sighed, loathing that Santos had heard our conversation, and Bee spun toward my eighteen-year-old apprentice. But he might as well be fourteen with his thin frame, shaved hair, and his maturity level. Then again, were Bee and myself any better?

"Hey, guys talk crap about girls all the time," Bee said. "What's the difference?"

Santos set the three boxes of tobacco leaves on the end of the counter. "You two are too old to talk about such things, and it's gross."

"Old?" Bee's voice climbed. "We're only a year older than you." She turned to me with a cocked eyebrow, expecting me to say something. I shrugged my shoulders.

"That's okay, Santos," I said. "We'll curb our tongues if it makes you uncomfortable." He worked his butt off, and I didn't need him leaving. He'd been working for me for a year and had just learned the names of all the dried plants we sold.

"It's fine." He didn't glance our way and instead opened the first box and scooped handfuls of tobacco into tiny satchels.

I marched to the opposite end of the counter. Bee followed me, probably ready to offer one of her smartass comments about Santos, but I jumped in first to change the direction of the conversation. "How come you're not wearing your new boots? The ones I got you for Christmas?"

Bee huffed. "Can't get them dirty, as I plan to wear them to the town ball. Might attract myself a prince in disguise. Besides, you live in the woods with lots of mud and—"

The front doorbell chimed, stealing her words.

We all glanced up to find Mr. No Pants bursting into the shop with a flurry, his breaths labored and his cheeks red.

"I need help," he wheezed.

"My, what do we have here?" Bee said, drawing the newcomer's attention to the three sets of eyes on him... mine lowering to his legs, and even with his tunic covering, he had a huge package. But I focused on the red bleeding through his tunic at his hip. How had he gotten injured? Animal attack?

At once, Mr. No Pants straightened his posture and flicked his raven hair over a shoulder, his sights sliding from me to Bee, then locking on to her curvy chest.

Okay, he was a womanizer. Score another point for Bee against Santos in the women versus men chauvinist race.

The newcomer could at least have had the decency to keep his eyes above neck level.

Bee pulled the elastic free from her braid and fluffed out her hair. Typical. I nudged her and raised my eyebrows.

"Geez, live a little, Scarlet," she whispered. "You've been too sheltered."

I tucked a lock behind an ear. "Brown as a deer," my grandma had once called my hair. Nothing sexy about that. Maybe the reason I never got a guy's attention was I stayed too safe.

My sights fell on the newcomer's blood. Was it a human who had shot him with a bow and arrow? I rounded the counter. "Are you all right?"

He stood at least six foot with a solid square jawline, studying me as if I might be an animal he'd crossed paths with in the woods.

"You're injured," I continued.

The man didn't say a word but scanned the room, and then looked out through the windows behind him. "I'm wonderful." Yet he stood there, a trickle of blood rolling down the side of his leg from under his tunic.

"Don't think so," Bee blurted out. "Unless you're a mutant who bleeds instead of sweating, you're about to dirty up Scarlet's floor."

He stared at me, and a brush of desperation shifted behind his eyes. The kind I'd seen when I'd first met Santos over a year ago, when he'd been sleeping on the streets, thin and pasty. Sometimes asking for help was the hardest thing to do.

"Come," I said. "We have a room out back, and I'll bring you hot tea to calm your nerves." I surveyed the dirt road outside and the woods in the distance for anything suspicious. My shop was located in the forest on the fringe of civilization, so I often saw strange things. But it was all clear.

A few weeks ago, in the middle of the night, another buff guy with no shirt had turned up on my doorstep asking for specific plants for healing someone gravely ill. Before that, another man had been at my door, his clothes torn and his butt exposed.

A loser in the town of Terra had scored Get Your Herb On with a one-star on the town review board. The priestess ruling over the Terra realm in Haven had introduced a new system. The Customer Approval Plank, she'd called it, insisting it would assist people in choosing the best shops for their needs.

So now, not only did the scoreboard sit in the main town square for everyone to view, but some troll kept marking my store with one star. Was that person spying on me and noticing naked men at my door? No wonder my business has slowed lately.

Mr. No Pants scoffed and folded his arms across his strong chest, then cringed and lowered them.

"So, you going to buy something or—"

I cut Bee a glare, cutting off her words, then turned to the stranger. And I recognized the desperate need for someone to reach out and make that connection, offer a lending hand. When my grandma had passed away of old age, I'd lost everything. She had been my rock, my family, and without Grandma's support, her tonic soups, her hugs, I hadn't been sure how to go on. She'd raised me after my parents had been torn apart by a pack of wolves. Bee had reached out to me, guiding me to find purpose in life again, so now I'd do the same with this man.

"Come with me," I said and headed to the back, his foot-steps trailing behind me. "Santos, can you show him a seat? I'll bring him some tea." Something to ease any pain he felt along with his nerves. Might even encourage him to open up about how he'd gotten hurt.

Without a complaint, the two vanished into the storage room. Bee shook her head, giving me a glare.

"Don't say it," I said.

I rushed to the pot with boiling water Santos had set up for samples. I collected a jar of valerian and arrowroot from the cupboard lining the wall behind me. Teapots, candles, and more tea containers filled the shelves. Together with a pinch of chamomile, the aromatic scent had my shoulders lowering.

Bee was in my ear, and I tensed again. "What if he's a guardian? Do you want to bring the priestess's attention to your business? You know she abhors magic. That's why I do my enchantment spells in the basement at home so no one ever catches me."

"This is just an ordinary tea store," I whispered, lowering my palm over the tea bag.

Bee snatched my wrist and lifted my hand, sparks of white energy dancing across my fingertips. "Right, so this is perfectly normal?"

I'd always had the ability to enhance plants, and my grandma had taught me how to harness the power she'd insisted I shared with nature.

"It's nothing." I lied, well aware that the priestess who ruled over the human district forbade anything non-human related. And punishment came in the form of imprisonment for life. Each of the seven territories in Haven were homes to various races, from wolf shifters in our neighboring land, to mermaids, and rumor spoke of a girl with magical hair. Yep, one day I'd explore Haven, but until then, I'd remain in Terra with other humans, pretending we were pure and everyone else was the freak... according to the ruling priestess. And leaving Terra or strangers entering was prohibited. Hence guardians captured any shifters or intruders in Terra for interrogation, never to be seen again.

"Don't kid yourself, Scarlet. I've heard the priestess infiltrated places like the bakeries in town, convinced their breads were too good to be true. And that the baker engaged in sorcery."

Her words left me jittery because I wanted to believe what I did benefited those in need. I drew on my ability to amplify the strength of herbs, so when people used them, they got the full effect. If chamomile calmed someone, then it put them into such a relaxed state, their anxiety slipped away. What was wrong with that?

"We'll be cautious, then," I suggested.

Bee nodded. "Smart idea. I'll be the bad enforcer and you the good."

"What? Wait, no."

Bee had already steamrolled toward the rear. I left the tea behind and rushed after her.

Santos appeared from the room, his attention sailing to the box of dried tobacco leaves.

"We'll be in the back for a moment," I said.

He nodded. "I've got this." He didn't seem worried in the slightest. Then again, he had no reason to believe the guy was anything but someone in danger, and he had zero idea about my powers.

Once I entered the storage room, I found Bee leaning over Mr. No Pants, who sat on a chair, her index finger pressed against his chest. "Where are your trousers? This isn't a peep show kind of store."

"Bee. Give him space to breathe." Without waiting for a response, I collected my medicine box from the shelves and flipped the lid open. "Now, let's examine your wound."

"How did you get hurt, hmm?" Bee towered over him, her hands gripping her waist. Geez, the girl should train as a guardian.

"I'm not here to harm you. You can relax." He lifted the tunic up and bunched it at his side.

My gaze dove to his midsection like a desperate hound dog. Except the guy wore black underwear.

Bee sighed.

He peeled away fabric stuck to the mess underneath, wincing, and I cringed at how much it must have hurt.

Three claw marks tore across his side, blood everywhere.

"Holy shiitake mushrooms," I said. "What did this to you?"

He cut me a strange look with a raised eyebrow as if he'd pull away from my touch if I tried to treat him.

"Crapping balls, Scarlet. This requires a fuck me, not mushrooms," Bee blurted out. "But really, dude." She turned to the stranger. "This is bad. Like you'll die, that kind of bad. If you want my friend to cure you, talk."

Bee was the queen of exaggeration. The guy only had a few scratches and would survive. "Bring me a bowl of boiling water," I asked her because tact wasn't her forte. I grabbed an old towel from the cupboard and cleaned around his wounds. They didn't require stitching.

"Don't listen to her," I said to Mr. No Pants. "What's your name?"

"Better you don't know." He didn't keep my stare, but instead studied the room as if attempting to appear busy. Yep, right there was the warning Bee had mentioned.

"Look," I said. "I'm happy to help you, but are we in danger if we do? Do you work for the priestess?"

He scrunched his nose. "Gods forbid."

Bee returned with a bowl of water she set on the table, and I drenched the stained fabric before continuing to cleanse the injury.

"Where are you from?" I asked. "The mountains? The wolf Den? Oh, maybe you're one of those desert dwellers." The thought had crossed my mind. The human world was comprised of a massive town with several hundred thousand people. Farms dotted the outskirts, but this man wasn't a local. There was an air about him every girl in Terra would have sniffed out by now, especially if he was single. And I would have heard about it at the monthly town gatherings. The ones where the priestess reminded us of our blessing to be pure along with the latest attempts by other factions to infiltrate our territory. In particular, Terra's number one nemesis, the wolves to our east. "Barbarians who attacked anything that moved," she called them.

"I'm not from Terra." He held his head high, as if having nothing to hide, and his admittance didn't surprise me because it wasn't the first time someone had snuck into Terra for help. And humans did the same all the time, leaving behind our land and entering others for various reasons like falling in love with a lion shifter, or at least that had happened to a bookshop owner back in town.

"Are the guardians after you?" I asked.

Bee gave me the *told you* look. But if you followed the rules, Terra was a safe place most of the time.

"No. There was a wolf. In fact, a pack chased me."

"In Terra?" I asked, squeezing the towel into my fist and returning to wiping his wound. I dabbed a mixture of my pre-made antiseptic onto his injuries, and he didn't grimace once.

"Nope. On wolf territory, in the Den. I was passing through and took a shortcut across their land and yours." He paused and wiped his mouth. "But a vicious pack found me and hunted me. I barely escaped with my life before they ripped my pants off."

Bee burst out laughing, her hand pressed over her stomach. "You sure it wasn't a pack of she-wolves?"

He straightened himself. "Girls throw themselves at me

all the time, so I'm guessing the wolves who attacked me instead of ravishing me were males."

Holding back the giggle in my throat, I placed a bandage on his wounds and wrapped it around his waist, then tucked the loose ends in on each other. "There—"

A piercing hoot sounded somewhere outside, and my feet cemented to the ground.

"Fuck," Bee said. "That's the guardians." She shoved a hand into Mr. No Pants' shoulder. "You said they weren't after you."

His face blanched, and he leaped to his feet, towering over us, his top falling over his hips "They aren't. But I have to go."

"Wait, you're still injured, and—"

He placed a hand to my mouth. "Hush."

I pushed his arm away. "Excuse me, who do you think you are?"

"Is there a rear exit?" he asked, his voice low and carrying an air of panic.

Bee stood in the doorway. "Tell us what's going on and we'll let you leave."

The man laughed deep and raw, almost terrifying. "Little girls, you cannot stand in my way. But I will leave you with a warning because you aided me. The wolves are at war amongst themselves. And one fight always spills over in other lands. I was attacked right on the Terra border."

"But we've got wolfsbane dividing our land. That'll keep the packs at bay," I called out as he stormed away from me and lifted Bee out of the doorway as if she were a doll. He then sprinted faster than anyone his size should have been able to.

Santos entered the storeroom. "Where'd he go in such a rush?"

Bee and I exchanged glances as dread threaded through

my chest. I glanced out through the front windows and spotted two guardians in uniform darting left. I sure hoped Mr. No Pants had escaped. It wasn't the first time I'd seen them chase trespassers in Terra, and if I kept my head low, the guardians left me and my store alone. "Well, he wasn't from Terra," I said. "No wonder the guardians are after him."

"He's a looney." Bee wove her arm around mine and guided me back into the main area. "You should consider a lock on the door and only let people in after you study them through the window."

I nodded. She had a point, yet in the back of my mind, I couldn't ignore Mr. No Pants' warning. It wasn't the first time the wolves had attempted to claim territory. They had entered our land before my time, and hundreds of innocent lives had been lost on both sides.

"Do you think the priestess knows about the wolf war?" I asked.

"For sure. Otherwise, what else would her job entail? Oh, right." She cocked a brow. "Controlling all of us. Anyway, I should return home before the sun goes down. Do you have any wolfsbane?"

For those few seconds, Bee's words didn't register as I remained caught up in the whole wolves warring thing and the half-naked stranger at my store, who hadn't even given us his name. Perhaps a lock on the door to protect us from crazy customers wasn't such a bad suggestion.

Bee poked a finger into my arm. "Hello, Scarlet, are you with us?"

Shaking, I hurried to the counter and pushed aside the fabric underneath, concealing the dangerous ingredients. Wolfsbane was poisonous, and I kept it out of view. I plonked the jar on the table, but it was empty and there were a few specs of dust inside. "Well, that's a problem."

Bee gripped her waist. "I thought only I bought the stuff?"

I scratched my head, then remembered where it had gone, but Santos stole my words as he headed into the storage room, calling out his response. "Last week, you added it to the concoction to clean the bird poo off the windows."

"Poo?" Bee paced to the door and back to my side. "But I need it this week. I'm hiking into the mountains to see a client. I assumed you had some." She leaned closer and whispered. "My client claims to have a curse put on him, and I need wolfsbane to create a counter-spell."

Bee practiced magic in secret and was known for her abilities outside of Terra. Here, the priestess would arrest her if she found out, so Bee often sought jobs in other territories for her services.

"Sorry, I'd been meaning to top up the supplies. I'm running out of a few other things too. When did you say you need it by?"

Santos reappeared with the bowl of hot water and bloody towel, heading to the front door to dump the contents outside.

"Tomorrow." Bee twirled a red lock over her shoulder.

"Sweet bolts, that's soon." I hurried to open the front door to hold it for Santos.

"Real sorry, Scarlet. It's just that I received the job this morning."

Santos interrupted. "I can collect some." His eyes were pleading, as he'd wanted to go out on a field excursion forever.

As much as I loved that he offered, I couldn't let him go. "No, it's all right. The plant's dangerous, and I don't want you getting harmed." Plus, I found if I applied my magical touch on plants while still fresh, their intensity worked a treat in spells.

"If it's too hard, I can ask my client if it's all right if we delay the appointment," Bee said, twisting hair around her finger, something she did whenever she was nervous. She and her father struggled financially, and her jobs kept them above the water. I didn't want to cause them any more strain.

"You know I'd do anything for you," I said.

She ran over and drew me into a tight hug, her citrus and vanilla perfume bathing me. "Thanks. And I've always got your back too."

"Sure do!" I giggled, and Bee broke away.

"Okay, I've got to go. Dad's finishing one of his new inventions, and I promised to be his assistant. See you tomorrow? I'll come in the morning?" Bee asked.

"Nah, I'll pop over to your place," I suggested. "You're always saying I spend too much time in the woods instead of society." For the past week, I'd been preparing a paste for her dad, who suffered from joint aches, and planned to finish it tonight to surprise him tomorrow.

Bee hugged me once more and kissed my cheek. She whispered in my ear. "Penis." With a giggle she picked up her satchel from the counter and strolled outside with a wave at Santos before vanishing down the dirt track through the woods.

Santos returned inside. "Yes, I'll watch the place while you're gone. And I promise I won't make any tea pouches and only take orders if anyone needs one."

"You know me too well." I took my coat and bag from the back. Looked like I was making a last-minute trip into the woods. Yet trepidation sat on my shoulders, reminding me of Mr. No Pants' words about the wolves at war. So I grabbed a new bottle of citrus bane mixed with water. The spray would deter any predator coming near me, and when sprayed in anyone's eyes, it made them temporarily blind, giving me time to escape.

ABOUT MILA YOUNG

Mila Young tackles everything with the zeal and bravado of the fairytale heroes she grew up reading about. She slays monsters, real and imaginary, like there's no tomorrow. By day she rocks a keyboard as a marketing extraordinaire. At night she battles with her might pen-sword, creating fairytale retellings, and sexy ever after tales. In her spare time, she loves pretending she's a mighty warrior, walks on the beach with her dogs, cuddling up with her cats, and devouring every fantasy tale she can get her pinkies on.

Ready to read more of Hunted and more from Mila Young? Subscribe today here.

Join Mila's **Wicked Readers group** for exclusive content, latest news, and giveaway. Click here.

For more information...
milayoungauthor@gmail.com

12271618R00197

Made in the USA
San Bernardino, CA
09 December 2018